I0723225

# CASUAL BUSINESS WITH FAIRIES

J. W. JUDGE

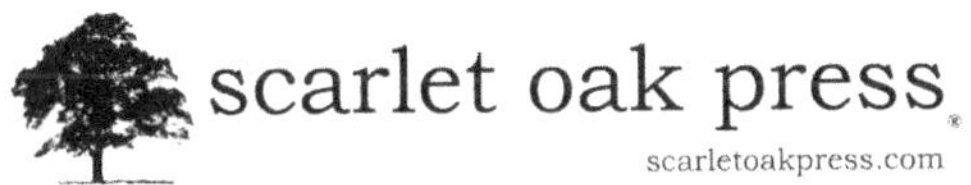

scarlet oak press

scarletoakpress.com

# Contents

scarlet oak press



For permissions and information about special discounts for bulk purchases, contact Scarlet Oak Press at contact@scarletoakpress.com.

ISBN: 978-1-954974-13-5 (Paperback)

ISBN: 978-1-954974-12-8 (eBook)

ISBN: 978-1-954974-14-2 (Hard Cover)

Library of Congress Control Number: 2022921902

Attribution for dagger image: knife art tattoo PNG Designed By Artilution from https://pngtree.com/freepng/knife-dagger-wing-illustration-art_7712254.html?sol=downref&id=bef

Published by Scarlet Oak Press (scarletoakpress.com)

# Works by J. W. Judge

*Fiction*

Casual Business with Fairies

Vulcan Rising (The Zauberi Chronicles, Book 1)

Seeking Sanctuary (The Zauberi Chronicles, Book 2)

Forging Bonds (The Zauberi Chronicles, Book 3)

The Murder Tree (A Short Story)

*Non-Fiction*

Write Your Novel One Day at a Time: How to Write a Novel While
Having a Career, a Family, and a Life

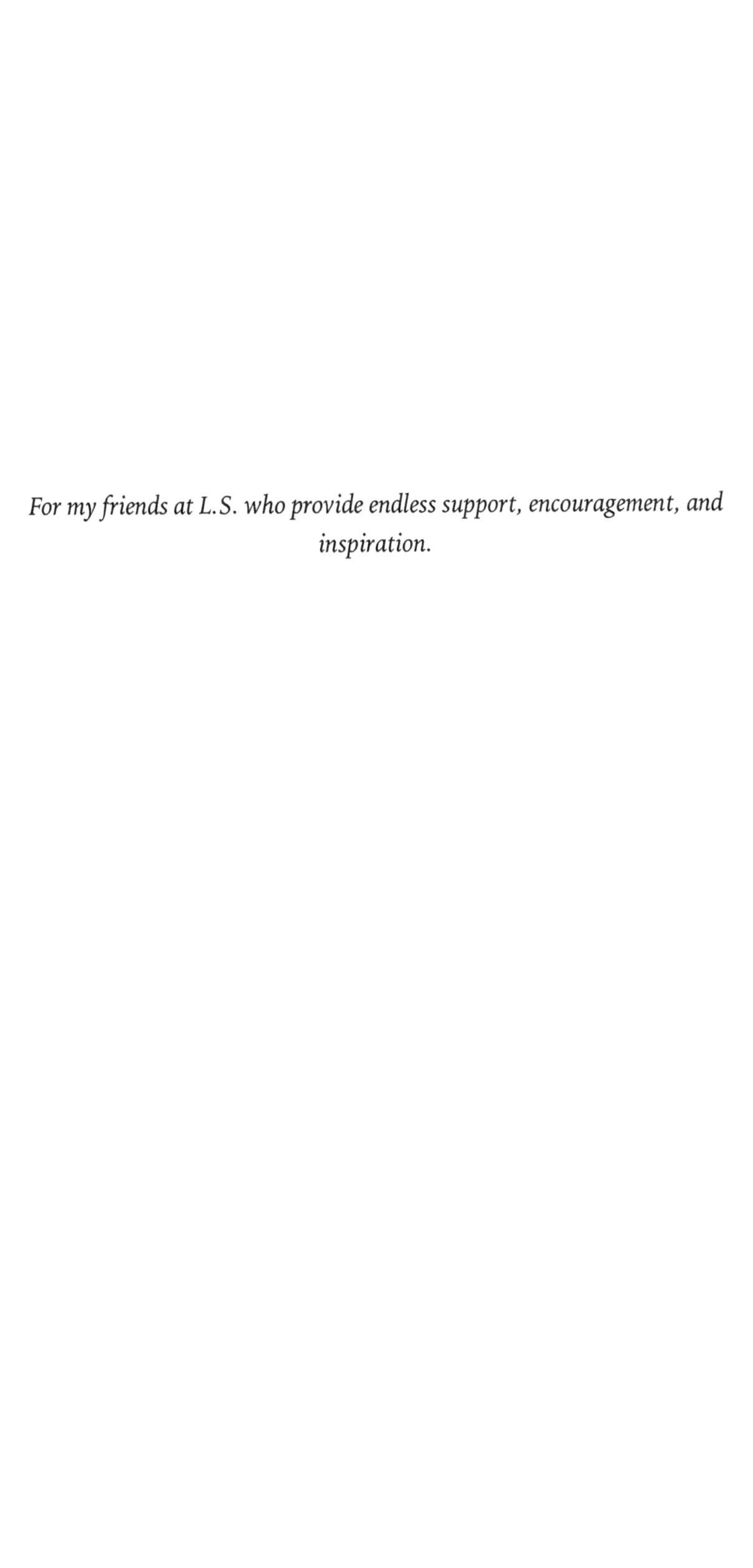

*For my friends at L.S. who provide endless support, encouragement, and inspiration.*

*Come away, O human child!*
*To the waters and the wild*
*With a faery hand in hand,*
*For the world's more full of weeping*
*than you can understand.*

The Stolen Child
William Butler Yeats

# Casual Business with Fairies

# Chapter 1
# Tooth Fairy Faux Pas

Even before I answered the phone, I regretted the decision to do so. Without any real enthusiasm, I said, "Hey."

"In a world where we worked out, you'd still call me darlin' when you answer the phone."

She was clever enough that I didn't know if she'd been hanging on to that line until the right opportunity or if it had just popped into her head. Regardless, I didn't have either the capacity or tolerance for it. "Please don't do this."

"Do what?" she asked in a tone dripping with nectar.

A weary sigh escaped my lips. "Please, Ashleigh. I just can't."

"Can't or won't?"

I tried to keep it in check, but my tone hardened anyway. "Did you have a reason to call?"

"I didn't get your child support this month." It stung her pride to make this call and ask for help. Like many Southern women, she had a backbone made of steel. But she was on her own now, and she was broke.

I cursed under my breath and pulled my phone away from my face to see the date. The eighteenth. She'd waited three days before calling. "Sorry. Work has been pretty wild. I'll send it to you as soon as we hang up."

"Okay," she said. It hung heavy in the air. We were both still getting used to this, and there were a thousand things we had left unsaid. "Are you doing alright?"

I disregarded the question. I wasn't even close to ready to go there. "I'm out of town this week. Headed to Amarillo."

"By morning?"

Deep furrows creased my forehead. "What?"

"'Amarillo by Morning.' George Straight. Keep up. Wait, are you driving? They wouldn't fly you?"

"They would have, but I decided to drive. I'm pulled over to eat some lunch." I mopped the sweat off my forehead with my arm.

"Are you on that stupid motorcycle? I still can't believe that's the first thin—"

"Ash, I'm not doing this. I've gotta go. I'm in the middle-of-nowhere Mississippi, and I've gotta get back on the road."

"Fine. Bye ... I guess."

"See ya."

"Wait," she said urgently.

My answer was clipped. "What?"

"What did you do with Ella's tooth that she lost when she was at your place?" She wouldn't call it the basement apartment that it was. Part of being Southern and divorced was the shame of a failed marriage that marked you like a scarlet letter. My apartment was a regular reminder of that. While I had let her keep the house, it was too big for just the two of them. We'd planned to fill the place with a handful of kids, until the pregnancies hadn't worked out and we had to make a little science baby. Something had broken along the way. A small fissure that a thousand grains of sand seeped into over time. Instead of forming pearls, they laid the groundwork for earthquakes.

The question about a tooth wasn't what I had expected. I

pinched the bridge of my nose, thinking. "I couldn't find it when I went to swap it for the money."

"Also, ten bucks for a tooth?"

"What was I supposed to give her?"

"I don't know. Not ten dollars."

"Whatever. I couldn't find the tooth. It never turned up. Maybe I vacuumed it up later."

"You vacuum now?"

I didn't answer. I didn't want a fight. The divorce was supposed to help us stop fighting, but instead, it gave us other things to fuss about. "What does the tooth matter? I would've just thrown it away anyway."

"You can't throw it away. It's her bone."

"Teeth aren't bones." Even as it slipped out, I regretted it. Now wasn't the time to be pedantic. "Sorry. If it turns up, I'll let you know. I gotta go."

"Okay. One more thing."

I grunted.

"Make sure you've paid your life insurance premiums."

"Not funny."

She snickered. She'd always been able to make herself laugh. Often at my expense. Her wit was quicker than mine. It had always been cute and endearing until it turned mean.

"Bye." I clicked the red button.

I had parked under an oversized oak tree when I stopped to eat my PB&J, but I had long since sweat through my tank top. I didn't even pretend I was going to wear my motorcycle jacket. With the way the asphalt was already boiling, the black fabric and plastic plating would have cooked my insides. Braised organs with a side of roadkill.

The heat that dripped from the sun was like molten lava, but it was nothing compared to what radiated back at me off the roadway. In the throes of July, the air was so laden with humidity that breathing and drowning were similar experiences.

I had left the interstate and picked up Highway 82 in Tuscaloosa. From there it ran due west for 700 miles all the way to Wichita Falls, Texas, where I would take Highway 287 for about another four hours until I got to Amarillo. I-20 would have been quicker, but sometimes I can't help but think of interstates as prisons with prescribed exits. Especially when I on I'm motorcycle, where it seems like cars go out of their way not to see you.

Besides that, Highway 82 was home to the idyllic Americana of a bygone era. Pine trees that led from one quaint setting to the next. Monolithic trees reaching for the sun by the thousands. Towns in which the exteriors of buildings had changed little over the last fifty years, except to have been sanded and painted a couple of times in the interim. And the cars that adorned the town squares had been steadily updated through the decades. If I tried hard enough, I could imagine these same towns being not altogether different in an era that predated motor vehicles.

As the afternoon waned and the sun attempted to force me to look it in the eye, I kept a lookout for a place to bed down for the evening. Before long, billboards pointed me toward an RV park beside Lake Columbia. As good a place as any.

I pulled off the highway onto a county road that eventually gave way to a packed gravel drive. The attendant at the park's entrance booth was accustomed to vehicles much larger than my motorcycle. I killed the engine when I pulled to a stop at her window. She immediately started talking, but I couldn't hear whatever it was she said, so I tugged my helmet off my head and took out my ear buds. "Ma'am?"

"Can I help you?" she asked.

I knew what I wanted, but since I didn't have any familiarity with RV parks, I didn't know the lingo. Even if I managed the correct terminology, I wasn't certain she would let me sleep there. I half expected to be dismissed outright with a grunt and a wave of the hand.

I placed my palms on the small of my back and stretched. "I need to rent a lot for the night."

She was as suspicious as I had expected. She looked me up and down, trying to decide if I was just messing with her. "You want to rent an RV space for your motorcycle?"

"Yes, ma'am. Just for the one night." I let the Texas drawl that I usually kept tucked away, sneak out just a bit. Maybe she'd find me more trustworthy if I wasn't some city slicker. Of course, there had never been any love lost between Texas and Arkansas, so this wasn't a surefire plan.

"There's a motel up the way." She nodded her head toward the west.

"Budget's pretty tight." That wasn't strictly true, but whatever.

She leaned toward the glass. "You got anybody else in your party?"

I looked around, unsure why I was doing so. I would've been as surprised as anyone to have seen somebody back there. "Nope. Just me. Party of one."

"You gonna need power?" she inquired.

I shook my head. "No power."

"Water?"

"Nope. No water either. Just a space."

"Uh-huh. Be ten bucks." The attendant shook her head slightly. Maybe she thought I was still yanking her leg, and telling me the cost would draw an end to the tomfoolery.

I reached into my pocked and pulled out a couple of sweat-dampened five-dollar bills.

She didn't make a move to collect the money.

"Should I pay you now?" I asked as the bills fluttered between us in my hand.

"Huh-uh. I'll send the super around later to collect it. But don't get too cozy 'til you talk to him. He may not cotton to this arrangement," she warned.

I nodded, thinking that my foam ground pad and sleeping bag weren't likely to lend themselves to too much coziness regardless. I was getting too old for cowboy camping and should have sprung for a motel, but I had a reason for it. Maybe not a good reason. But it was still a reason. Trying to prove something to myself. "Alrighty. Expecting any weather tonight?" I asked.

"Nope. Be fine. But the skeeters are pretty fierce. Rained a couple days ago."

That may prove problematic. Mosquitoes down here can carry off small children, and I hadn't brought a tent or bug spray.

She pointed me through the entrance. "You can go on to Lot 37. Super'll be by in a bit."

# Chapter 2
# Leering at Lake Columbia

I bounced my way through the pitted gravel driveway and found the wooden marker numbered 37. I parked and dismounted my motorcycle for what I hoped would be the last time that day, then walked around like a saddle-sore ranch-hand for a bit and tried to work out all the kinks.

I took stock of the lot that the attendant had assigned me. Despite her skepticism concerning most everything about me, she had given me a scenic space close to the shoreline and, more importantly, in proximity to the bathroom. So I had that going for me.

I'm not much of a planner. Well, that's not entirely true. When things involve other people, I'm a meticulous planner. No, that's not true either. Sometimes, I'm good about planning things. Other times, I wing it. The results are mixed.

Within about an hour of my arrival, I began bearing the brunt of my personal failing. Dinner consisted of a couple of granola bars while folks around me cooked on barbecue pits and over open fires. It was nearly intolerable. I buried my nose further into Stephen King's *Wizard and Glass*, but even that was insufficient to keep me from being drawn back to the smells that inundated the park. Birds and sausages of all sizes sizzled over fires in every direction.

I began re-evaluating everything in my life that had led me to that hungry place and realized that I had drawn someone's attention. Their pity followed. A beefy man walked toward me with a plate in his hand. He was backlit by the setting sun, so I couldn't tell what was on the plate. But it didn't much matter.

"Looked like you were a little low on provisions," the man said as he got closer.

I hung my head in shame. "That obvious, huh?"

"The wife noticed you over here. Our boys are grown, so she's always keeping an eye out for someone she can mother."

Feeling inhospitable, I said, "I'd offer you a seat, but as you can see, I haven't even got one for myself."

"I'm good," the man said. "Been sitting most of the day. Eat up while it's still hot."

I inspected my plate, which was complete with plasticware and a paper towel. Barbecue chicken, green beans, mac and cheese, and cornbread. I shoveled several bites into my mouth and made sounds of approval. He smiled and patted his belly. "She's a looker and cooker."

I paused my chewing, trying to figure out whether that's an expression I'd heard before or something he made up. I picked up the cornbread. "You got an oven in that camper?"

"Nah. The missus cooks it over the fire. Don't know how she tolerates it in this heat, but I'm sure as hell glad she does."

With a mouthful of the stuff, I grunted my agreement.

"Alright. I'll leave you to it … well, I was gonna call you by name, but I realize now I didn't even introduce myself. I'm Clarence. Wife is Evelyn."

I stood to shake his hand, wiping the crumbs and chicken grease onto my pants. "Scott Warren."

"Nice to meet you."

"Same," I said. "Thanks for the grub. And the company."

Before he walked away, he asked, "What're you gonna do about the mosquitoes?"

"Are they really that bad?"

He raised an eyebrow. "I don't expect you'll have a drop of blood left in you come morning."

"Great."

He gave me a half smile and feigned tipping his cap as he turned and ambled back toward his campsite.

My eyeballs fussed at me about being suffocated by my contact lenses for too long, so I peeled them off and popped them into their container. Surely, the solution would cleanse them of the grime from my fingers that hadn't been properly washed all day.

The RV park was more vibrant and communal at night than I'd expected. This place was a people-watcher's paradise. People didn't stay within their family groups. They migrated from one fire to the next, meeting the folks who would be their neighbors for a week or maybe only a day.

At first I thought it was a socioeconomic difference, but was soon dissuaded of that. People in mobile mansions that cost more than my house — scratch that, Ashleigh's house now — were as generous with their company and food as those dragging aged pop-up campers behind their bedraggled pickup trucks. It was a difference in lifestyle, and I could see the appeal.

The bathrooms, on the other hand, left something to be desired. The sweetheart at the front didn't seem to prioritize attending to these facilities. I guess, when most everyone else brought their bathrooms with them, I was in the minority of folks making use of them anyway.

After what was hopefully my last foray of the evening away from my campsite, I flipped on my lantern and read *Wizard and*

*Glass* for as long as my eyes could tolerate the strain of the limited light.

With everyone else still going full tilt and me getting an early start in the morning, I stuck my foam ear plugs in and scrunched into my sleeping bag. Within minutes, I was pouring sweat. It was still over eighty degrees outside, and I'd brought a winter bag.

This wasn't going to work. But I couldn't lie here uncovered either, or the hordes of mosquito would drain me of my blood. Besides, lying in bed — even when the bed is just a ground pad — totally uncovered is one of the most exposed feelings I can imagine.

As I sat contemplating my situation, I noticed a man halfway across camp, leaning against a tree. He was unmoving and appeared to be facing me, watching me. But between him being back-lit by a streetlight and me not having my glasses on, it was hard to be sure.

I scooched over to my motorcycle and felt around in the saddlebag for my glasses case. I was about half sure that once I got them on, I'd discover that the looming figure was a shrub or a cutout like one of those cowboy silhouettes.

It wasn't.

Without looking away from him, I removed my earplugs. The muffled din returned to full volume as my brain struggled to compensate for the sudden change. I tugged on my jeans and boots. Still, the man leered my way like we were in a Western. I pushed myself to my feet and walked toward him. I don't know why. It went against all my conflict avoidance tendencies.

He wasn't more than a dozen yards away when a flock of middle grade kids sideswiped me as they migrated across the grounds. Profuse and well-mannered apologies followed the collision.

When I looked up again, the man was gone. No disappearing into the shadows. No vehicle skittering off through the gravel.

Gone as in vanished. No sign that he'd ever been there. Just gone.

I kept walking toward the tree where he had been only seconds earlier, most of my senses on high alert. I did a lap around the tree, even being so thorough as to peer up into its boughs in case he was some kind of freak tree climber.

No sign of him.

I strode back to Lot 37 and packed up. Between the mosquitoes and the ... whatever that was, I was done with Lake Columbia. My watch told me it was just after 9:00. There were 550 miles between me and Amarillo. I was pretty darn wide awake now. I could put a couple more hours in tonight before turning in, again. Next time would be at a roadside motel.

# Chapter 3
# Meeting Fiachra Sid

**Six Days Later**

My legal assistant leaned into the doorway. "I've been meaning to ask, but it's been a hectic few days — how'd the trip to Texas go?"

"Kind of a disaster on most fronts, but I had a good meeting with the clients. We should keep getting plenty of work from them."

"Glad to hear it, James Dean. Your ten o'clock is here."

I finished the paragraph of the brief I was working on and looked up. "I don't have anything at ten."

"Your calendar says you do."

I definitely hadn't scheduled anything, but I went to my email calendar and checked anyway. Sure enough, I had an appointment on there. "Did you put this on here? Who the heck is Fiachra Sid?"

Annie said, "No, and he's the tatted-up guy in the lobby. When you're done with him, I may take him home with me for my lunch break. I think he's in need of some attention."

"Nice. Super helpful. Also, no … uhh … cavorting with clients."

"Is he a client?" she asked.

I raised my arms out to the side. This wasn't going to be my best meeting, on account of I didn't know what I was walking into.

A minute later, she walked the man who was apparently Fiachra Sid to my office. As he walked past her, she checked him out from head to toe, and there was no doubt about her intentions for him. When I really looked at him for the first time, my jaw fell open. "You."

"Yes. Me," he said and stuck out a hand that might as well have been a bear's paw. "Fiachra Sid."

I recovered my decorum. "Hi, Fiachra. I'm—"

"I already know your name," he said abruptly.

Okay. This was not getting less weird. "I think I owe you an apology, Mr. Sid. I didn't have this meeting on my calendar, so I'm not entirely sure what we're doing here."

"No apology is required. I set the meeting."

His brogue was so thick, and his words tumbled out so fast, that I could hardly understand what he said. My Southern ears were accustomed to much slower speech patterns.

"With Annie?"

"No."

I clenched my jaw. I had a thousand things to do, and none of them included meeting with someone who was being intentionally vague. "Why don't you tell me why you're here since you seem to be the only one who knows what's going on, and it seems an awful lot like you might have been following me around halfway across the country?"

"I can explain."

"That would be nice."

"This will take a while." He reached into the front pocket of his pants and retrieved a pipe and pouch of tobacco. "Do you mind?"

"There's about a half-dozen laws against smoking indoors."

"I did not agree to abide by them."

I cocked my head to the side. "That's not ... how laws work." If he turned out to be one of those sovereign citizen quacks, there was no way I was taking this case. There's not an hourly rate high enough to deal with that bunch of hogwash. Actually, that's not true. There's almost always a big enough number.

"You will find that I'm not beholden to them," he said.

I scratched at the crown of my head, not that it itched. I needed something that I had some semblance of control over, because this thing was spinning. And we hadn't even gotten to the question that should have been the first thing out of my mouth. "Why have you been following me around?"

"I needed to know that I could trust you."

"Trust me? I'd have been glad to send you some references."

He smiled grimly. "I do not think you will have the right kinds of references."

"Then I may not be the right person for ... whatever this is."

"I have considered that possibility."

I rubbed my eyes with the heels of my palms, then shook my head. "I've got to tell you, man, this has been peculiar. I know that's not polite. But it is what it is."

"My apologies. I am unaccustomed to interactions like this with huma—with people."

A tingle hurried down my spine.

When you're cross-examining witnesses, the key to extracting more information from them than they want to give (aside from kindness, which is a hugely underrated asset) is silence. People are really uncomfortable with silence. I like to just let it hang in the air after they think they've finished answering my question. That silence will get thick as a castle wall. And people can't help but to fill it. Anything to alleviate the discomfort and awkwardness.

But not this guy. He seemed more at ease when we stopped talking. I was the one who couldn't let go of him using *human* in that way. The inference was clear. He recognized that. It's why he had gone with *people* instead, but he'd already let the cat out of the bag. Except him being non-human wasn't possible. So the real revelation here was that he's totally nuts.

"I need to know what that means."

"I misspoke," he said.

I cocked my head to the side. "No, you didn't. Someone who misspoke would've offered an excuse and a clarification. But not you. You spoke some iteration of the truth, or at least what you think is true. However, my plate's pretty full right now, so I'm going to extricate myself from this situation and call an end to this meeting. Then I'm gonna have an early lunch and play Call of Duty for about an hour." I stepped forward and gestured toward the door. "Annie will show you out ... happily."

"I need your help."

I didn't want to take the bait, but I could hardly help myself. "Why me particularly? You haven't even begun to tell me what it is you need help with."

"Words matter. I need someone who chooses their words with care and says precisely what they mean. That is the first thing."

"And the second?"

"You have a child. A daughter."

The hair on my arms and neck bristled. "Walk carefully."

"I am not threatening her. She is already in danger, but not from me."

I took another step forward so that I was uncomfortably close. He stood several inches taller than me. His tobacco-laden breathing remained even and unperturbed. The jets of air from his nostrils cascaded across me. "You need to leave."

He turned and walked out of the office without another word.

I gave it several minutes before I dashed out of my office and across the street to where I had parked my car on the third level of the deck. My degree of breathlessness by the time I sat in the car and had it cranked reminded me that I hadn't started running again like I'd been promising myself. I broke a bunch of traffic laws on my way through downtown Birmingham and into Homewood, but at least had the decency to slow down once I was in the neighborhoods.

My car wasn't even fully stopped in the driveway when I threw my door open and popped out. I rushed to the door and tried the handle. Locked. So I whipped out my key and fumbled it into the deadbolt.

In the entryway, all was quiet and still. Until a banshee in a charcoal skin care mask and a bath towel nearly bludgeoned me with a flashlight. I caught her by the waist and tried to keep her at arm's length. "Ashleigh! It's me!"

She dropped the flashlight onto the rug. The loud clank suggested the tiles underneath didn't appreciate it. She'd always hated the tile entry anyway.

"What the—what are you doing? You can't just let yourself in."

She'd gone from scared to angry. Of course, she was right. I couldn't just let myself in. It wasn't my house anymore. I hadn't considered that. Hadn't considered anything beyond Ella being threatened. "I just—"

I just ... what? Had a meeting with someone who was possibly not human and thought our daughter was in danger? That wouldn't do.

"Just what?" she insisted.

"Forgot something for work. I came here out of habit, I guess."

"Uh-huh." She wasn't buying it. "Listen. Whatever you

thought was going to happen here in the middle of the day while Ella's off at school is absolutely not happening."

Oh no. She clearly had the wrong idea about my intentions. "No, no, no," waving my hands in protest.

"Hold on. I have to take this mask off." She squatted down to get the flashlight, holding onto the top of the towel so it wouldn't come untucked. She pointed it at me and, with a tinge of anger still in her voice, said, "Don't go anywhere."

She retreated to our bedroom. Nope. *Her* bedroom.

After the water cut off, she returned with pinkish cheeks and still wrapped in her towel. Now she was just messing with me. She could've changed if she'd wanted. But she knew I liked it when she strode around the house in a towel. It was as much about what you couldn't see as what you could.

Sometimes, it *was* about what you could see. It wasn't all that long ago that the best part of my day was when she would run naked through the house because we'd run out of clean towels in our bathroom. I would stop what I was doing to make sure I didn't miss the second pass, and couldn't be more disappointed when she returned with a towel wrapped around her. She would grin at me with a twinkle in her eye, knowing what she'd deprived me of.

Not anymore. That wasn't the world we occupied. There were no twinkles.

"You can't come over unannounced and let yourself in."

"I know," I said with the appropriate tail-tucked tone in my voice.

"Well, if you know, why did you do it?"

I've heard her use that some line on Ella dozens of times, and I didn't care for being treated like a child.

"You're sure Ella's at school? She's okay?"

"Yes, she's at school. Don't be weird. You know that if she's not, we get a text, phone call, and email simultaneously at like three seconds after ten o'clock."

She was right. That didn't occur to me. I looked at my watch. It was well after ten now. If something was wrong, we would have known. If I hadn't gone off half-cocked, I'd have realized that.

Besides, Fiachra Sid hadn't actually threatened her. He said she was in danger. But how did he know anything about her to begin with? So many more questions than answers.

Now, I was here in what was becoming an increasingly uncomfortable situation from which I needed to remove myself.

"Listen," I said. "Sorry. I just … you know. Sorry." Nice. Very eloquent.

She gave me a patronizing smirk. "You'll show yourself out?"

I nodded and turned toward the door.

"Scott …"

I paused, watching her through the reflection in the frosted glass on the door.

"Call before you come by next time." Even though she said it as sweetly as she could, it still stung. But not nearly as much as when she dropped her towel just as she turned the corner, knowing that I could still see her. The woman still had my heart, despite everything. She'd promised nothing like it would ever happen again. But it shouldn't have happened in the first place. That was the whole point. And I was unwilling or unable to forgive it, as much as I wanted to.

So I made a choice. If I couldn't forgive her, I better let her go. I still don't know if it was the right call, but there was no going back.

# Chapter 4
# Absurdity Abounds

I swung the front door to the office open a few minutes before nine. Annie was already behind her desk, fingers flying all over the keyboard. She looked … different. When I set her coffee on her desk, I asked, "Why are you dressed like that?"

"Like what?" she said, suppressing a grin.

"Well, for starters, it's not jeans and a sweatshirt. You look like you going out with your girlfriends after work and don't plan to leave the club until the sun's already coming up again."

"That sounds like a compliment, though I'm certain you don't mean it that way."

"I bet you're even wearing your shoes," I said, adding, "And I bet they're heels."

"As a matter of fact, you're wrong … sort of. They are heels, but I already took them off. I can't be expected to be confined to foot prisons all day."

"Alright, hillbilly. You still didn't answer why you're in a little black dress."

"Do I have to have a reason?"

"Yes."

She turned her attention back to her monitor. "It definitely

19

doesn't have anything to do with the scrumptious man you're meeting at nine o'clock."

The church bells tolled the hour as she said it. "I don't—daggumit. This again?"

She shrugged. "He asked me to set it up as he left yesterday. You'll be glad to know I didn't jump his bones on the way out. I'm a person of great restraint."

I looked her up and down. "Clearly. You didn't think to mention that he was coming back?"

"He said you requested it."

"Great." I turned toward my office and pushed the door open. I nearly spilled my coffee all over myself when I found a hulking figure waiting for me in the high-back chair I kept in the corner for reading.

He stood to greet me. "Maidin mhaith."

I plastered a smile on my face and said hello. I set my coffee on the desk and dropped my bag onto the floor before excusing myself from the room.

As soon as the door latched behind me, I growled at Annie. "Don't you think you should have told me he's already here? And why is he in my office without me? That should never happen."

She got up out of her chair and stood a little closer than was comfortable. Her cheeks flushed as she pointed a finger at my chest and said in a low tone, "Mr. Warren." She never called me that. I knew I was in trouble. "You need to check yourself. I work here at this firm with you precisely because you don't talk to me, or anyone else, in the way you just did."

"It's not the great pay and benefits?" I tried some humor. It didn't land.

"I could do better at Trader Joe's," she said flatly. "Second, I didn't let him in. I didn't know he was in there."

I'm sure the surprise showed on my face. Nothing happened

around here without her fingerprints on it. The paralegals resented it, but this was Annie's house, and she kept it in order.

"Then how did he get into my office?"

Now that my tone had softened, Annie took a step back and sat in her chair again. "Dunno. I went and peed earlier. Maybe he let himself in."

I turned around without saying another word and headed back to my office. "I accept apologies in the form of sweets," she called.

I pushed my office door open and stalked in. "You shouldn't have let yourself in."

He stood up as I entered. "I agree it was improprietous, but you would not have met with me otherwise."

"Yeah, and I have a good reason for that — you brought my daughter into this."

"No. We need to make an important distinction. I brought your daughter up, but I didn't bring her into anything. Others have done that, but no more or less than they have done with other children."

"Stop." There was more force behind it than either of us expected. I was sure Annie had heard it, too. "If this conversation is going any further, you're going to tell me who you are and what you want."

He gestured at the chair he'd been sitting in. "May I?"

I nodded and seated myself in one of the chairs on the visitor side of my desk. It wasn't comfortable. That had been intentional. It kept people from staying an unreasonable amount of time, but now I regretted having sat here instead of in my desk chair. I'd wanted to keep the desk between my guest and me, but the comfort the extra space and large obstacle provided was undermined by the stupid chair.

Fiachra Sid sat quietly, watching me fidget. I stilled myself. "Ready when you are."

"Do you consider yourself an open-minded man, Mr. Warren?"

"Like about religion or politics or what?"

"In general. Are you generally open-minded?"

I shrugged. "Without more context, I'll have to give you a frustrating lawyer answer — it depends."

Fiachra nodded. "Are you willing to suspend what you think you know to broaden the scope of your understanding?"

"Listen, for the sake of brevity, why don't you just say whatever it is you have to say and then I can decide whether I buy it, okay?"

He looked directly into my eyes for an uncomfortably long minute. Once he'd sized me up, or whatever he was contemplating, he mumbled an affirmation and leaned forward, resting his elbows on his knees. "I'm a fairy."

I laughed. It wasn't malicious. It's a coping mechanism in tense situations and has caused me innumerable problems my entire life. "You built that up pretty big for a small payoff. My wife's cousin is gay. You'll get no judgment from me. But I probably won't use that word. It has a negative connotati—"

"No. You misunderstand. I am a literal fairy."

"Uh-huh." I rubbed at the scruff on my chin. "Just so we're clear — literally literal or figuratively literal?"

"Literal."

"Okay." This was why I hated impromptu client meetings. It's why we used questionnaires. So that I could familiarize myself with the issues ahead of time, and not sit here stumped while the client waited for my synapses to fire. Not that the form would have addressed this particular issue.

"For what it's worth," he added, "fairies are asexual beings."

Annie was in for some disappointment.

I set aside the extraordinary skepticism that resided in the chair with me and to ignore every instinct that told me to shed myself of my visitor. Instead, I dug in. I've examined lots of witnesses I don't believe. You can't uncover the holes in their story unless you dig. "I don't mean to be insensitive, but you're not really what I expected a fairy to look like."

"You expected Tinker Bell or Cinderella's godmother?"

"I mean, *expected* is probably the wrong word altogether. I hadn't *expected* to meet a fairy at all. But yeah, that's definitely the depiction I have of fairies."

"That is to be expected. Disney has done both humankind and the Fae a great disservice in that way. It has encouraged people to deal casually with fairies, which couldn't be a more treacherous undertaking."

"And let's not forget the tooth fairy," I added with irreverence.

"Let us not forget the tooth fair*ies*. Plural. They are what brings us together."

"Tooth fairies? Sorry, that's a bridge too far."

"Is it? You created them."

"*I* did?" I didn't bother to be polite and hide my incredulity any more. My thoughts painted themselves all over my face and in my inflection.

"Not you specifically. More of a general you. Americans."

"Okay. Americans have been blamed for a lot of things, but this is a first."

"You all created the tooth fairies. They are a uniquely American invention."

I held up my hands. "Wait. We made up the idea of the tooth fairy — if that's even true. I've never thought about it before — but we didn't create any actual tooth fairies."

Raising an eyebrow at me, he said, "You think you bring the idea of a thing into the world without creating the thing itself? That is rather a rosy perspective of a world without consequences."

"Come on." I stood up and paced around the room. "This is absurd. I don't even know why I haven't asked you to leave yet."

He ignored my skepticism. "Humans and fairies have lived adjacent to one another for millennia. Sometimes in harmony, other times as adversaries. But in all that time, there were covenants, rules of engagement that most abided by. Detractors were ... dealt with. Only since the so-called Enlightenment have humans disregarded the knowledge they've harbored since Creation because they've found that it no longer comports with the limited worldview with which they have encumbered themselves. And now this new breed of fairies is not beholden to the old covenants, are not beholden to anything other than their own selfish whims. Much like their American counterparts."

"Uh-huh. That was very ... practiced. Have you been working on that for a while?"

A grin crept up on one side of his face. "I have. Did I oversell it?"

"Yeah, a bit."

He nodded. "That doesn't make it not true."

"So ... what? This new brand of fairies — tooth fairies — doesn't do things like the old guys want, so y'all want them to get off your lawn. Is that about the sum of it?"

"Would that it were," Fiachra said with a pained expression. "What do you know about the Fae people?"

"Who?"

He sighed at me. "Fairies. Fairy culture."

"Oh." Finally, a question with a straightforward answer. "Basically nothing."

"As I said, there are rules. They exist for a reason. One of these rules is that you never give a fairy your true name, as names carry great power."

I connected a couple of dots. "Is that why you interrupted me when I started to tell you my name yesterday?"

"Indeed," he said, nodding his head. "Before I finish making my point, let me ask you a question."

I waited, neither giving permission nor denying it.

"Has your daughter begun losing her teeth?"

I gave a tentative yes, entirely uncomfortable with her being brought up again.

"What happened to it? The tooth?"

I thought back a couple of weeks. "Don't know. Never found it after we put it under her pillow."

Even though I knew that was the answer he expected, a dark expression crossed his face. "If a name carries power, how much more lives within a bone? The tooth fairies used to be a breed of mischievous wildlings. More recently, they have organized and cast off the moniker *tooth fairy*. They have taken to calling themselves The Bone Collectors Guild."

"Teeth aren't bones," I said for the second time in a week.

He held his arms out. "Nevertheless."

I sidled around my desk and dropped into my chair. "I think that's about all I can do for today. I've got a fair bit to consider, not the least of which is whether I'm losing my mind."

"You are not losing your mind."

"But of course, you would say that, right?"

He shrugged noncommittally.

"Can you meet tomorrow? I've got court at nine, but we could meet for breakfast before that. The Pancake House at eight?"

"Ay."

"Look, if I don't show up, it's because I've decided this is nonsense and checked myself into a mental institution."

Fiachra nodded with a smirk and showed himself out. My body slumped further into the chair, unwilling to support both itself and the weight of all this new information.

I wasn't kidding about not knowing whether I'd meet him the next day. But being true to my roots, I also thought it would be rude to ghost him without telling him in advance of that possibility.

Several minutes later, Annie stepped into my office. She had changed into her standard office attire and cut off any comment I might make. "I don't want to hear it. I only came in here to ask what the insurance company thought of your virus exclusion idea."

"Well, they didn't love losing hundreds of millions of dollars because of some missing language, so they were pretty receptive to my proposals. We have another meeting in a couple of weeks to finalize the policy language."

# Chapter 5
# The Virus Exclusion

**Seven Days Earlier**

This wasn't the first time I'd stood in front of a boardroom of insurance executives telling them why they were hemorrhaging money, but it was the first time to have one of these meetings in person since the onyx flu brought the world to a standstill. Everything old felt new again. The jitters were a little more exaggerated than I remembered them being before, and I was glad that I'd gone with half-caff coffee at breakfast.

Before I started my presentation, I looked around the room at the folks whose company had been hit hard in the last couple of years by payouts it had to make because of the onyx flu, while its competitors were able to deny the same claims and just sit back on their laurels collecting premiums. I made eye contact with as many as were willing to do so.

"Let's talk about this in general terms before we identify the specific problem and what we can do about it. Insurance policies include two important parts: the terms of the policy and any exclusions that apply. There's other stuff in there too, but that's not what we're here about today. When you started getting hit with onyx flu claims by the businesses you insure, you had to determine whether there may be coverage under the insurance policy.

"Since your policies are occurrence-based policies, you had to decide what an *occurrence* is under your policy language. Basically, your policy defines *occurrence* as an accident. While the onyx flue isn't an accident in the traditional sense, when your policy later defines accident, it includes 'continuous or repeated exposure to the same type of harmful conditions.' Everybody with me so far?"

Heads bobbed up and down. That was good. We'd have big problems if I'd lost anyone this early on.

"Here's where we get to the kinds of claims that gave y'all fits. Your policies provide coverage for lost business income. This usually results from some kind of physical loss or property damage. Like, if there were some kind of accident that happened to a business that caused it to close temporarily—"

"Like a fire?" one of the junior executives offered with helpful optimism.

"Exactly. When that happens, you have to cover the lost business income. So when claims started coming in for the onyx flu, the first question you had to to ask to figure out is whether onyx flu caused a physical loss or property damage to a business you insured."

Some neighbors murmured to each other as they leaned heads together. Others exchanged knowing glances with cross-table counterparts. We were getting to the crux of the problem.

"Now, your policies include insurance coverage for pollutants, and in some ways, the onyx flu is similar to a pollutant. Think in terms of fumes and vapors. Like them, the onyx flu can cause physical damage to the property that isn't visible to the naked eye.

"Because you didn't have the benefit of knowing how courts would answer the question in this brand new context, you had to assume that courts would allow the virus to fall within the definition of a pollutant."

I didn't see anyone mentally checking out yet. This stuff was dense, but we had to get through it so they could understand how to fix it.

"Even if a claim triggers coverage because of an occurrence, it must still contend with any applicable exclusions. To combat having to pay out on these types of claims, many policies specifically exclude claims that involve the transmission of a communicable disease, and specifically viruses or bacteria. Your policy doesn't have a virus exclusion, so when those claims started rolling in as businesses shut down, you didn't have any reasonable grounds to deny the claims, and you lost your shirts."

One of the mid-level execs in a white shirt and no tie raised his hand. I pointed at him. "Why didn't we have a virus exclusion?"

"That's a good question and not one I can answer. I'm kind of like the middle innings relief pitcher. I'm here to force a couple of outs and get you out of a jam. But if I had to guess, it's because your company wasn't around during the previous pandemic, and it didn't occur to whoever developed these policies to include it. A simple oversight."

"An awfully damn expensive one," one of the gray hairs grumbled.

"Undoubtedly," I agreed. "But we will draft a virus exclusion to insert into the policy so that if future variants shut things down again, or if there are other similar events that come down the pike, you'll be in good shape."

Mr. No-Tie said, "What about other things? Like things we don't know about yet?"

A woman across the table rolled her eyes. "That's what reinsurance is for, Gordon."

The meeting went on like this for a while with back-and-forth about other exclusions that should be considered and what the language would look like. I promised to have a draft within ten days. I could have had it within the hour, but this wasn't the atmosphere for it. Too many folks (like Gordon) who would want to offer their unsolicited and uninformed input.

Annie scrunched her face up. "No, that's super exciting. I'm glad you told me in so many details. If I have any trouble sleeping tonight, I may give you a call and ask you to tell it to me again."

I turned to my computer and waved her off. As she returned to her desk, I reread the virus exclusion that I had drafted to be included in my client's now-standard policy. It would probably next come in handy in a hundred years or so whenever there was another global pandemic. In the meantime, it would sit in the policy, completely ignored, like most other coverage exclusions.

I revised section under Exclusions to include viruses, bacteria, and communicable diseases. That should help them preclude coverage for the things they want and keep anything from falling through the cracks.

It's funny how one little paragraph (or its absence) can be the difference in so much capital changing hands. A lot was riding on those words.

# Chapter 6
# Meeting at the Pancake House

The next morning, I got up with the sun. The birds were already telling their neighbors about having made it through another dark night. Squirrels scoured the pecan tree for any opportunity for an early harvest.

With a legal pad tucked under my arm and a cup of coffee in hand, I went out to the enclosed back deck that overlooked the woods behind my rental house. Of course, *rental house* was overstating it a bit, but telling people I was renting out the basement apartment of a house while the family lived on the top two floors sounded weird. Paying for two households was more than my law practice could sustain, so sacrifices had to be made. The one redeeming quality about the place was that it backed up to the woods that were home to a spring-fed creek.

I set my coffee and paper on the side table and myself on the dew-covered chaise lounge. I groaned. Summer down South coated everything in a layer of condensation in the mornings, and I was so consumed with Fiachra Sid that I hadn't paid any mind to it.

I grabbed my yellow legal pad and tried to refocus my attention, though with every movement, my clinging shirt served as a constant reminder that it was wet. Setting that aside, I scratched notes about everything I could remember of my conversations with Fiachra over the last two days.

Three pages later, I reached for my coffee to discover it was now approximately the same temperature as the stuffy air around me. Ashleigh still would have dra=unk it, but I wanted my coffee hot as hell's pepper patch. If it wasn't on the threshold of burning my lips, I wasn't interested. The mug sat unattended while I returned to my legal pad, reviewing what I had written and filling in blanks.

When I thought I'd captured all the relevant information, I checked my watch. If I jumped in the shower right away, I would have time for a walk downtown before meeting with Fiachra. I was a firm subscriber to Nietzsche's idea that all great thoughts are conceived while walking. And I could use as much greatness as I could muster right now. Weird things were afoot.

No one else was in my office building when I got there, a time of day I usually coveted. No incoming emails or phone calls. No one to pop in and ask a question or give an opinion. But today, I just dropped my bag in my chair and walked out again, locking the door behind me.

I tapped the screen on my watch and pressed a couple of buttons so it would be sure to give me credit for going on an outdoor walk. I always wanted proof of any exercise I did. It helped keep my doctor off my back. Thanks to some bad genetics, my blood pressure was high enough that he doubted I ever ate anything green or intentionally elevated my heart rate. That made me a good fit for the legal profession because an inordinate percentage of us are given to dying at our desks.

I struck out on the sidewalk, crossing one empty street after another, not even bothering to slow at intersections because the morning traffic hadn't made its appearance yet.

I stopped mid-stride when I noticed red lights staring up at me from below the sidewalk grate. Normally, I walked around the grates. I'd read an article once — Or was it a scene in a movie? It doesn't matter — about the number of people who fall through grates each year. Admittedly, it was a small number when you consider the number of people who walk on city sidewalks. Even so, there was some chance of it happening. An avoidable chance. My recent motorcycle acquisition aside, that should tell you most everything you need to know about that state of my risk aversion.

Most days, I sidestepped and went around, or course-corrected, as I approached one of the grates that littered the city sidewalks. But not today. I must have been feeling adventuresome considering recent events.

Regardless, as I walked across the sidewalk grate, I watched the ground, waiting for signs that it would buckle under me and I would fall to my death. I saw something I had not seen before. Could not have seen before because I didn't have the right angle of view — two red lights in the tunnel that ran under the sidewalk.

They were peculiar enough that when my feet hit the pavement again, I circled back and took another lap. This time, as I walked, the lights blinked. Not blinked in the way that a light flicks off and comes back on. They blinked the way something does when an eyelid closes over it and reopens.

I'm a rational person, so I talked myself into the most obvious solution. I had walked past something that had momentarily interrupted my view of the lights, and my imagination had taken off at a sprint. Cutting my walk short, I headed directly to the Pancake House a few blocks away. I needed to shed myself of Fiachra Sid before I got too wrapped up in his craziness.

He had been seated already when I arrived. The largest

western omelet I've ever seen hung over the sides of his plate. I looked at my wrist. I was early. Fiachra gestured at the chair across from him, so I pulled it out and sat.

"Morning," I greeted.

He gave me a thumbs up. The server returned to the table ostensibly to get my drink order, but she had eyes only for Fiachra. And hands too, apparently. She kept one on his shoulder the whole time she was at the table. I ordered a coffee, and Fiachra ordered a Nutella crepe for me with promises that it would literally change my life.

When the server left, I asked, "What is it with you and women? Is it part of your fairy thing? Annie was about ready to take you home with her the other day."

"It's not only women." He grinned unapologetically. "I've it dialed back as much as I can, but it's the nature of things. Fairies are an evocative lot."

"Do you ever ... uhh ... capitalize on the opportunities?"

Fiachra furrowed his brow. "That is rather a personal question. Particularly as it comes from someone who doesn't believe most of what I tell him."

I grimaced. "Sorry. You're right. My apologies."

He flashed another smile. "But I will answer it. Asexual, remember?"

"Ah." I'd forgotten that part of our conversation from the day before. Another thought crept in and escaped my mouth before I could censor it. "Then how do y'all procreate?"

"We are begotten," he said. "Are you familiar with that word?"

I was, but only in one context. "As in John 3:16? 'For God so loved the world that he gave his only begotten son...'?"

"Yes, exactly."

"I'll be honest. I don't really know what the word means."

He appeared unsurprised. "To produce as an effect."

I shrugged and shook my head. The definition meant nothing as applied to what we were talking about.

"You need to connect the dots. Fairies do not reproduce. I have already told you how the tooth fairies were created as a consequence of evolving human mythology. However, we are not all manifestations of human imaginations. The earliest of us have been around since the dawn of time, and for better or worse, we are inextricably tangled up with you lot."

I considered that for a while before asking what seemed to be the natural follow up. "And if we quit believing? What happens then? You cease to exist?"

He smirked. "We are not so fragile as that."

We sat in silence while he ate his omelet and I waited on my crepe. After it arrived, Fiachra decided he was ready to talk again. "I feel like our interactions have been rather one-sided."

He wasn't wrong, but I wasn't sure what he was prompting me for either. "Yeah, that happens when you tell somebody fairytales are real and there's allegedly a whole other world they know nothing about."

He cocked an eyebrow. "Allegedly?"

I nodded.

"We'll come back to that," he said. "Right now, here's what I want from you."

"I guess I knew this was coming."

"Explain baseball to me."

I sputtered and nearly choked on the bite of crepe I had shoved in my mouth. That's not what I was expecting. I pounded my chest a couple of times with a closed fist, but waved off the concern that he showed. After I took a drink of coffee and recovered myself, I shook my head. "Can't be done. I once took a group of Brazilian lawyers to a Birmingham Barons game and spent the whole time explaining to them what they were watching. They were totally baffled by the sport."

"Sport?" he scoffed. "Fat men are playing. How is that a sport?"

I shrugged, disinterested in arguing the merits of baseball as a proper sport.

"You do not believe me," he said.

I took another bite of my breakfast and considered how best to answer. "It's just rather unbelievable, in the most literal sense. What you are saying is so far outside my own experience that I have no context for it. Besides, I am a lawyer. I am trained to follow the evidence, and so far, there has been no evidence that anything you've said is real."

"Fine. Let's provide you with some evidence." He motioned for our server.

I hadn't exactly expected him to slink away when I demanded evidence, but I hadn't thought he would play along either.

The server handed me the bill. Of course. God forbid we inconvenience Fiachra with it. I skimmed the ticket. "A six-egg omelet?" I asked, turning it toward him.

"I was hungry."

Leaving the money on the table, I stood up to leave. Fiachra followed suit. Once we were out on the sidewalk, the peculiar fountain of a goat reading to the other woodland creatures stared at us from across the intersection. I'd always thought of it as uniquely representative of Five Points South. But maybe it was a more literal depiction than I'd ever presumed.

My skepticism was losing its foothold on the idea that the world was as relatively normal as I'd always believed it to be. But before the walls could come tumbling all the way down, I needed evidence.

My career was built around the ability to prove my arguments. Or more accurately, since I'm usually on the defense side, my opponents have the burden of proving by a preponderance of the evidence that what they're saying is true. They have to show that a thing is more likely than not. If you had to put a percentage on it, it has to come to anything more than fifty percent. That's what I would hold Fiachra to — can he prove to me by some form of evidence that it's more likely than not that he's a fairy? If not, I would try to put this entire episode behind me, which would require the skills of a *very* open-minded psychologist.

What if he did give me adequate proof? I reckoned we'd cross that bridge if we came to it.

# Chapter 7
# The Proof Is in the Bread

Fiachra looked at me with open contempt. "So what do you want me to do, find a pumpkin and turn it into a carriage?"

"Is that on the table?"

"No. There are several kinds of fairies, but none of us does that nonsense."

When we turned from 20th Street onto Highland Avenue, I asked, "Are we headed somewhere particular?"

"Yes and no. You know the round building a couple of streets over?"

"The abandoned one with bars all the way around it?"

"Yes, that's where we are going."

"Is it ..." I didn't even want to say it out loud. It felt ridiculous. "Is it magical or something?"

Fiachra smirked and looked at me quizzically. "No, it is abandoned. If you are demanding a demonstration, I thought some isolation would be preferable."

We passed the next three blocks in silence until we arrived at the round building. I'd always thought it odd to have a circular building, particularly one this small. I had assumed the offices inside would all be pie-shaped. Nothing about it seemed practical.

Fiachra stopped at the ground level entrance on 21st Place and retrieved a key from his pocket. I was mildly annoyed, having expected magic to accompany everything. So far, my fairy friend had been extra ordinary. The first floor had only a bathroom, a reception desk, and an iron spiral staircase. The air was thick as molasses and still stifling from the prior day's heat. It was so stagnant that I was sure this was the first time anyone had disturbed it in weeks, maybe months.

I followed Fiachra up the stairs, which he ascended without placing his hands on the rails. When my head popped up to the second level, I found that I'd been wrong about wedged offices. This floor was one large room that, because it being of a round building surrounded by windows, gave its occupants a 360-degree view. Unfortunately, this was no longer one of Birmingham's finer areas.

When I'd finished taking in the panorama of empty parking lots and vacant buildings, I turned to Fiachra, who was ... no longer human. To be fair, he'd never been human. But now, he didn't appear human.

His skin was a teal hue that undulated slowly between green and blue. He was still imposingly tall and muscular, disabusing any notion that fairies were dainty things. As best I could tell, there weren't any wings bound under his clothing.

"Well?"

I gathered I'd been gawking for a minute. "Whoa," I said in an awed whisper. "How did you do that?"

"Which part? What you had seen until now was an illusion of sorts. A form that I can take upon myself. Humans have a hard time coping with the alien and unexpected." As if anticipating my thoughts about whether this was sufficient evidence the Fae were real and he was one of them, Fiachra said, "The proof is in the bread, no?"

My head tilted to the side. "That's not how that expression goes."

"But the expression makes no sense. You proof bread. Even alcohol is described in proofs. But pudding? No."

I had no answer for that. He wasn't wrong. "I assume it's a British thing. Aren't you from that part of the world?"

His skin tones darkened and took on a red flavor, making it more purple than anything else I could identify. This was a whole new level of wearing your feelings on your sleeve. The change was more than just visible. The air prickled with intensity, almost like a static charge. "There are many layers of ignorance in your question."

"My apologies," I said, trying to diffuse things. "I'm still finding my way around with all this. Maybe you could enlighten me?"

His demeanor cooled. "Many hundred years ago, there were no British. What you call British is a muddled confluence of conquerors and oppressed peoples. There is an evil that dwells in the southern half of that land. It compels its inhabitants to subjugate and establish their dominion. They attempted the same with us, so we vacated the land. We maintained relationships with the peoples you know as the Scots and the Irish, and to some degree, the Germans. But again, a unified Germany is a modern invention. Those who dwelt there were once as diverse as the land itself. It was a simpler time, uninhibited by a drive toward homogeneity. Unencumbered by a need for sameness and uniformity."

"This may be a weird thing to say, but you speak beautifully. Nobody talks like that anymore."

He seemed pleased. "I have had a long time to practice with the language."

Fiachra's youthful appearance made me contemplate whether he was an ancient being that he claimed to be. Even if fairies didn't age like us, you'd think gravity would still have its effects. If I could bottle some of that up, I'd have it made.

"Now, as for the question of where I am from … we call it Sidhe Baile."

"Never heard of it," I said.

"I did not expect that you would have."

I shifted my weight from one hip to the other and wished that whoever had last leased the space would have had the decency to leave some chairs behind. It was awkward to have this long of a conversation standing in an empty room. But it would have been even more awkward to plop down on the floor.

"So where is it?" I asked when Fiachra wasn't forthcoming with more information.

"Adjacent to your plane of reality. Never too close, but neither is it too far."

"Could you take me there?"

He nodded. "I could, and perhaps the time will come that I will. It is a hazardous place for any stranger, and particularly those who do not abide by our ways. Humans have not fared well in Sidhe Baile. They have a way of being extraordinarily arrogant about whose customs should be observed."

I pursed my lips. "Yeah, that checks out."

"We still have much ground to cover, but that will have to suffice for now. Are you convinced that I am who I say I am?"

"I guess. But I have more questions. What's the hurry?"

"I am in no hurry, but you indicated that you have an appointment at the courthouse at nine. And as it stands, you are going to be late."

An icy ball of panic formed in my belly. I looked at my watch. I had gotten caught up in this madness and totally lost track of time. I was absolutely going to be late, which never sits well with any judge, but particularly this one, who rules his court-room like a tyrant.

I hurried toward the stairs without any kind of farewell.

From behind me, Fiachra called, "The judge has run into some obstacles this morning and will be late for court."

My eyes widened, and I turned. "Did you—"

He was gone. I stood alone in an abandoned circular building, completely awe-stricken. Presumably, that was the effect he was going for.

# Chapter 8
# Pillow Fight

As soon as the credits started rolling, Ella asked, "What are we gonna do now?"

The clock sitting on the side table read well past nine. "What do you mean? It's already past your bedtime. We've got to clean up this disaster of a room and turn in for the night."

Popcorn bowls and candy wrappers littered the floor around us. And not far from them was a half-assembled Lego set. "I hate cleaning up," she whined.

"You and me both, kiddo."

"So I don't have to do it?"

Her youthful optimism was endearing, but it was my dad-duty to crush it. "That is not at all what I said."

A glimmer skittered across her eyes. "I have an idea."

I was skeptical. These ideas always ended up being pretty one-sided. "Go on."

"How 'bout you clean up while I go brush my teeth and get my PJs on?"

I pitched a throw pillow at her. "How 'bout no way, Jose."

She launched herself across the sofa, leading with the pillow as both a shield and a weapon. Her war cry was more adorable than fierce. I fended her off with one hand while I floundered around in search of another pillow that I knew was on the floor.

Ella's tiny fist slipped off the pillow and smashed into the bridge of my nose. My hand that fended her off instinctively went up, and the full force of her six-year-old self fell on my already searing face. The cackle that burst out of her reinforced my belief that all small children are sociopaths.

My free hand finally found the pillow on the floor. I swiped upward and smacked her in the face. She dropped her weapon and covered her mouth with a look of shocked dread. When the blood seeped between her fingers, the dread transferred from her to me. She pulled her hand away from her face and the sight of blood evoked a scream. From her, not me.

"Let me see," I said.

She clamped her mouth shut and covered it with her hand, smearing blood across her lips and cheek.

Anxiety gave rise to panic. How bad was it? Ashleigh was going to kill me. "You have to let me see."

She shook her head, but there wasn't any conviction behind the gesture. I peeled her hand away.

"Open," I instructed gently.

She scrunched her face and spit into her hand. A tooth landed amid a puddle of bloody spittle.

My eyes widened in surprise.

A gappy smile broke out on her face. The hole in the bottom row had doubled in size. I pulled my phone off the side table and turned the camera on selfie mode so she could check out the new development while I went to get a couple of wet paper towels.

As I wiped the blood from her face, I asked, "Was that one loose?"

She nodded.

"Head to the bathroom. We've got to rinse it in warm saltwater."

"Why? No. It'll hurt."

"It doesn't hurt," I reassured her, even though I couldn't remember whether or not it hurt.

Ella protested. "We didn't do it last time."

"Last time, it was so loose it came out without even bleeding. Go on. I'll meet you in there."

In the kitchen, I poured a measure of salt into one of Ella's plastic cups and filled it halfway with warm water. When I got to the bathroom, she was leaning in toward to mirror jutting how lower jaw out like a shih tzu, with the tooth on the countertop beside her.

"It stopped bleeding," she said. "We don't need the saltwater."

"Move your tongue."

She rolled her eyes. When she moved her tongue out of the gap, blood seeped out of the newest opening.

I held out the cup of saltwater, which she grabbed reluctantly. "Why do I have to do this?"

"It stops the bleeding and kills the germs. Or something." I couldn't remember if that was right. It was just the thing you did because that's what your parents did to you.

She took the cup with a sigh.

"Don't swallow it. Just swish it around and spit it out."

I should have been more specific with my instructions. Ella didn't lean down when she spit, so as much red-tinged saltwater went into the sink as coated the mirror and countertop. "Nice."

I reached into the cabinet for a washrag that I dampened and handed to Ella. "Here. Wipe the blood off your face before it dries and we have to scrub at it."

I was wiping down the wet surfaces with a hand towel when Ella asked, "Have you ever had to scrub dry blood off someone before?"

Kids have no idea how messed up the innocent questions they ask are. Or at least how screwed up the answers are. I wasn't ready for the sweet little six-year-old with a smattering of freckles splashed across her nose and cheeks to hear the answer to her unsuspecting question. "No, baby girl, I don't recall having to do that."

"I'm not a baby. Babies don't lose their teeth."

"Fair."

Mercifully, that seemed to distract her from any follow-ups on the previous topic.

"Still got your tooth?" I asked.

She held it up. "Can we call Mommy and show her?"

Guess we're about to find out if Mommy was really having that quiet night of sappy movies and a self-administered mani and pedi. I pressed the video chat button. When Ashleigh answered on the third warbly ring, I already had the camera pointed at Ella.

"Hey, Mommy."

"Is everything okay?" Her voice was thick with concern.

"Daddy knocked my tooth out!"

"Awesome," I muttered.

"Oh?" Ashleigh said.

"Maybe give her some context, Ella," I suggested from off camera.

Ella giggled. "We were having a pillow fight, and he whacked me in the face. Blood was everywhere."

I whipped the camera around to reassure Ashleigh. "Blood was not everywhere."

She smirked. *My Best Friend's Wedding* murmured in the background, and nail supplies were strewn around her. "Did it bleed? How'd she do?"

"It bled some. She was a champ. Definitely handled it better than you would have."

"Turn the camera around," Ella demanded. "I want to show Mommy the hole."

## Casual Business with Fairies

I swiveled the phone toward Ella, who had her jaw unhinged as far as it would go. Ashleigh's squeamishness at the sight of blood was clear, even through the phone. When Ella held the tooth up to the camera, I knew that Ashleigh would have looked away.

"Let's let Mommy get back to doing her nails. Then you and I have to clean up and get you in bed?"

"I still have to clean up?" Ella fussed.

"Well, yeah."

"You're going to make that poor girl pick up after you knocked her tooth out?" Ashleigh piled on.

"I don't need you to tag-team here," I grumbled. "Alright, Ella, tell Mommy night-night before she gets in trouble."

Ella giggled. "Night, Mommy. Love you."

"Love you too, Butterbean. See you Sunday."

Ella waved.

I clicked the phone off without turning it back toward me.

"Okay, little one, hop up and go brush your teeth. Be super careful not to poke the place where you just lost the tooth."

"Can I just brush the top ones?" she asked.

"Sure."

While she brushed, I tidied up the living room with the minimal amount of effort I could spend and still see a result. After I heard the toilet flush, I went to Ella's room. I set her tooth on the nightstand and turned back the bed as she narrowed down which stuffed animals would accompany her. Once she'd jumped onto the bed, she lifted her pillow.

I placed the tooth on a specific design under the outer quarter of the pillow, where I knew I could find it in a couple of hours.

I turned off the lamp and kissed Ella on the forehead.

"Prayers," she reminded me.

After we said our nighttime prayers, she asked, "Do you think I'll get ten dollars again?"

"I think the tooth f—I think you get more for the first one than for the others."

"Say goodnight to my stuffies."

By some miracle, I remembered all their names as I worked my way from closest to furthest in proximity to Ella.

I pulled the door closed, but not clasped, and returned to the couch, where I collapsed and searched for something to watch for the next hour until I could handle the last of my dad duties for the day by swapping out a tooth for some cash.

Three episodes of *Seinfeld* were just what I needed to pass the time without too heavily engaging my brain. I stood up and stretched before heading to my room in search of a five-dollar bill. When I started working downtown, I quit carrying money in my wallet. That way I wouldn't be lying to the panhandlers when I told them I didn't have any cash. But now, when I needed it, it was always an effort to scrounge up some cash. I remembered having some Susan B. Anthony's tucked away in a baggy inside a pickle jar where I'd stored spare change for years.

Before I went into Ella's room, I readied the coins in one hand and held my phone in the other with my thumb over the flashlight. I nudged the door open with my shoulder and was pleased to find Ella cuddled on the opposite side of her pillow from where I'd stashed the tooth.

I sidled up to the bed and gently raised the pillow. Nothing was under it. My heart beat faster. I passed my hand over the sheet in case it had just been lost in the pattern, ready to scoop up anything solid that I touched. When that yielded no results, I kneeled on the floor and shone the light under and around the bed.

But I knew the deal. I wasn't going to find anything.

Ella's tooth had been scavenged by the Bone Collectors Guild.

# Chapter 9
# Losing Touch

I didn't sleep. Not a wink. It wasn't for lack of effort. I'd much rather have been asleep than saddled with my new reality, in which I could no longer disregard Fiachra Sid as some trickster with extraordinary abilities.

At some point in the night — I don't know exactly when because time kind of melted there for a while — I rummaged through my work bag and dragged out the legal pad that I'd scribbled my notes on two days earlier. As I read through them, I became starkly aware of how much they sounded like the ravings of a madman. If Ashleigh ever found this, I'd never be allowed unsupervised visits with Ella again. I could always tell her I was working on a novel. That would certainly be more believable than the truth. Lots of lawyers are convinced they have a story inside them. It's just that most of them write legal thrillers and courtroom dramas, not fantastical stories about evil bands of tooth fairies.

When Ella got up a little before seven, two sports show hosts were arguing about rookie quarterbacks that no one had seen perform yet. The volume on the television was set just north of audible. I wasn't really paying attention to it, but more silence was intolerable because my brain was filling the vacuum with a bunch of racket.

Ella walked up to where I was lying on the couch. "You look really bad. Are you sick?"

"Thanks. That's very kind of you to point out."

She shrugged. "I'm just saying."

Easily my least favorite expression of the last twenty-five years. As if you could justify any remark by tacking that to the end of the sentence.

"No, I'm not sick," I said.

"Why do you have the same clothes on as yesterday?"

I gestured at her princess nightgown. "So do you."

She scoffed at me. "These aren't clothes. They're pajamas."

It's amazing how certain kids can be that the adults in their lives are morons. Makes you question yourself. Especially when you've spent the entire night contemplating the reality of tooth fairies and why they're stealing kids' teeth. She was just pitching more fuel on the fire.

The clock was a couple of ticks shy of eight when I couldn't wait any longer and called Annie.

She answered with a husky voice. "Someone better be dead for you to be calling me this early on a Saturday morning. No, scratch that. Not dead. If they're already dead, then there's nothing anybody can do for them anyway. So this better be the last resort call that saves their life. Is that what this call is?"

"Umm … no?"

The line went dead.

I returned to the couch, noting that magical cartoon ponies had overtaken my sports programming. I had barely sat down when the phone rang. It was Annie.

I answered by saying, "No swearing. Ella is close enough to hear you."

She sighed at me. "Well, I'm awake now. What do you want?"

"I need Fiachra Sid's contact info."

"That's it?"

"Yes."

"It's really this pressing that you called on a Saturday morning?"

"Annie, have I ever called you this early on a Saturday before?"

"Are you gonna tell me why?"

"No."

"Okay. Give me a couple of minutes."

The line went dead again.

Ten minutes passed. Then twenty. I was getting fidgety when Ella said she was hungry, so I went into the kitchen to pour her a bowl of overly sweet cereal. The phone rang in the living room. I dashed in to grab it.

"Daddy, please don't talk in here. I can't hear."

I gave her a thumbs up and waited until I reached the kitchen to answer. "Give me a sec to get to a pen and paper."

A dejected Annie said, "You don't need it. I don't have any information for him. He's not even in the system."

"How is that possible? Intake is the first thing we do, even before we set up the meeting."

"I know how we do intake. I'm the one who does it."

"Do you though?" I said, letting my frustration get the best of me.

"I know you still don't believe me." I could hear the restraint in her voice, as she was trying not to fight my snarky comment with her own, "but I didn't put that appointment on your calendar. And as best I can tell, no one else did either. So there wasn't any intake."

"I believe you."

There was a pause on the other end. She was considering why I was willing to believe something that couldn't happen.

"Did you do it?" she asked.

A reasonable conclusion. Just not the correct one.

"No. Not only did I not do it, I wouldn't know how if I had to. Between that and issuing subpoenas, there are just some parts of this operation that I leave entirely up to y'all."

"It doesn't make sense. Like, it can't happen. Someone can't just show up on the calendar like that."

It can when there's fairies involved. But I wouldn't burden her with that knowledge. "It's fine. Don't worry about it. I'll figure something out."

Another pause, before she asked with a quiet voice, "Can I ask you something? Are you involved in something, like, bad?"

I laughed. Sort of. Maybe? But definitely not in the way she was thinking. "No, everything is okay."

"But that's what you would say, even if it wasn't."

Ella traipsed into the kitchen with an impatient expression on her face. I held up a finger for her to wait, but she shook her head. She poured the milk into her cereal and carried the bowl into the other room.

"Look, things are a little wonky right now. But it's fine."

"If you say so."

"Can you just do me a favor and check again to see if we have any kind of way to get in touch with Fiachra?"

"I will, but we don't."

She had already double checked. Thoroughness and attention to detail were among her best qualities. They were how she'd become my right hand, by filling the gaps left by my weaknesses. I'm the twenty-thousand-foot guy, not the minutiae guy. Actually, she was more than an appendage. I'd cope better without a right hand than without Annie. The only problem was that she knew it.

"Just humor me," I said. "See you Monday."

I returned to the living room and plopped onto the couch. How could I find Fiachra Sid when I had no way of contacting him? I racked my brain for the most fairy-like place in Birmingham. It's not something I'd ever thought about before, and I didn't immediately come up with any place more likely than another to host a congregation of fictional creatures.

I pushed myself up and announced to Ella that I was going to take a shower. On the way to the bathroom, it struck me. What I was looking for wasn't in Birmingham. It was in Montevallo.

"Hey, Tiger Lily, when I get dressed, we're taking a field trip."

"Where to?"

"A park?"

"Is there a big slide? Slides are my favorite."

"Maybe? I'm not sure. That's not why we're going. We're gonna take a walk in the woods."

"Great," she mumbled. "Sounds like fun."

I thought I had a half-dozen more years until the sarcasm took root. Guess not. She is her mother's child, after all.

"It's pretty cool," I said, trying to talk her into some interest. "A long time ago, someone carved a bunch of faces and figures into the trees."

"Uh-huh."

I wasn't making any headway, but I had one last card to play. "It's supposed to be magical."

A glimmer of interest kindled on her face, but it didn't last. "Whatever."

# Chapter 10
# An Extraordinary Patch of River

After I dropped Ella off with her mother on Sunday morning, I knew that I'd make myself stir-crazy if I went back to the apartment and puttered around. I needed something to do to distract myself from the urgency I felt about reaching Fiachra and the total impotence that came along with having no way to do so. The magical park in Montevallo was a bust. Just a trail where someone had carved whimsical faces into trees.

I grabbed my fishing gear and went out to my motorcycle, tossing the slingpack and water bottle into one saddlebag and stuffing the waders and boots into the other. When I had finished strapping my fly rod holder and landing net across the back seat, I readily conceded that a motorcycle wasn't the most utilitarian choice for transporting gear. But nobody ever bought a motorcycle because it was practical.

By the time I got my helmet on, I was already sweating. With this kind of heat and me not having a boat, there was really only one place to go. The most extraordinary patch of river in Alabama is Blevins Hollow at the base of Smith Lake Dam, where the water is a crystalline teal and cold as glacier runoff, even in the summer. The state stocks it with trout, so it's become a haven for fly fishermen in northern Alabama who would otherwise have to go north into the Smokies to find waters cold enough for trout.

The trouble with this spot on the Sipsey Fork is that it's run by the power company, who opens the dam on a schedule. It's necessary for generating electricity, and it's how the river stays so cold year round. But if you don't check the schedule before planning your trip, you may have your outing wrecked by torrential floodwaters.

I realized as I turned off the interstate onto Highway 69 that I'd forgotten to check the website. I'd just have to hope for better luck than I had any reason to expect. Another twenty minutes of riding through rural countryside filled with mobile homes and signs for half-million-dollar lake houses brought me to the river and my turnoff toward the dam.

I drove slowly past the prescribed landing sites, where there was roadside parking. I kept going until I reached the power substation, deciding to park here and hike to the shallows closest to the dam. I could always fish my way back down toward the parking area, shortening the hike back, which was always the worst part of any outing.

The mile-long hiking trail from the parking lot to the tailwaters of the river just south of the dam is mostly unremarkable. It is almost as though its true purpose, beyond physically transporting you to a beautiful place, was to give your mind about twenty minutes to relinquish its cares and prepare for immersion.

Maybe that's overstating things. I was in kind of a weird head space. And it needed decluttering. Who was that lady on Netflix who helped people tidy their places up? Maybe she was a head shrink, too.

I emerged from the woods into a clearing, and the Sipsey Fork opened up in front of me. Shallow and rocky, with plenty of fallen trees and boulders to give the fish a place to hang out while they waited for a meal to float by. Most trout are opportunistic predators. They aren't actively hunting — except for the young ones, who haven't quite figured out that if they'll just wait long enough, dinner will come to them. Patience has never been a virtue possessed by youth.

I was counting on the juveniles today. I didn't need a trophy, just some entertainment.

As I picked my way carefully across the rocks alongside the river, I noticed a woman ahead of me sitting on a small boulder. Her pack was open beside her, and she was tying on a new fly, a midge by the looks of it.

She looked up when she heard the scraping of my feet and the swoosh of my waders. I offered a "Howdy" and a half-smile.

Her auburn hair framed her face and was held partly at bay by the sunglasses she'd pushed back on her head. "Caught a tree," she said.

I scrambled for something to say. "Did it put up a fight?" Immediately, I began figuratively punching myself in the face.

With her chin, she gestured down at the box of flies and tippet in her lap. "The tree always wins. It's a of law of nature."

I smiled and moved on downriver before I could say anything else regrettable. Given the opportunity, I would invariably do so. Worse than the doing was my intractable memory for such instances. They could fill a notebook. I was smart enough to know that I wasn't witty, but not smart enough to quit trying to be. Ashleigh had found it endearing, though I was mostly galled by it. I suppose that's how most of us are about our quirks and shortcomings.

I picked out a spot with a large flat rock, where I could set my stuff down and get situated. The rod that I brought with me was an old fiberglass rod I was given when my Papaw died. I'd never known him to fly fish before. He'd taken us grandsons fishing plenty of times, but he spent most of those trips corralling us and untangling lines. When he did get to fish, I got the sense that he didn't want to be bothered with catching anything. He just wanted to be out there casting and reeling and tending to his thoughts.

At the time, that seemed awfully boring to me, but I have come to understand it. Most of the time, it was enough to be out there on the river. But not today. Today, I needed the rush and distraction of catching, which effectively guaranteed that I wouldn't.

I looked at the olive woolly bugger that was tied on to the end of my line and decided to give it a go. It was usually a fly that was better for catching bass and sunfish, but there was no accounting for what fish would decide looked tasty on any given day.

I used my landing net to corral the trout without losing him. I soothed him with some soft words as I jostled the hook out of his lip. It probably wasn't any consolation to him that I'd flattened the barb on the hook, but I felt better about it.

I got my phone out of the chest pocket of my waders to snap a couple of pictures of him. He wasn't all that big, but any fish is noteworthy when it's the only one you catch. I'd been out there an hour or so and had a few nibbles, but nothing bit. The most frustrating part of fishing waters as clear as these is being able to see the fish swim up to your fly, nudge it with their nose or take a non-committal nip and swim away.

After those pictures, I decided that the trout and I needed a selfie together. But I didn't want to take him out of the water because oxygen is already so scarce for them when the weather is hot, and I didn't want to distress him. I turned the phone ninety degrees in my hand a couple of different times and couldn't figure out how to get both of us in the frame. I wasn't doing a very effective job of working within my constraints.

"You need a hand?"

I about jumped out of my skin. There was a snicker behind me. I turned around to see the woman I'd spoken to earlier.

"You got a guilty conscience?"

I was totally confused. "Excuse me?"

"Anybody that jumpy is either Catholic or carrying around a guilty conscience."

Having caught up, I nodded my head. "I don't want to speak out of turn on account of I'm Baptist — or at least my parents raised us that way. I don't know what I am now — but I think those two things go hand-in-hand."

She smiled and pointed at my net, which miraculously still held a fish. "You still want that picture?"

I nodded. "Sure."

She gestured for me to hand her my phone. She pointed it at me and pressed the shutter button a few times, then started thumbing at my phone. I thought maybe she was taking a lot of time to make sure she got a good one. When she handed the phone back to me, she said, "I'm Sam."

"Sam?"

"Sam, as in Samantha. But nobody calls me that except my mother. And then only when I'm in trouble."

I raised an eyebrow at her. "Aren't you a little old to be getting in trouble?"

"I don't think that's something you outgrow."

"Fair enough."

"Anyway, my name and number are in your phone now. Sam Roberts."

"Just like that? You don't even know my name."

She shrugged. "Anybody that goes to the trouble to make sure they don't hurt a fish can't be all bad. Besides that, I have a theory that fly fishermen are abnormally conscientious people."

"Interesting. Got any data for that one?"

"Not yet. It's more like a working hypothesis. Text me. Let's get dinner."

Then she just walked away. As gracefully as anyone I'd seen walking in felt boots. She picked her way across the rocks with the nimbleness and precision of a cat.

The fish had finally wriggled its way to freedom. For it to have taken him that long, he definitely wasn't the brightest his species had to offer. I decided to pack it up and head back to the bike. There was nothing that could happen now that wouldn't somehow spoil the day. And there was no way I was going to turn off the side of my brain that analyzed and critiqued my involvement in a truly unexpected flirtatious conversation.

# Chapter 11
# The Eight Commandments

I finished breakfast at the kitchen table as I perused news headlines on my phone. War, pestilence, and famine. Repeat. It was like something out of the Old Testament.

The first thump on my door startled me nearly to death. By the second, I was on my feet and nearly to the door when the third resounded in my ears.

The peephole showed an imposing but familiar figure. I yanked the door open. "What the heck, man? Are you trying to knock the door down?"

He brushed past me into the apartment.

"Come on in," I grumbled. "Make yourself at home while you're at it."

"It is time," he said.

That was sufficiently vague that I had no idea what he was talking about, but I had something I wanted to address. "Where have you been? I've been trying to get ahold of you for a couple of days. But I don't have a way to reach you. I went all the way to Orr Park to find you."

"Gross. No. That place is an abomination," he chastised me. "It is time for you to go to Sidhe Baile."

That shut me up momentarily.

"Before you go, we must discuss the eight commandments of interacting with the Fae, else there is little chance of you returning."

That one sentence left a lot to unpack. I started with the most obvious. "Eight? You know there's like four thousand years of precedent for ten commandments?"

Fiachra wasn't interested in chatter. He was far more serious than usual. I took my cue from that, but there was little chance of us getting through this without wisecracks.

I got out my phone and opened my notes app, ready to type.

"What are you doing?" he asked.

"I don't want to forget these commandments."

"Your devices will not work in Sidhe Baile. You must commit them to memory." He jumped in without further interlude. "One. Never eat fairy food. The food of the Fae will force you to stay in Sidhe Baile indefinitely and make you intolerant of human food. It cannot satisfy the needs of your human body, but it will keep your from dying. So you will live a miserable, craven existence until you choose not to live any longer."

"Geez. Are all eight of them this uplifting?"

He ignored me and continued his delivery. "Two. Do not accept a gift from a fairy. You do not want to become beholden to one of us. They will require repayment, and you will not know until they come calling what price they will require."

I wondered if Yahweh took inquiries from Moses when he was delivering the Law or if it was a forty-day monologue while Moses scratched everything out on tablets.

"Three. Never give a fairy your name. Names hold power — we've already been over this one. Either deflect, or if you must give a name, give a fake name you can remember. They likely won't give you their name either. Are you still with me?"

I nodded.

"Four. Always be polite to the Fae, but do not conflate

manners for kindness. They are not the same. You will be expected to conform to our morals and social norms, or you will offend someone. Punishments for selfishness, rudeness, and impropriety are swift and severe."

In my head, I sang the tune of a Bon Jovi song. *"Woah, we're halfway there ..."* And I might need to catch up on my prayers if I was going to make it through this.

"Five. Do not stand in a fairy fainne. When a tree dies and its anam departs, it creates a temporary portal to Sidhe Baile, marked by a ring of mushrooms. As long as the fainne persists, the portal can be accessed. If you attempt to use it without a chaperone, you could get stranded for centuries. If you are fortunate enough not to get stuck, you will proceed to Sidhe Baile, where you will be treated either with great deference as a guest or you'll be imprisoned, depending on who you encounter first.

"Six. Never go back on a promise or lie to one of the Fae. Fairies cannot lie, and they will expect the same of you. Not that you should take what they say at face value. There is a significant difference between not lying and being truthful."

I jumped in with a question. "Didn't you just tell me to lie about my name? I feel like I'm getting conflicting advice."

"Not advice," he corrected. "Commandments. Advice is a recommendation. These are so much more dire. But about your name, note that I told you to deflect first. In this case, between being dishonest about your name or giving it, lying is the less hazardous option. Seven. Do not apologize or express gratitude. Both indicate indebtedness, which you must avoid at all costs."

I am a person who always wants the *why* of things. It's the reason I decided not to join the military. I got the distinct impression no one would be compelled to answer *why* questions about the orders I was given. Turns out, judges aren't always inclined to answer that question about their orders either. Fiachra was falling into the same camp — here's what you need to know, but not the reason behind it.

"Eight. There are always strings attached. Always. To everything."

I raised my eyebrows. "That's it?"

"It is imperative that you commit these to memory. We are not humans. Your rules are not our rules. Your ways are not our ways. You would do well to think of us as aliens and yourself as entering an alien land. Though, in fact, it is rather the opposite."

"How are we going to get there? To Sidhe Baile? Use one of those mushroom rings?"

"Fairy fainne," Fiachra reminded me of the term. "No. They are too fickle. It is more a question of how we are going to get *you* there. I can come and go as required. For this, we need a totem." He walked around the room, scrutinizing any knick-knack he could find. These were sparse as the place was spartanly decorated. "Do you have something small that is closely associated with your family lineage?"

"What size are we talking?"

"Able to be carried in a pocket."

I ambled over to my desk, pulled something out of a coffee mug, and held it out for Fiachra to see. "A letter opener my grandfather brought back from Germany after World War II."

Fiachra reached for it and shuddered as his hand approached the object. He swiftly retracted his arm. "What is it made of?"

"Not sure. Maybe steel. They made a lot of that in Germany back then. Still do, I guess."

He shook his head. "That will not do."

I thought through everything that might be lying around and came up empty. "I don't think I've got anything like what you're talking about."

"Do you have anything pertaining to rabbits?"

My confusion must have been transcribed all over my face, because Fiachra repeated himself. "Rabbits. Fluffy, bouncing creatures."

"Yeah, I know what they are, but why rabbits?"

"Warren. Your family name. Warren is a place where rabbits breed."

Did I know that? I don't think I did. At the very least, I'd never put it together before. Regardless, it sparked something. I held up a finger and walked out of the room.

On the small bookshelf I kept for Ella when she stayed the night was a pocket-size edition of *The Tale of Peter Rabbit*. I tipped it back and snatched it off the shelf.

When I presented it to Fiachra, he nodded. "That will work." Before taking the book, he reached into a pocket and withdrew a small leather pouch. He unknotted the strap that gathered and closed the pouch's top.

"Open the book."

I held it in one hand and flipped it toward the middle with the other.

Fiachra withdrew a pinch of a shimmering substance from the pouch and sprinkled it over *Peter Rabbit*. The air became effervescent and danced as the fine powder flitted onto the exposed pages.

He tucked his pouch away and took the book into his hand before pronouncing it good.

I was incredulous. "You were giving me a hard time about Tinker Bell when we met, and now you're just going to sprinkle fairy dust over this? It's basically the same thing."

He shrugged. "Some legends are born out of reality." He handed the book across to me, but didn't release it when I gripped it. "Do not lose this. Do not let it leave your person. Without it, there is no guarantee of you getting back."

Only when I expressed my understanding did he let go. I shoved the now-glittery book into my back pocket and lamented that cargo pants had never come back into style. Ashleigh had gotten rid of mine shortly after we got engaged and forbid me from buying more. I gave her my most compelling argument about their utility, but she wouldn't be swayed by my reasoning. She never fully subscribed to the idea that form follows function.

"Ready?" he asked.

"I guess. How does this work, exactly?"

# Chapter 12
# Inside Sidhe Baile

Fiachra clasped my hands with his own. "Close your eyes. This will be disorienting." I did as instructed, and moments later, my stomach lurched like we'd driven over a hill at high speed.

When he released my hands, I opened my eyes to see that he had reverted to his native variable coloring. He blended in with the shadows of the trees that surrounded the mountain meadow in which we stood. It was immediately apparent that he was more a part of Sidhe Baile than apart from it.

"This way," Fiachra said, starting down a path that led from the meadow into the woods. The mountains that rose around us weren't the towering, stony peaks of the Rockies. These were much older, worn smooth by time. They reminded me of North Carolina but wore a more brilliant green than even those mountains.

Under the canopy of trees, the forest wasn't shy about displaying its grandeur. Strewn about everywhere were ferns large enough to lie across and patches of any kind of berry you could want. I stopped in my tracks at the sight of a black bear not twenty yards from us picking berries and putting them in a basket. Putting *most* of them in a basket. Every third pawful went to her mouth.

Fiachra must have sensed that I was no longer following him. He returned to my side. "That's Cassandra. She has a place at the market. It would be a much more profitable venture if she didn't … hang on … you have an expression for this."

Still mostly speechless, I pointed at my chest and formed a question on my face that said, *Me?*

"Plural *you*. Humans. Just remembered it — she gets high on her own supply. Literally. She sells rhododendron honey. She and the bees have arranged a split commission. I don't know the finer points of the deal. But it's amazing stuff. The most vivid hallucinations."

I wasn't sure someone hadn't already slipped me some.

"Come," he said. "There is much for you to see."

He wasn't wrong. Even the things that he found ordinary were popping with colors so vibrant it was as though the artist who created the place bumped the saturation levels several degrees past normal. When the Fae visited our world, they must have found it terribly drab. Or maybe it was refreshing to be somewhere that their senses weren't being overloaded.

The path we were on broadened into a lane, and before long, the forest began giving way to structures. The buildings increased in frequency and complexity as we entered a town. Children with purple and orange coloring peered at me with curiosity from inside doorways and around corners.

"Is it unusual for someone like me to be here?"

"Unusual, yes, but not so unusual, as if I were to appear in my own skin in your world. Still uncommon enough to be a curiosity for the young ones. You will note the sideward glances you receive from the elders among as. That is because your visits are ominous. Most humans do not come here as a matter of course. You do not trade with us like the trolls or other woodland creatures. When humans come here, it is because you want something."

"And me? What do I want?"

He stopped in front of an extraordinary hut, whose thatch-work was much more intricate than I'd seen before. Not that I was an expert in the field. He turned to me with a wry smile. "More than other humans, you are a bit of an oddity here, in that I have brought you here because I need your help." He opened the door. "Please come in."

Fiachra kept the tidiest house I'd ever seen. Everything was in its place. Fastidious was the word that came to mind. It wasn't altogether different from what a cabin built from stone would have looked like in the decades before electricity. I must have made a noise upon noticing the stone walls.

"What is it?" Fiachra asked.

I gestured at the walls. "I'm surprised you use stone. It seems cumbersome."

"What else would we use?"

"Wood," I suggested.

He scoffed. "I suppose we could, but that seems awfully inconsiderate. 'Oy, Mr. Juniper, I know you've been growing there for the last sixty years, but would you mind if I cut you down and chopped you to bits? You and your children?'"

I was bewildered. "Your trees are sentient?"

"I do not know. But why should I assume that because they cannot communicate with me that they are incapable of great intelligence? Maybe it is we who are insufficient. Did you know a grove of aspen trees is a single organism? Imagine what a collective conscience like that is capable of. A single tree can live up to two hundred years. A copse would have thousands of years of life experience. And you would have me turn it into floors to be tread upon."

Nicely done. I'd been in Sidhe Baile for less than an hour, and I had already offended my host.

"Sorr—"

"Do not apologize. Remember the commandments," Fiachra said hurriedly and with authority. Then he sat on a large cushion on the floor and spoke more softly. "We occupy different worlds, and though they share many commonalities, the rules and customs will differ. We must both remember that. Besides, are you not familiar with thermal mass? A stone home heats efficiently in the cold winter months."

I plucked up some courage. "Can I ask you a question? It might be personal."

"Proceed."

"If you don't … uhh … procreate, why is it that you still appear male?"

The color in his face shifted several degrees. Was that embarrassment?

"We are not male and female as you are. But that does not mean we are not without variation. I am masculine. Others are feminine. We were created so. It is a spectrum that provides for optimal companionship."

"Uh-huh."

"Now, can I ask you about your penis and testicles?"

"Excuse me?" I said in surprise.

A smile played at his lips, but his eyes showed he was tired. The way an entire day of parenting is exhausting and unrelenting. All the way down to your bones, and there's somehow still another hour before bedtime. I was definitely contributing to it, but I suspected there was more to his weariness than dealing with me.

Despite his condition, he recalled his duty to be a good host and offered me tea.

A wry smile crossed my lips. "The commandments?"

He hung his head in mock shame. "Of course."

I sat down across from him. "Why did you bring me here today?"

"You know, most people would have asked that question much sooner."

"Maybe I'm a simpleton."

"That, you are not. There is a gathering I want you to attend with me. We will have to cover you. It would be problematic if someone perceived you to be human."

I considered what kind of gathering he would want me to see. There was only one answer. "The Bone Collectors Guild?"

He nodded.

"Are there enough folks in your village for a rally of any size?"

"It is elsewhere, quite some distance away. A city much larger than ours."

"When?" I asked.

"Just after sunset."

Several hours away still, but if it was far, it seemed to me that we should already have been heading toward it. When I suggested that to Fiachra, he shook his head. "We will get there the same way we got here."

"Teleportation?"

"We do not think of it as such, but yes. It is a great luxury. We have monthly allotments, so we use it sparingly. But when you have been invited to a dinner party and do not want to appear travel weary upon your arrival, it is a good option to have."

"Or if you have a human with you and don't want everyone else to know about it."

"Ay, that too," he said. "Now, how shall we pass the time until we must go?"

If I couldn't eat, I would rather not be idle. "Can you show me more of your village and the woods?"

"That I can do," he said, pushing himself to his feet and reaching down for my hand with his cool, blue skin.

# Chapter 13
# A Gathering

After a time, Fiachra looked toward the setting sun. "It is time we get ready for the gathering that brought us here."

"That's pretty non-specific. Anything else you can tell me?"

He turned and headed back toward his home. "The Bone Collectors Guild is holding a rally in Lár Na Cathrach to spew their rhetoric and drum up more converts. But we must pick up some items first. You cannot go dressed like this, where you will be so easily identified."

At the house, he handed me what looked like a hooded burlap poncho. When I pulled it on, I discovered it was every bit as uncomfortable as it appeared to be. "Is this used as a torture device on other occasions?"

"It is best that I not give you anything that might be deemed a gift."

So many rules. And I thought my insurance coverage practice dealt with a highly regulated industry. At least, if I screwed up there, I only had to put my malpractice insurer on notice. Here, I might get stuck in a foreign land where I can't eat or drink anything. Or worse, find myself under the control of some other being, however that works. Fiachra hadn't been at all clear about the mechanics of that.

He looked me over and said, "You'll need to get rid of your shoes. In the warmer seasons, most do not wear them. In the darkness, no one is likely to notice that your hands and feet are the wrong color."

I slipped off my shoes and socks and flexed my wrongly colored feet. As a kid, I'd only worn shoes when required. From Spring to Autumn, the soles of my feet were calloused and tough as bison hide. My mother had called me her "sweet, little hillbilly." Not anymore. Adulthood had made me soft ... in many ways, feet included.

"How do I look?"

He reached across and pulled the poncho's hood over my head. Because he was so much taller than me, it felt very much like a parent bundling his child.

"Ordinary enough, as long as no one looks too closely." He grabbed my wrist and said, "Close your eyes."

With a burst of sudden acceleration, I felt like we'd left most of my vital organs behind. Just as abruptly — not more than a blink — we stopped.

A clamor of raised voices and cheering. But it was not jovial cheering like at a child's dance recital or a sporting event. There was something nefarious about it. More jeering than cheering. Even before I got my bearings, I smelled the stench of a mass of people. Different from that stink of a congregation of humans, but not altogether dissimilar. Sweat, hormones, and dirt make a pungent combination regardless of the species involved.

I wondered if the Fae had created scientific categories for themselves and the other creatures of their world. Even as I thought it, I realized that was a distinctly human thing. We were created to be the stewards of our world, and while we'd generally done a piss-poor job of that over the last couple hundred years, there was still a part of us so deeply ingrained with our calling that we couldn't help but to continue to identify and name the life forms of our world, just as the First Man had done at the Beginning. Maybe Fiachra would know if the Fae were the stewards of their world as well.

I was drawn out of my rabbit hole by an increase in the noise of the raucous crowd. For the first time, I took in the scene ahead of me. We were on the outskirts of a town constructed of stone buildings. Lamps lit the streets at regular intervals.

Hundreds of fairies gathered around a central figure, who stood on a boulder. Her features were more feminine than Fiachra's, but she was no less imposing. She nearly glowed with energy in the lamplight.

As the clamor died, she resumed her speech. "If the Fae wish to live, to truly live, then we are forced to subjugate others. To kill if it comes to that. The struggle for survival is the struggle for conquest over others. This may, in turn, result in the elimination of others. As long as there are Fae and humans, there will be dominion of one people over another."

Another roar of approval.

Fiachra leaned down and spoke into my ear. "Stand at the back of the crowd. We will be less conspicuous than keeping a distance."

I saw then that there were dozens who stood away from the crowd, at the edges of circles of light. They were more readily identifiable than those congregated in the throng. His last instruction before the speaker picked up again was to keep my back to the light, so my face remained a shadow.

"We must protect our collective rights in the same way one is compelled to protect their individual rights. One is either the hammer or the anvil. The Fae have been the anvil for too long, subject to the whims and fancies of humans."

The crowd voiced its agreement. The speaker was very

compelling. I'd heard these kinds of speeches before at protests and political rallies. The most evocative of speakers had an innate sense of when to pause for their constituents and when to resume so as not to lose momentum.

"We confess that it is our purpose to prepare the Fae for the role of the hammer."

The congregation roared, and each raised a hand above their head formed into a fist. Fiachra nudged me with his elbow. He raised his fist, and I followed suit. The best camouflage was compliance.

"We freely admit that if we are victorious, we will concern ourselves daily with governing humankind, rather than cowing to them. We will cast off the yoke of responding to man's demands and expectations. Rather, it is we who will set the tone."

Thunderous applause broke out, bracketed by a synchronous stamping of feet.

Watching her, she reminded me of someone. I couldn't quite place it in the moment, but later realized that it was Mystique from X-Men, but without the cat-eyes and weird markings. She was enthralling and magnetic.

"Everyone among us is a scoundrel if they do not try day and night to overthrow the bonds by which we are held." Her voice was strong and clear, and she spit the words out as though they left a bitter taste in her mouth. "Your ancestors made covenants that you allow to bind you still. Why are you beholden to promises made in antiquity?"

Most of those in the shadows slunk further away from the light at the accusations. For that's what it was. One bold detractor asked, "What of the Godmother?"

The first words of her response drew gasps. "The old crone has too long been complicit in the tyranny of men. She can either stand aside or be overwhelmed by the changing tide."

There was no questioning her belief that you were not with them in the march toward a new world order, you were with the enemy, a part of the old order that they would overthrow.

I had to push the cadence of Eminem's lines out of my head as the words *move toward a new world order* invaded momentarily.

The speaker's next words hammered home her point.

"Not so with us. We are freely begotten. We who collect the bones of men. But we would not leave you behind. We would bring you with us. With every step we take, we strengthen our arms, augment the numbers of our constituency, and increase the strength of the Fae. We will dash to pieces any who dare to hinder us in this undertaking. Our rights will be protected only when man is held at bay by the point of the Fae spear."

I expected a deafening roar. Instead, the speech's climax was punctuated by silence and raised fists. It was a terrifying and incredible moment, but not nearly so terrifying as what happened next.

The person on my other side nudged me, presumably wanting to share the moment with another. I ignored it. But when they jostled me harder, I had little choice but to look their way. Ice formed in my belly.

Lamplight fell on my face as I looked up.

My neighbor's expression morphed from riled up anger to awe. He opened his mouth to yell. I punched upward, driving my fist into the underside of his jaw. I reminded myself of Little Mac in Mike Tyson's Punch-Out on the Nintendo. The fairy stumbled backwards, though I have to concede, it was much more likely surprise that caused the outsized reaction, rather than the force of the punch.

I turned to Fiachra, who had caught the tail-end of the tumult.

"Run," he mouthed as he pulled his own hood up over his head.

I bolted for one of the five streets that emptied into the plaza where the gathering was being held. As I put distance between myself and the crowd, I heard cries of "Human!" emerge.

I glanced over my shoulder. To my dismay, Fiachra wasn't behind me. But neither was anyone else.

# Chapter 14
# Displaced

I ran through street after street, making one random turn after another. If I were going to be caught by a mob, it wasn't going to be for lack of effort. When I was convinced that I'd put enough distance between myself and the rally-goers, I ran between two buildings where there was barely enough light, and stopped.

My heart banged against my rib cage, and my lungs protested about the effort being required of them. I probably hadn't sprinted that long or that far since childhood. But now, I was pent up like prey, with no sense of where I was or in which direction I might find my only ally in this whole world.

Or at least someone who presented himself as an ally. It still wasn't clear why he had involved me and what he wanted out of this. I guess it was my fault for getting this far into things without raising that issue. I would never have done that in my law practice. As a lawyer, I needed to know what a client wanted so I could moderate their expectations while trying to resolve their issues. It was something I raised in the initial consultation and that Annie reinforced with almost every client call she fielded.

Yet here I was, a week into this nonsense — literally in another world — without having sorted out my purpose. Assuming I got out of this little pinch I was in, I would have to settle that. But for the time being, I felt a bit like George Clooney and crew stuck in a burning barn with the devil lurking outside: "Damn! We're in a tight spot!"

Once my heart reverted to a normal rhythm, my feet notified me of their displeasure with recent events. Checking to the left and right first, I sat down against the wall of a building to inspect their condition.

Even in the dim light, I could make out the patches of blood from a dozen nicks and abrasions, making its way through a layer of dirt and grime. Great breeding grounds for any number of bacteria that would do their level-best to set up an infection. When people asked how I lost my foot, at least I'd have an interesting story — "You see, I was being chased by a band of murderous fairies...."

With that behind me, I recognized my need for a getting to a different location. I couldn't see anything where I was. I needed to find some higher ground. As it was, I didn't know whether I'd run clear across the city or run in a big circle, putting myself nearly back to where I'd started.

As I thought through what I'd seen as I ran, I realized that almost all the buildings I had passed were single story. That would have to do. Fortunately, I appeared to have run to a more commercial part of town, which was vacant at this time of night. I stalked the shadows of one thatch building after another, which were little more than kiosks, until I came to a stone structure.

It was made from flat river rock that made it moderately easy to climb. It also indicated that there was a river in close proximity. I hadn't seen any beasts of burden yet, but the Fae must have them. Either that, or they were much stronger than the human-like qualities I had superimposed on them would imply.

Of course, it was absurd of me to make any assumptions about these people. I had too little actual information to go on.

I pulled myself up the wall of the building and was glad to reach its top about ten feet off the ground. The roof was a single enormous stone, set at a shallow pitch. I stood on it without fear of causing any damage.

I wasn't high enough off the ground to get a good feel for the city, but it was enough to serve my purposes. It was laid out like a wheel, with the streets either set in concentric rings around the obelisk that served as the city's center, or serving as spokes that cut through the rings to carry traffic in or out. I was in one of the middle rings. Behind me, a dark ribbon interrupted the city's construction. I didn't remember having seen a river on the way in, but I was a little preoccupied, so it's not like I was actively taking in my surroundings. Besides, we'd teleported in pretty close to the square where the meeting had been held.

Although the town was mostly quiet, there was a section to my left that a din arose from and permeated the air. I couldn't see down into those streets from my vantage point, but I could see roving points of light reflecting off the faces of buildings.

Torchlight. People were searching. Was *people* the right term? It would have to do. This wasn't the time to worry over the best use of language. My ability to fret over the minutiae of language at a moment when I was literally being hunted didn't speak well of my survival instincts.

It was time to skedaddle, which led immediately to questions about where to go and how to get there.

I laid on my belly and scooched backwards toward the edge of the roof, letting my toes gain purchase against the river rock I'd climbed up a few minutes earlier. Just before I stated my descent, I felt something in my back pocket. My eyes widened with hope. The book. *Peter Rabbit.*

I pushed myself back onto the roof and stood to my feet. My hand got tangled in the poncho as I reached for the book.

Huddling it close to protect it from any wind, I opened it carefully and found that the sparkly totem was still intact. Glittery dust covered the interior pages.

I found myself almost disbelieving the situation. Of course, that felt rational. All of it was unbelievable. Every bit of the last couple of weeks had such an unrealness (not a word, I know) that I kept expecting to wake up at any moment.

The open book in my hands brought me back to the present circumstance. Real or not, I needed to extricate myself from the situation. Looking at the shimmering pages, I realized I had no idea how this worked. Fiachra hadn't explained it. He had just done it. Neither of us anticipated a situation where I might need to know how to transport myself apart from him.

I decided to give it the ole' *Wizard of Oz* treatment — think about where I wanted to go and hope it took me there. Except that I didn't think I could get all the way home. I needed a waypoint, and the only one I could put my mind to was Fiachra's village. So that's where I fixed my focus while I traced my hand over the fairy dust covered pages.

My stomach was sucked up into my ear canals, and I was yanked out of my place in time and space. When my brain stopped being wrung like a sponge, I stumbled forward with my eyes still closed, and fell against a mountain of fur.

An angry roar deafened my ears, as hot breath and saliva spewed onto my face.

# Chapter 15
# The Bear Minimum

It took a lot of effort to keep my eyes closed, but I was pretty sure I didn't want to see the predator I'd just run into that was about to remove my face from my head. Only later did I have an opportunity to appreciate that I'd just fairy dusted myself from one place to another.

"I am so sorry," I heard. "How terribly rude of me. Are you alright?"

I opened one eye to a squint and found a dark, furry torso in front of me. I looked up. The face of a black bear stared down at me expectantly. She continued, "It's just that you surprised me. You were not there a moment ago. I would have smelled you. I'm certain of that. And you stepped on my paw. But that is no excuse for such behavior. Please accept my apologies."

She reached out toward my head. I flinched, as would anyone in that situation. She slid my hood back off my head. "That's what I thought. You do not smell like the Fae."

For the second time in the last hour, acute terror subsided down to a moderate buzz of fear and anxiety. Apparently, I went a while still without responding because Cassandra poked me in the chest with one of her curved claws.

"Ow." I immediately rubbed at the place she had prodded, but the gesture did have the intended effect of bringing me out of my funk.

Cassandra dropped to all fours and walked past me, presumably in the same direction she'd been going when we had our run-in. I stood where I was on the path for a moment, feeling very much like a lost child. "Excuse me," I turned and called to the bear. "I don't know where to go."

"Come with me," she offered as she continued walking.

I wasn't convinced, but I began walking in the same direction she was going. "Shouldn't I go to Fiachra's house?" It was the only place I knew in Sidhe Baile, and I didn't know where it was in relation to where I was.

"Fiachra is not home."

If I were taking her deposition, I would've had to point out that she didn't answer the question I'd asked. But since she was a gargantuan bear and I was a lost human, I let it slide and jogged to catch up to her.

The only bears I'd ever seen in person were at the zoo when we took Ella, but they were rarely close enough to watch with any level of scrutiny. Based on her size, I would have expected Cassandra's gait to be cumbersome. Walking beside her, though, I saw how lithe she was. Even as the moonlight filtered through the canopy of trees and reflected off her fur, the muscles working beneath it made themselves evident. I nearly reached out and touched her, but treating her like a pet struck me as an extraordinarily bad idea.

Now that I was well on my way to wherever Cassandra was taking us, I realized I hadn't asked the most glaring question. "Where are we going?"

"To my den."

I caught a hitch in my step as what should have been obvious caught up to me. Visions of a dank cave littered with the bones of fish and small mammals crashed into me. Not that I thought she intended to make a meal of me. But still, that seemed a rather uninviting atmosphere. Instead, I found a more practical question to ask. "Is there room for both of us?"

She had an edge to her voice when she answered. "I am not your average bear."

I didn't ask any further questions as we sauntered through the woods. It turned out that I didn't have long to wait to discover what I was in for. A faint glow emerged out of the forest floor just off the trail we were traversing.

As we closed in on it, I noted that a circular wooden door with a small window covered the den's opening. I tilted my head and asked, "You aren't worried about the trees?"

"What do you mean?"

"About them being ..." It felt absurd saying this out loud. If she'd been a snake instead of a bear, she would've been able to sense the blood rushing to my cheeks. "... being conscious, intelligent."

Cassandra stopped and swung her head around. She looked directly at me for a long time, the same way my mother did after I'd done something peculiar — a frequent occurrence — when she was trying to figure out whether there was something wrong with me.

"No," she said as she shuffled the last few steps toward the den.

I felt I needed to explain myself. "Fiachra said he thought the trees might be sentient. That's why the houses are made of stone. I thought that might be a thing here."

Her head bobbed up and down. She stopped at the door. "Fiachra has his own ideas about things. But did you notice that his home has a fireplace? What do you think he burns in there? Rye grass?"

I closed my eyes for a moment so that I could mentally peruse his stone home. There in the center of it was a fireplace with a stone hearth and chimney. It was so commonplace that I hadn't even taken note of it. My cheeks grew warmer still. I opened my eyes and said, "Oh."

Cassandra was gracious enough not to drive home the point of my foolishness. "Do you know how long fairies live?"

I shook my head.

"They are nearly immortal."

Sooner or later, these kinds of revelations would quit catching me by surprise. "How is one 'nearly immortal'?"

"Their natural life spans are measured in centuries, not decades. It is why their homes are made of stone. If you're going to be occupying it for the better part of forever, you might as well build it out of something that's likely to survive most of that time."

"Ah." It's all I could muster. I was still taking things in. Slowly.

She opened the door of her den and motioned me to enter. The home was dug out under an enormous tree. Looking up, I could only just see where the boughs opened up into a canopy of leaves that were swallowed by the night's darkness.

The only bear dens I'd seen before were cramped things they had dug out to hibernate for the winter. This was not that. It was a proper home. Deep enough that both she and I could walk upright. The ceiling was a domed collage of roots. An oil lantern sat to one side of the space near several baskets of berries, nuts, and root vegetables. There was not a bone to be found, unless they lay in the basket that was covered by cloth.

The space where she slept was clearly identifiable by the deeper impression in the ground, almost like a shallow bowl. I noted that there was no fireplace here. When you're closing in on half a ton and covered in fur, you're basically a walking furnace.

The soft light and the window in the door kept the den from feeling murky and claustrophobic. The sight of the food cache sitting on the floor set my stomach to grumbling. It had been a long time since I'd eaten.

Cassandra must have heard the complaint. She flicked her snout toward the food. "Please help yourself. Winter is many months away, and I do not think you will put much of a dent in my stores."

A couple of handfuls of berries and mixed nuts (even without being roasted and salted) would be amazing. But I hadn't so much as moved toward them when a less short-sighted part of my brain reminded me that I wasn't supposed to eat anything in Sidhe Baile.

"That's very generous of you to offer, but I'm not really hungry."

"Yes, you are. Do not lie."

# Chapter 16
# A Prophet and a She-Bear

That was a commandment, too. Not to lie. I'd been caught and called out. These things needed nuance. In Alabama, it's better manners to lie than to hurt someone's feelings or be an ingrate.

Besides, I wasn't even sure whether these rules applied to bears. That hadn't come up earlier.

"My apo—" I cut myself off. I wasn't allowed to apologize for lying, either. What quagmire of etiquette quandaries. "Fiachra said I can't eat anything here."

"That is not what he said. He told you not to eat fairy food, which is not what I offered."

I raised my eyebrows. "How do you know what he said?"

"I know the Commandments."

I sat down against a wall of the den and nearly melted with exhaustion. My forehead rested against my knees while I tried to sort things out. I parsed words for a living. Their specificity makes all the difference between outcomes. Mark Twain is quoted as saying that the right word and the almost right word is the difference between lightning and the lightning bug.

The problem was, I couldn't remember precisely what words Fiachra had used. Had he told me not to eat fairy food, meaning food prepared by fairies? If that's what he'd said, then Cassandra was right and I could eat what she'd foraged.

On the other hand, if he had said not to eat any food that came from Sidhe Baile, then I would be signing my death certificate by eating the offering. That seemed like rather a colossal risk for some berries. Good thing she hadn't offered a ribeye, though. That kindled a question. "Do you eat meat?"

"Ay, if fish are meat. There is a creek nearby that runs with the plumpest brown trout. Catching them is often the best part of my day."

"What about other mammals?"

"Usually not. The lynx and I do not meet paws on that front. While we often fish together, I will not hunt with him. Not only do I find it a distasteful practice, it is also a great deal of trouble. All the fur. It's a mess."

I decided to tempt fate. "I don't have much fur, and I wouldn't be much of a hunt."

Her expression soured. "I would not eat a human." So much contempt in that statement.

"We don't taste good?"

"I would not know. It is not the way of things. I too am subject to covenants."

An uncomfortably long silence settled over us. I had twice offended my host apparently and was ready to turn the conversation away from food, so I took another gamble. "Can I tell you a story about a couple of she-bears?"

Her eyes shone with delight. "Let me get comfortable." She shuffled toward the place where she slept and slid in. There was a bit of grunting as she found the position she was seeking. She settled down with her chin resting on her forepaws. When she breathed out, two streams of hot air blew across my legs.

"Several thousand years ago, there was a prophet in Israel named Elisha. Do you know what a prophet is?"

She rocked her head from side to side without lifting it off her giant paws. She really was much larger than I thought black bears were supposed to be. But it seemed uncouth to ask her about her size.

"A prophet is a religious figure ordained by Yahweh to speak the truth to his people."

Cassandra nodded slightly, so I moved on with the story.

"The Israelites were in rebellion against Yahweh, from the king down to the lowest peasant. So Elisha walked from town to town, preaching to the people to repent. On Elisha's way to a city called Bethel, which was one of the most offensive cities to Yahweh, because the people were raising asherah poles and worshiping false gods, a gang of young men started harassing the prophet.

"They yelled, 'Go up, bald head!' On its face, that sounds pretty harmless, but I'll give you some more context."

Cassandra cleared her throat. "Where are the bears you promised?"

"Soon. Elisha's mentor was Elijah, and years earlier, he had been taken up to heaven in a chariot of fire. So when the mockers were telling him to *go up*, they were telling him to die. And at the time, baldness was associated with sickness or some kind of skin disease. I don't think the context fully translates into English. That reminds me — how is it that you speak English?"

She turned the question back around. "How is it that *you* speak English?"

I frowned. A sarcastic bear was interesting, but not helpful. "I wouldn't have thought that English would be the native language here."

"Why is it you think English is the only language I speak just because I am speaking it with you?"

A multilingual bear. I was dumbstruck.

"Can we get back to the she-bears?"

"Yes. Sorry. Almost there," I said. "As Elisha passed by the guys who were harassing him, he spoke a curse in the name of God. Two she-bears came out of the woods and attacked them. Scripture tells us the bears tore forty-two of them to pieces."

I waited expectantly after finishing my story.

"Why did you tell me this story?"

"It's about bears. I thought you would like it?"

"Do you like all stories about men, regardless of their actions?" When I didn't answer her question, she followed up with another. "What was the moral of the tale you told?"

I shook my head. "I've been wondering that for a long time. When I was a boy, my teachers said it showed why we should be respectful to priests and ministers. But I don't think that's right. On the surface, they were mocking Elisha. But that was just a manifestation of their lives that were in open rebellion against Yahweh, who had formed a special relationship with them and made a covenant with the people of Israel. So he struck them down. Or something like that. I don't know."

She only grunted. It sounded like disagreement. But I didn't know enough to want to carry the conversation further. It had already gone differently than expected. But I was curious about something. "Can I ask you a personal question?"

"Go on," she said.

"Do you believe in God?"

She considered the question for longer than I would have expected. It had seemed like a simple one.

"This question is not personal," she said. "The Creator's existence is unaffected by my belief." She flicked an ear toward the door, and her nose twitched as she sniffed at the air. "Fiachra is back."

"That's a neat trick. I have to rely on my video doorbell to tell me who's coming."

She made an expression that seemed to resemble a sneer, though that didn't quite fit the tone of the conversation. "It is a miracle your kind has survived this long. Do you not wonder why the Creator's did not gift you with more effective, less fragile bodies?"

"I didn't before. I will now." But a more dangerous human seemed like something we were all better off without. "To be fair, we've caused quite enough harm in our present state."

She made a low-level rumble. The sound of assent.

# Chapter 17
# A Petition for Aid

"Is he coming here?" I asked.

"He is not yet on his way, but I suppose he will be soon. But we should have time to tend our remaining business."

My eyebrows shot up. "What business is that?"

"Tell me about the bears where you are from."

It was the first time she had exhibited real curiosity about me. She had tried to sound demure, but there was too much earnestness behind the request.

"Are you not able to go there?"

She huffed indignantly. "Am I a fairy that I can travel between worlds? No, I have not been there. I have only been in this world with other bears, who are morons. The males are only interested in making cubs, after which I have to keep them from killing their own progeny for a couple of years until they are big enough to go out on their own. And the females are little better."

"Right," I said. "Well, where to start. I think you would be equally disappointed with our bears. We have many different kinds, and they are incredible creatures. Smarter and more resourceful than most other animals. But they are dumb. No offense. I mean it literally. They cannot speak. They're nothing like you."

As I spoke, the spark of interest snuffed out. I could almost see her deflate, so I did not continue. I hadn't considered how lonely it must be as the only one of your kind. The First Man felt the same way. After he had given names to the animals, he was lonely and asked his Creator for a companion. It didn't appear that Cassandra's creator was as conscientious of her condition.

In the flattest of tones, she said, "Fiachra will be here soon." Then she turned to face the wall of her den, her chin resting on her paws.

I was inclined to go give her a hug — a bear hug? — but didn't know whether that was appropriate. So we waited out his arrival in silence.

When Fiachra knocked at the door, Cassandra pushed herself to a sitting position, adopted a demeanor that more closely resembled her posture than what she had been showing a moment ago, and said in a lilting voice. "You may enter."

It was really quite a turnaround. Regardless of what species we are or the world we hail from, we all put on airs for company.

Fiachra swung the door open and crouched to enter. His skin undulated between midnight blue and rich ebony, making him all but impossible to see in the dark. I looked at my watch. Assuming it still worked properly here, we had crossed the threshold of midnight some time ago.

Fiachra spotted me and grasped the hilt of a knife that he kept strapped to his thigh. I hadn't noticed it before. He stared intently for several seconds. I couldn't decide whether I needed to watch his hand or his eyes, so I darted my attention back and forth between them both. I'm sure I looked frantic. Very slowly, I stood from my reclined position against the den wall and steeled myself for whatever was to come next.

His grip shifted on the knife. The coloring in his hand and

arm betrayed the tension he experienced, as cords of muscle rippled in preparation for action.

With my peripheral vision, I took stock of anything that might be available for me to use to defend myself. There was precious little.

Cassandra watched, apparently disengaged, as events unfolded around her, until she spoke and belied her interest. "If you shed my guest's blood under my roof, I cannot let it stand."

Fiachra chanced a fleeting look her way. "Can you be sure that your guest is the man he holds himself out to be?"

The bear swung her gaze my way and tilted her head.

"Tell me something only you and I would know," he instructed.

I considered it and a smirk pulled at my lips. "On your second visit, my assistant Annie wore a black mini-dress, hoping it would capture your attention and you would whisk her away to … give her a new perspective on life."

He nodded, and his hand relaxed.

"Now your turn," I said.

He scoffed. "One fairy cannot take the form of another."

"Says you." I shrugged. "How do I know that?"

"Tell him, Cassandra."

She shook her sable head. "I do not know your limitations. Answer him."

"Fine." When he returned his attention to me, I saw that his coloring was returning to the aquamarine that I thought of as his natural state. "Much like Annie, you too are curiou—"

"Forget it! We're good. I believe you."

As the stress of the resolved situation bled from his shoulders, Fiachra stepped to the middle of the room and squatted on his haunches. The posture of someone who rarely allows himself to fully relax, always ready to spring. As opposed to my slovenly sprawl, born out of a life of relative leisure.

I folded my legs into what Ella called criss-cross-applesauce.

I resented whatever preschool teacher had come up with that. It took entirely too long to say. Maybe they experienced some self-loathing about it too, since they had to say it forty times a day to a bunch of rowdy three-year-olds. That's what justice would require.

Fiachra stared at me for a long minute before he spoke. It became uncomfortable, and I looked away. "I need your help."

I nodded. I already knew that much, but it was about as far as we'd ever gotten. "Why?"

"The Bone Collectors Guild is a scourge on this land. They are growing in strength and numbers. And now they are campaigning to bring others into their fold. You heard the speech tonight. Did you recognize the language?"

I shook my head. "Should I have?"

"Mark her words, and search it out when you get home."

"You could just tell me the answer to the question you asked, which you obviously already know."

"I could. I won't."

"Whatever," I said with a huff. "But you didn't answer the *why question I was* intending to ask. Why do you need *my* help? I mean, I understand why you picked me. You already said that before. But why do you need a human at all?"

"Only a human can bind a fairy with a covenant. It is like the checks and balances with your government. Each branch has some authority over the others. It is the same with humans and fairies. The commandments restrict your actions here in Sidhe Baile. And the covenants govern our conduct there."

"But the Bone Collectors are not subject to any covenants because they were created later?"

"Ay," he said with a nod.

"You want me to draw up new covenants for y'all?"

He nodded again.

"And somehow force them to agree to it?"

"We cannot compel them. They must do it willingly."

A harsh bark of joyless laughter escaped me. "You're not asking for much, are you? I don't suppose you have copies of the old covenants that I could borrow from?"

Fiachra looked down at the packed earth floor of the den. He shook his head.

"Hell's bells," I whispered.

A silence followed.

Cassandra snored gently. Apparently, she'd finally lost interest in the line of conversation. It forced a smile to my lips to realize my circumstances, which a mere two-and-a-half weeks ago would have been entirely incredulous.

"I forgot to ask how you got back to these woods."

I shifted my weight and pulled my weathered copy of *Peter Rabbit* out of my pocket.

His eyes lit up with a smile. "Well done, Scott. I was rather concerned for you."

"It was touch-and-go for a minute."

He stood and stuck out a hand. "Let's get you home. There's someone I need to introduce you to."

# Chapter 18
# Making an Introduction

Normally, when someone says they want to introduce you to someone, they don't mean right that very minute. It's more of a the-next-time-we're-all-in-the-same-room kind of thing. But not Fiachra. He meant immediately.

We were closing in on twenty-four hours since I'd last slept or had a meal, so I wasn't super keen on socializing. But I wasn't being given much choice either.

He ported us back to my apartment and hurried me to the car, hardly giving me time to grab my keys and wallet.

Once I was behind the steering wheel, I was in control again. Or at minimum, I had some small semblance of control. It felt like I hadn't fully been in control of anything since my trip to Amarillo.

I whipped the car out of the parking lot and onto the roadway.

"Would you like to know where you're going before you take off like a sprite chasing the wind?"

"I know where I'm going." The last of the fast-food places closed in about fifteen minutes. I'd figure out where Fiachra wanted me to go after I had some food in hand. Stealing a glance to my right, I realized for the first time since we'd landed back earth-side that he had put his human facade back on.

*Earth-side* didn't sit right. As best I could tell, Sidhe Baile was a version of earth too, just on a different plane or in a different dimension. Science fiction isn't a category where I'd score many points in Jeopardy. As I pulled into the drive-thru line behind a couple of other people, I asked. "What do you call this place?"

He looked at me quizzically. "Taco Bell."

I smiled. That was a poorly worded question. "No, the earth where the humans live."

"Ah. Cré Duine."

I nodded, then gestured at the menu. "Want something?"

He wrinkled his nose and shook his head emphatically. It felt kind of judgy, but it was probably the appropriate response.

A flat voice came through the speaker. "Welcome to Taco Bell. What can I get you?"

"Two bean burritos, no onions. And two soft tacos."

"Will that complete your order?"

"Yes, thanks."

"Please pull around to the second window."

I drove forward a couple of car lengths. "What does it mean — Cré Duine?" Pretty sure I butchered the pronunciation.

"It translates to *human clay*."

At the drive-thru window, I traded a couple of bills and some change for a bag of food. I dropped the bag beside me and entered the roadway.

"It is odd here," Fiachra said. "Everyone says 'please' and 'thank you' and all manner of niceties, but no one really means any of it."

A bellyful of laughter exploded out of me. I nearly had to pull over to the curb. After a moment, the laughter subsided, and I wiped the tears from my eyes. He had totally nailed our entire sub-culture. "Welcome to the South, man. Wait until someone says, 'Bless your heart.' Then you'll know you've been properly insulted."

As the smells of refried beans and melting cheese wafted their way toward my nose, I asked, "Where are we headed?"

"Gardendale."

I did a double take. "Gardendale? There's hardly anything in Gardendale."

"Hardly-anything-there is kind of the point when you're a giant who wants to be inconspicuous."

I refrained from my second double take in as many seconds. But just barely. While I wrangled with whether he meant *giant* literally, I drove the car toward I-65 North.

As I hit the entrance ramp, I remembered the only thing I knew about the town we were headed to. "Did you know Gardendale was founded as Jugtown? They changed the name about a hundred years ago. I think it was the right call."

When Fiachra didn't offer any commentary on the subject, I shoved the last bite of my second burrito in my mouth and considered how displeased my primary care doctor with be with my food choice.

We traveled north on the interstate for about twenty minutes, with Jason Isbell crooning at a low volume and no words passing between Fiachra and me. I had more questions than time to ask them and get proper answers. But more than that, I needed time to think. The volume of information I'd ingested was the equivalent of the food that gets shoved down at a hotdog-eating competition. Except I didn't have the option of purging it. My brain needed an opportunity to sort through everything and conduct some analysis.

Oh, and sleep. I also needed sleep.

As we neared Gardendale, Fiachra gave me the address, and I plugged it into my GPS. We took the prescribed exit and hung a right, passing a Mormon temple, followed by a sports complex whose immediate neighbor was a cemetery. The juxtaposition amused me. Eventually, the computer told me to turn left at a long and winding road that turned out to be possibly the world's longest cul-de-sac.

At the end was a home that was nestled into the woods in a way that made it feel almost a part of the landscape, rather than an intrusion. I would've liked to have seen it during the day, but as it were, I could easily have been convinced that I was somewhere in Appalachia, instead of a dozen miles north of downtown Birmingham.

I parked on the street, parallel to the front of the house. Fiachra offered no last-minute instructions on the way to the door, and I still didn't know who we were visiting or why.

Fiachra knocked lightly at the door. I didn't hear footsteps approaching from the inside, but when the door opened, I found it nearly impossible that the occupant had trod so quietly.

Looking straight ahead, as I had been, brought me eye-level to his chest. I craned my head upward to see our host's face. Childhood memories of watching old wrestling videos on the couch with my dad flooded my senses. If the Junkyard Dog were about sixty years old and north of eight feet tall, this would be him.

He spoke in a velvety baritone voice. "Fiachra. It is disquieting to see you. As always, I assume something has gone wrong."

The fairy, who looked small compared to the giant, doffed a hat that he wasn't wearing and bowed deeply. Fiachra took a half-step forward but stopped when our host (or maybe he was just a potential host at this point) didn't move aside for him to enter the dwelling.

Fiachra looked up to meet his eyes.

"You going to introduce your guest?"

"This is Scott Warren. He's a lawyer in town. Giving me a hand with something." Fiachra turned to me. "This is Oberhaupt."

"Not any longer. I'm retired. You can call me Athos. Now, fairy, tell me why you're here."

Fiachra strained to maintain his polite demeanor. "Perhaps we could go inside so we don't get carried off by these birds you call mosquitoes?"

The giant put a heavy hand on Fiachra's shoulder. I was certain I would have sagged under the weight. "No shenanigans."

Fiachra put his palm to his chest and feigned offense. "I would never."

Athos grunted and stepped to the side.


Once we'd settled in — no, settled is the wrong word. I was sitting in a room with a fairy and a literal giant. I'd recently been in the den of a talking bear. And before that, I'd been chased by a hoard of angry nationalist fairies who wanted to get revenge on humans for … something. No, I was all kinds of unsettled.

By way of further introduction, Fiachra explained that Athos had been the head of a magical paramilitary outfit based in Birmingham. My head had truly begun to swim.

"Time out," I said, making the corresponding T gesture with my hands, before running those same hands through my hair. The other two waited quietly but impatiently. "Y'all are telling me that there are actual witches and wizards and stuff, and they have an army?"

Athos shoved himself up out of his massive chair with enough force and suddenness that it scooted backward several inches. He stared down Fiachra. "You brought an unterlegen to me?"

I didn't recognize the word and switched my gaze to Fiachra, who grimaced and whispered. "It's not a nice word, but he didn't mean it."

He sure looked like he meant it.

The giant continued. "The last time I got involved with … a non-magical person, it did not end well."

"I know the events you're speaking of, and that was always going to go poorly, regardless of the involvement of any outsiders. Besides, I'm not asking you to get involved. I just need you to be a liaison for my friend here. He doesn't have a way to reach me when I'm on the other side."

Well, this was awkward. I felt like the child in a divorce case whose custody was being discussed by the adults in the room.

"A liaison? That's it?"

Fiachra nodded emphatically. "Probably."

The giant rolled his eyes and addressed me for the first time since we'd been introduced. He pointed sharply at Fiachra. "Do not trust the Fae. They may not lie, but they're never telling you the truth, either."

The fairy shrugged it off. It wasn't the first time someone had leveled these kinds of allegations at him.

"I've agreed to what you asked. Are you ready to go now?"

Fiachra weighed the question for a minute, as if disregarding its rhetorical nature. "I suppose we are. Besides, Scott ate a large quantity of food on the way here, some of which contained beans. We should get him out before his flatulence presents itself."

# Chapter 19
## Not Your Average Murder

The next week passed more-or-less normally. That said, no week with an elementary school kid is entirely normal. They're not capable of normalcy. As best as I can tell, they get progressively weirder over the next several years, though girls generally get less peculiar more quickly than do their male counterparts.

In the days that followed my meeting with Athos, I checked the contacts in my phone from time to time just to reassure myself that there was evidence that all this was real.

The six o'clock news was well into its broadcast as I sat my desk eating a pulled pork sandwich and attempting to catch up on emails. It was a never-ending game that you couldn't actually win. There were times I was tempted to erase everything in my inbox under the theory that if something was important, I'd get another message about it. But the thought of having to explain that to my malpractice insurance carrier kept me from acting on the impulse.

I closed out my email, having made enough headway to feel like I wouldn't drown, and instead turned my attention to the insurance coverage denial letter that I needed to draft. It was a close call whether coverage applied, but I had landed on the side of the facts aligning with exclusions in the policy that prevented coverage. I hated it when it was a close thing. Somebody was about to have to go out of pocket for something based on my analysis. I would much rather it be super clear cut, but making calls like that is why I get paid the medium bucks.

I wasn't more than a paragraph into the letter when a news headline caught my attention. PROMINENT ANIMATION STUDIO EXECUTIVE FOUND DEAD IN GRUESOME MURDER. I snatched the remote control off my desk and unmuted the television so Becki Donaldson of Channel 6 News could fill me in on the story behind the headline.

"—is unfolding at this moment. All we know right now is that the CEO of our parent company was found dead in his home in an apparent murder. There is some thought that because of the grisly nature of the murder, it may have involved a ritual sacrifice." She no more finished reading the words off the teleprompter than she broke character and said, "Oh, come on. Are we serious?" Her eyes widened and her cheeks immediately reddened as she realized her thoughts had escaped her lips.

Her co-host, Joshua Saffold — he was one of those insufferable people who corrected anyone that shortened his given name — attempted to help cover for her. "Uhh, that's right, Becki. We're all a little shocked to hear this."

He sounded more like a robot when he was impromptu than when he was reading.

Joshua continued as Becki pecked at a device that was just below the desk. "We understand that photographs have been released, but because of their graphic natu—"

Becki blanched, her still-reddened cheeks draining of all their color. She turned to Joshua with tears in her eyes and held out a tablet for him to see the screen. He flung a hand toward his mouth, but not in time to stifle the "Son of a b—" that resulted in the station cutting to the no-signal screen.

"Oh, my gosh!" I said aloud to no one. It was the most astounding minute of television I had ever witnessed. The kind of thing that would keep social media abuzz and give birth to memes that would never die. Self-important Joshua had just created the legacy that would outlive him.

Annie stepped into my doorway, startling me nearly to death and interrupting my schadenfreude.

"You say something?"

"What are you still doing here?" I asked.

"What are *you* still doing here?"

"Working. Well, I was working until the nightly news went haywire." In my excitement, I talked way faster than normal. "I've told you that you don't have to stay late just because I do."

"I know."

"Fine. If you're going to be here, you might as well see this." I swiveled my monitor and opened my web browser. TMZ was almost certain to have the photographs.

Annie walked around behind my desk and sidled up beside me, her hip against my shoulder. It probably wasn't intentional, and it certainly didn't mean anything, but I couldn't not notice it.

I diverted my attention — most of it — back to my screen. True to my expectations, the story was at the top of their homepage. But so was something else, which I'd never seen from them before. Not that I frequented gossip rags. They had blurred out the photographs and embedded a GRAPHIC CONTENT warning over them.

*Geez, how bad could it be?*

Before I clicked on the image, Annie said, "Are we sure we want to see this?"

"No. But also, yes."

"Okay," she said with some uncertainty and leaned forward, flattening her palms on the desktop.

I clicked.

And immediately regretted having high-speed internet. In the old dial-up days, it would have come in fourteen pixels at a time. I could have closed the browser or at the very least looked away. The state of current technology meant I had time for neither.

"Oh." Annie whirled around. She leaned against the desk. With one hand, she covered her mouth while the other white-knuckle clenched my arm. Her nails dug into my skin, leaving divots I didn't notice until later.

My stomach lurched, but I couldn't look away. I wanted to. It's just that I couldn't make myself.

The words spoken by the woman on the box at the political rally — Liadan, according to Fiachra — leached back into my brain like they were coming from a slow-drip coffee maker.

*If the Fae wish to live, to truly live, then we are forced to subjugate others. To kill if it comes to that.*

*One is either the hammer or the anvil. The Fae have been the anvil for too long. …We confess that it is our purpose to prepare the Fae for the role of the hammer.* I had thought she meant that figuratively. Apparently not.

*We will dash to pieces any who dare to hinder us in this undertaking. Our rights will be protected only when man is held at bay by the point of the Fae spear.*

Upon further reflection, perhaps I should have considered the literal meaning of those words. Easy to say in hindsight, though.

Not that it would have made any difference here. It's not like I could have done anything to stop this.

"You okay?"

Annie nodded her head curtly, her hand still at her mouth.

But at least she removed her talons from my arm. All she could get out was, "What the hell?"

I was pretty sure the tooth fairies had just murdered one of Walt Disney's successors. Of course, I couldn't and didn't say that.

# Chapter 20
# Point of the Spear

I grabbed my phone and fired off a text to my new liaison. "Have you seen the news?" When I laid the phone back down, I sat back in my desk chair and closed my eyes. Unfortunately, the dead executive's image was engraved on the backs of my eyelids.

His bloody jaw fell askew as he hung by his wrists from a rope strung around the chandelier in the foyer of his Orlando mansion. They must have hanged him after they did all the other work on him, because they never could have mustered enough leverage to have done it otherwise.

There was no doubt where the blood that covered the lower half of his face and most of his torso had come from. He didn't have a tooth left in his head. That's not true. He just didn't have any teeth left in his *mouth*.

From the looks of it, they had ripped every tooth out. They'd had to break his jaw to get to the back ones. Hopefully, they killed him first. If the wet stain on the front of his pants was any sign, maybe they hadn't even shown him that small mercy.

The Bone Collectors Guild had taken each of the extracted teeth and driven them root-first into his face and head. They left him looking like the mutant offspring of a lamprey and a human.

For their closing act, they had impaled him through the chest with a spear.

*We will dash to pieces any who dare to hinder us in this undertaking. Our rights will be protected only when man is held at bay by the point of the Fae spear.*

Literally.

When I remembered that Fiachra had gotten me involved with these people and some of them may have seen my face, I jumped up and ran to the bathroom.

After I'd finished emptying my stomach of its contents, I went to the sink and splashed water on my face. The mirror showed me that I wasn't looking my best. I opened the door and was dismayed to find Annie standing there. She had definitely heard that. And possibly smelled it when I opened the door.

"You should have quit looking while you were ahead."

I nodded.

She handed me a manila envelope. "The documents for your meeting with the Ramseys tomorrow. I logged you out of your computer. Time to go."

I wasn't going to argue with that. It's not like I had any productivity left in me. All my feelings had been replaced by a cold dread that crept from my core to my extremities.

Annie and I exited the building and walked to the parking lot without speaking. Before we went our separate ways, she tugged at my shirtsleeve. "You alright?"

"Yeah, fine. You?"

"Sure," she said with faux cheerfulness. "Just another day at the office, right?"

I scoffed. "Something like that."

When she got into her car, I walked to mine and opened the door. I looked around warily to see if anything was going to creep out of the shadows made more dense by the failing evening light.

Seeing nothing, I got in the car and started the engine. Before I put it in reverse, I checked to see if Athos had responded to my text. Nothing. But he had his read receipts turned on — Who does that? — which showed that he'd read it. Nice.

Against my better judgment, I opened Twitter to see what the reaction was to the miserable death of the CEO of the company that brought us Cinderella and Peter Pan and any number of other fairy tales. The first thing I saw was that #toothfaced was trending. I closed the app. The worst humanity had to offer had outdone itself again.

# Chapter 21
# I'm Confused

When I finally heard from Athos a few days later, he told me to meet him at the Lynn Henley Research Library. The name rang a bell. But since I'm not a history major at any of the local universities digging through all the city's archives, I didn't know where it was.

A quick map search told me I'd walked past it at least a thousand times. Being directly across from the Birmingham Public Library, it was basically next door to the courthouse.

The next peculiarity at the instruction was the timing. He told me to meet him at 10:00pm. I was sure that the research library was normally closed at that hour.

Naturally, when it came time, I waited at the back entrance that faced the park. The vagrants and other regulars who inhabited the park at this late hour eyed me suspiciously, knowing that I didn't fit in. I kept my head down and tried to appear to mind my own business, though I was deeply curious about the lives of these folks whose experience with this city was so different from my own.

After checking my watch for the fourth time in ten minutes, I texted Athos. "Are you here?"

Three dots told me he was responding. "Yes. Inside."

*A man of many words, this one.* "At the back door?"

"???"

I was starting to feel like a moron.

"Come to the front."

The nice thing about texting with an older person was their use of complete sentences. A stark contrast to the nearly indecipherable abbreviations that Ashleigh or Annie used when I traded messages with either of them. I could only guess that by the time Ella was old enough to have a phone, her word usage would hardly resemble English as I knew it.

Sure enough, I found the front door unlocked and went in. A behemoth and a comparatively tiny woman awaited me. If she tucked herself neatly enough, she probably could have fit inside one of his legs.

Athos asked, "Why did you go to the back?"

I shrugged. "You had me meet at a peculiar place at night when it's usually closed. I thought I was being … clandestine." It felt dumb even as it come out of my mouth. And since I'm a person who dwells on and frets over conversations long after I've had them, I knew this one was going to nag at me for a long time to come.

Athos said, "Do you know the key to getting away with almost anything?"

I shook my head.

"Act like you belong."

That made sense. That's what Fiachra had done when we went to the rally. Dressed me like I belonged.

The small woman spoke up. "When I was a younger woman, I snuck backstage at a Slayer concert. When the first person looked at me a little too long, I was certain the jig was up. But rather than take off, I bent down and picked up the box that was beside me and started walking purposefully in a different direction. I carried that box around until the concert started, and no one ever gave me a second glance."

"Slayer, Madeline?"

"You don't like thrash metal?"

"I do not," the giant said. "But that demonstrates my point well." He turned his gaze to me. "Madeline is a research librarian … among other things."

"Does she …" Not only was I not sure if I was allowed to finish the question, but it also seemed rude to be asking Athos questions about Madeline that she could more readily answer for herself. "Sorry. Do you kn—"

"Yes, I know about fairies. The Fae. Fair folk. Whatever you want to call them. Yes."

"Another question, if I can." I grimaced. I already regretted everything about this entire interaction.

"Of course," she said, as chipper as anyone I'd ever met.

"Are you … magical?"

She snickered. "Nope. Just plain old boring human. You?"

"Same."

Athos cleared his throat.

"Don't be so pushy, old man." Madeline turned toward the interior of the library.

"Wait." I held up a hand.

Athos glowered.

"Is the Bone Collectors Guild going to try to kill me?"

He took far longer than I would have liked to answer, but then, I didn't much care for his answer when it arrived. "I don't know."

"Great. You have a very comforting presence. Has anyone ever told you that?"

Madeline laughed again.

Athos growled. "What they may attempt to do and what I will allow to happen are two very different things."

I raised my arms in mock triumph. "Well, see, you should have led with that. That was a much better answer."

The giant turned and proceeded into the heart of the library. "The more you run your mouth, though, the closer the alignment between what the BCG wants and what I want."

I refrained from even considering any clever retort.

Madeline grinned like she hadn't had this much fun in ages. She lilted down the corridor toward a door that required a keycard for entry. She swiped the card that hung from a lanyard at her neck, receiving a green light and affirming beep. Athos ducked into the doorway after her, and I followed in his wake.

A set of marble stairs led to a basement cluttered with books, old documents encased in glass, and several surprisingly new-looking computers. Based on the ramshackle nature of everything else, I'd have expected machines running Windows XP and attached to old CRT monitors that could serve a dual function as a boat anchor.

"Here we are," Madeline announced with the air of one who'd arrived at the end of a voyage.

I looked around, uncertain of her meaning. "We are where?"

She held her arms out and swiveled back and forth. "This is where we will do our work."

My gaze shifted from her to Athos, who watched me intently.

I shook my head. "I'm confused."

The other two looked at each other, then back at me. "As are we," Madeline said. "Fiachra said you would help us figure out what to do about the BCG."

"What?" My head shaking became more fervent. "I never said that. I never agreed to that. He never even asked."

"I would have expected that given your involvement and the gravity of the situation ..." Athos trailed off without finishing his thought.

"Uhh ... the gravity of the situation is exactly what has given me doubt. I'd rather a coroner not be extracting my teeth from my face and having my daughter standing in front of my casket."

Athos brushed past me, nearly sending me sprawling. "I did not take you for a coward."

Sudden introspection told me I'd never been in a situation to test whether or not I was a coward. For whatever reason that I would later have to explore with a psychologist, the whole thing made me angry and resulted in an eruption. "I didn't choose any of this! Some guy just showed up in my office one day. Mind you, that was after he stalked me halfway across the country. And then he came back a second time after I made him leave the first time."

Athos shrugged and spoke softly. "You are free to go at any time. Particularly, if your participation hasn't been voluntary."

I recognized that tone. It's how I placated Ella when she was being difficult. "Leaving? Nobody said anything about leaving. I just … give me a minute. Is there a bathroom around here?"

Madeline pointed to a door on the other side of the window-less library basement.

"Thanks. Just … I need a minute."

The innumerable shelves and tables full of bound documents I had to circumnavigate lengthened the already long walk to the bathroom, during which their stares burrowed into the back of my skull. I was pretty sure I also saw a scroll, however improbable that seemed.

In the bathroom, I strode to the sinks, leaned on the vanity top, and gave myself a hard look in the mirror. People talk about inflection points, most of which they recognize only after the fact. I had no doubt this was such a moment. There had been several leading to this point. When I invited Fiachra to have breakfast with me after our second meeting. When I had him prove he was one of the Fae. And most recently, when I went to Sidhe Baile. Upon further consideration, my participation may have been more voluntary than I'd allowed a minute ago.

But this moment now was loaded with consequences, as yet unforeseen and unknowable. If I went forward, I was putting myself at risk, but I might also put Ella in the path of danger. That wasn't quite right. Ella was already in danger. The BCG had bad intentions for her and everyone else whose teeth they'd been collecting.

A dozen contradictory axioms mingled with my brainwaves. Discretion is the better part of valor. The coward dies a thousand deaths, while the brave dies but one … or something like that. Then there were the words of Mark Twain, who could be found to have said something memorable for most any occasion. I don't know why this one had stuck. Perhaps, for this very occasion. "The human race is a race of cowards; and I am not only marching in that procession but carrying a banner."

While I was mostly indifferent about the banners of cowardice and valor, I was invested in having a say about my own fate. Now that I knew the players and had a pretty good idea about the stakes, I couldn't leave the problem for someone else to deal with. In the immortal words of NSYNC, "It's gonna be me."

# Chapter 22
# Company Comes to Town

"Your girl there is a total smoke show," one of the junior executives, whose haircut suggested he wasn't far removed from living at a frat house, said after Annie had left the conference room and shut the door. As was typical of guys who'd gone from kindergarten straight through to an MBA program, he had more student loans than sense.

I tilted my head and bit my upper lip, but not for long. "Let me tell you a bit about *my girl* there. She worked herself out of the trailer park one crappy job at a time. She basically raised her younger siblings because her parents were too strung out on some combination of uppers and downers to recognize what planet they were on most of the time. She's smarter and savvier than most of the people in this room, including me, but with none of the privilege. So if we could maybe address Annie with a little more respect, that would go a long way."

The offender shrunk into his chair. "Sorry, man. I didn't mean anything by it."

My reaction probably didn't make for a good business decision. I tried to rein it in. I took a deep breath to give myself a moment. "Don't worry about it. We're on the other side of it now. Probably best Annie didn't hear you, though."

"Why's that?" he asked meekly.

"She's usually like the humans in *Hitchhiker's Guide*, but sometimes she bites."

Most of the room looked at me blankly. But a youngish woman cackled and filled the rest of them in on the joke. "Mostly harmless. Good one."

I stood up. "If y'all will excuse me for a minute, I'm going to step down the hall. Then we can get started."

As I left the room, Jerry started telling his underlings. "And that is why we have all those human resources semina—"

When the door closed, Annie was waiting on the other side of it, arms crossed. She didn't say anything.

"What?"

"I have never been so offended in my life."

"I know. I handled it. He shouldn't ha—"

"Not that clown, dummy. I deal with his kind all the time. You."

I recoiled. "Me? What did I do?"

"Mostly harmless," she repeated back to me. "Mostly harmless? How dare you." Finally, she smirked and let me know she was just messing with me.

"I was trying to diffuse things. I got a little riled up. And I couldn't very well tell him he was lucky you didn't come in there and field dress him like a buck and leave his guts on the table."

"Can I tell him that? Or better yet, do it? Gotta get ready for deer season."

"It'd really be best if you didn't."

"That's not a no."

"I'm asking for a favor."

"Fine. I'll let it slide this time, but if he so much as speaks to me, the knives come out."

I nodded. "Fair."

"Okay. Where do you want to take them for dinner?"

"Let's do The Whole Hog."

"Reserve the back room and tell them you want the Big Daddy?"

"Perfect."

As she headed back to her desk, I turned my attention back to the insurance policy language we were there to finalize.

Some of the younger guys made no effort to hide their disappointment that we weren't at some fancy-pants restaurant. I could only imagine the disparaging remarks I'd been on the receiving end of during the drive over. But it didn't matter. And you know why? Because Jerry was in charge, and Jerry was pumped about some whole hog barbecue. Though, I'm not sure he knew exactly what he was in for.

I sat at one end of the table with Jerry and my *Hitchhiker's Guide* compatriot, Heather. The underling bros congregated as far from me as they could manage. I'd have to figure out a way to make good with them. If anything happened to Jerry or he went somewhere else, I'd be hard pressed to keep their business at this point.

"Do you like fantasy books or just sci-fi?" Heather asked.

"I used to read a ton of fantasy," I said. "But lately … this is going to sound weird. Are you ready?"

Her eyes glittered with curiosity.

"Lately, it's felt a little too real for me to enjoy fiction."

"How so?" she asked.

"Well … do you believe in magic and mythical creatures? Like real ones?"

Jerry raised an eyebrow at me.

Even Heather was skeptical now.

A bridge too far, I guess. "Nah," I grinned. "I'm just messing around. I haven't had a lot of spare time for reading lately."

"Good one," Jerry said, clapping me on the shoulder. He leaned forward and said conspiratorially, "*The Amber Chronicles* by Roger Zelazny changed my life."

Heather flung herself backward in her chair and raised her hands to her head before expanding them outward. "Jer, you're blowing my mind right now! I had no idea."

He wore an embarrassed smile.

"Any confessions from you?" Heather asked.

Keeping the same tenor, I looked over my right shoulder, then my left. "I love *Harry Potter* and listen to the audiobooks about once a year. Can't wait 'til my six-year-old is old enough for me to share them with her."

"Well, aren't you two a couple of saucy minxes?"

I snickered at that. I didn't really know Heather, but I was happy for her that she'd found her people. That makes almost anything tolerable.

Two servers walked out of the kitchen bearing a large … I'm not even sure of what the right word is. Tray connotes something too small. What they had was about the size of a folding table, but made of bamboo. And it bore a hulking animal carcass. The Big Daddy that I'd had Annie order for us was literally the entire pig on a platter. It was an extraordinary experience, as long as you could get over the idea that the animal's eyeballs were still looking at you while you ate it. Equally alarming (and I was sure they weren't prepared for this) was its teeth still being secured to its jaws. That fact made me shudder more than it might have a few days ago. The BCG had been living rent-free in my head for a while now.

Regardless, I was as excited about the reactions as I was for the meal.

My only disappointment was that as the servers delivered the hog, they pointed the tail end toward us. I thought it would be more symbolic for its backside to have been directed toward Mr. Smokeshow and the gang.

The disappointment didn't last. Groans and gasps arrived quickly.

"What the heck?" croaked the guy I remembered from the first meeting, Gordon.

"It's teeth, man. That's messed up."

My amusement turned to dismay. I hadn't expected the reactions to be this over the top. I stood up and noticed something white scattered in front of the pig's snout. When I walked around the table, I found that all its teeth had been extracted and piled on the tray in front of it.

My head popped up, and I scanned the room. The servers had left. It was just our group. I strode out and into the kitchen. Dozens of people bustled around. No one paid any attention to me, except for a couple of bus boys who jostled me as they scooted through the doorway.

I had taken another step into the kitchen when a somewhat familiar voice asked, "Is everything okay, sir?"

One of our servers stood behind me.

"Yeah, uhh. Could you bring another pitcher of tea when you get a sec?"

"No problem, sir. Be right there," he said with all the cheery hospitality of a person who knew that his livelihood depended on promptness and likability. I'd been there too. Heck, that's not far removed from my present line of work.

I saw nothing amiss on my way back to my guests. I went straight to the foot of the table and swept the pig's teeth into my hand. "Sorry, guys. That's not usually part of the experience."

Not knowing what else to do with them, I dropped the teeth into my pocket.

# Chapter 23
# The Old Covenants

"How do we even start?" I asked, back in the cozy confines of the library. So far, the thing I most appreciated about it was the lack of florescent lighting, whose constant buzzing and inevitable flickering were beyond irksome. The lamps and sconces were from a bygone era, and the basement was far warmer because of it. They seemed more appropriate for the topic of our research, which would take us back thousands of years in human history.

"Like anything else, I guess. What's your search engine of choice?" Madeline asked.

My mouth fell open. "I want you to know — you have single-handedly destroyed my entire belief structure about the superior knowledge of librarians."

She shrugged and opened a web browser. "We use the same tools as you mere mortals. We're just better with them."

An hour or so of inputting various queries — "history of fairies," "covenants between fairies and humans," "origins of fairies," and the like — yielded very little of substance. I wasn't entirely sure why I needed to be here for this.

After a while longer, we compared our meager notes. The

ancient Greeks referenced the equivalent of fairies. We found nothing noteworthy on the topic from the Hebrews. Genesis mentioned something about a people called the Nephilim, the offspring of relations between angels and men. I suggested maybe that was something to come back to. Madeline was convinced it was unrelated, but didn't want to get into it.

We discovered fleeting references to something in the British Isles about two thousand years ago, then nothing until the Middle Ages. Lore arising from that time eventually gave rise to modern fairy tales. It wasn't a lot to go on.

Madeline rubbed at her eyes with the heels of her hands. I knew that gesture well. It's what happens when all the letters on the screen lose their edges because your eyes and brain have made a pact to quit functioning until they can renegotiate their contracts.

"I'm not gonna lie," I said. "I thought we'd be looking through scrolls of parchment or something."

"Those on the shelf?"

I nodded.

"Nah. Those are relics that a German contingent brought with them when they immigrated here. Left them with us for safekeeping."

"And you just have them out in the open like that?"

She smirked. "Go give them a look-see … if you can."

I stood up from my chair and strode toward the bookshelf where the ancient documents rested. There didn't appear to be anything that would keep me from reaching out and picking one up. But there must have been, or she wouldn't have said it the way she did. I craned my neck to peer at the shelf from an angle. Still nothing.

When I stuck my hand out, I expected a shock. Like the one I got from the electric fence for the cattle at my grandparents' farm when I was helping my chubby cousin sneak under it, but he got tangled up in it and I got the worst of the electric bite.

Instead, it felt like I'd shoved my hand into warm bread dough. I jerked my hand back. Then tried it again. Same result. It was strange. I pushed my hand outward as hard as I could until it felt like the invisible goo had fully engulfed it. The force I applied and resistance I encountered reached an equilibrium well before I touched the scrolls.

I withdrew my hand and swiveled to look at Madeline.

She raised her eyebrows at me. "Yes?"

"What the heck is that?"

"Magic."

"Huh." I'd like to think I was beyond surprise by now, but mostly I was just speechless. My brain was redlining its engine, adding to the rapidly expanding repository of things it hadn't previously known existed. After I collected myself, I asked, "Isn't it kind of risky to have that where anyone can encounter it?"

"First of all, you have to have a key to get down here. And it turns out I'm the only person whose keycard works. Everyone else's malfunctions, and they've mostly forgotten the door to this part of the basement even exists. Second, and more importantly, when most people encounter things they can't explain, they either ignore it and their brain redirects attention elsewhere, or they contrive a rational explanation and move on. Humans are beings inherently bent to avoid confusion." She narrowed her eyes at me. "Except for lawyers and engineers. Y'all just keep poking at things that don't make sense to you. It's problematic."

I couldn't very well disagree with her. That poking was among my best or worst qualities, depending on the circumstance and who you asked.

"So, what's in the scrolls?"

"This is going to sound rude, but I don't mean it that way."

She wanted permission to say the not-rude thing. I waited.

"You're kind of on a need-to-know basis, and that's not really in the parameters of what you need to know. Sorry."

She was more sorry that she was the one who had to deliver the message than about the message she delivered.

"Why do you get to know?" I nearly cringed at how petulant the question sounded. It's not that I *really* wanted to know, but more that I didn't like not being allowed to know.

"I'm the librarian," she said as if that were of itself an explanation.

"And?"

"And we have been the holders and curators of knowledge for as long as humans have been writing things down. We have kept the world sown together when others have done their damnedest to tear it apart."

"Uh-huh." And here I'd thought lawyers were self-aggrandizing.

Madeline gestured toward her monitor. "Can we get back to this?" She tapped her watch, and the face illuminated. "I've got plans before too long."

I checked my watch. It was closing in on eight o'clock. I could remember a time when I didn't think that meant I was out late, but I'm fairly certain that was before I had a kid. "Sure." I added a bit of surliness so she'd know I hadn't forgiven the earlier slight.

"Do you watch football?"

That's not where I had expected us to start. "Is this us getting back to the covenants thing?"

"Yes-ish."

"Alright, yes, I watch football. But I don't pull for Auburn or Alabama."

She waved me off. "I don't care about that. You know how every year all the sports news outlets put out the way-too-early rankings like months before the season starts?"

"Yep."

"Well, I'm about to give you my way-too-early analysis about the covenants."

I shook my head. "That seemed like the long way around there."

She shrugged. "I don't think the covenants have anything to do with the Greeks. If they did, we'd already know about it. They always wrote about everything and like structure too much to have left something like this out."

"I'll take your word on it."

"And I don't think it came up during the Middle Ages in Europe. For similar reasons. Too much writing. We'd know something."

"Okay. That tracks." I looked down at my notes and ran a finger down the yellow legal pad. "So the British Isles then?"

"Yes. Maybe. I've got to do some more research to narrow it down a bit. Saying something is in the British Isles is like saying something is in Alabama, except if Alabama had ten times as many people and spoke four different languages."

"Okay. What do you want me to do?"

"Just go lawyer people or whatever. I'll holler at you in a couple of days."

I groaned. "The verbifying of words will be the demise of the English language."

"Don't care." She pointed to herself. "Librarian, not a philologist. Take it up with Tolkien."

# Chapter 24
# I Promise Not to Hurt You

To the west, cotton candy clouds (as Ella often called them) were backlit by the last of the lavender and orange rays left in the sky. Every step away from the library brought more relief. It wasn't like I was Frodo carrying a ring to Mount Doom, but this thing was weighing on me.

I waited at the traffic light for the signal to change and considered jaywalking because no cars were coming. A young woman stood on the opposite side of the street. She was tall enough that I wondered if she played volleyball at UAB.

When the light changed and the orange hand turned into a white figure frozen in mid-stride, I stepped into the street. As did the woman across from me.

We were about to pass each other when she stuck a hand out and planted it firmly on my chest. I can't imagine the surprise that played out on my face. Her stern demeanor never shifted. She was slightly taller than me, so I had to look up to meet her gaze.

"Do you know me?" she asked with an air of expectation.

I looked her fully in her very striking face. Not one that I immediately recognized, but when the recognition hit, it struck hard. The last time I'd seen her, she been addressing a mob, and her skin had been a fiery red that had wavered into purple and back as she delivered her monologue.

"No."

"Yes, you do." She wasn't arguing.

My face had betrayed me. I looked up and down the street. There were no cars or people.

"It's just us chickens, Scott Warren."

Her using my name brought my eyes back to hers. "Are you scared?"

"No."

She smirked and tilted her head. "Did Fiachra not teach you not to lie to the Fae? We take great offense to untruths."

I let loose a short string of swear words. The sound of it brought her joy.

Liadan latched onto my arm. "Let's go somewhere we can talk."

I yanked my arm free of her grip.

She pouted her lip out. "You don't want to take a trip with a pretty girl?"

"You're a bit young for me to be gallivanting about with."

"Let's at least get out of the street, then. I believe there is a coffee shop just around the corner." She threaded her arm through mine. "No tricks. Promise."

I walked in step with her. If I remembered my commandments correctly, she couldn't lie to me, but the truth could wear pretty thin before being perforated.

The coffee shop wasn't the cozy, low-lit place I liked near my house. It was bright and industrial and uninviting. But it was also empty, because it catered primarily to downtown foot traffic during normal business hours.

Liadan's order of steamed milk with caramel caught me off guard. It would have put me to sleep within the hour. I went with a decaf something-or-other that was a little more neutral on the drowsy-to-awake scale.

"I have some questions," I said quietly, though it wasn't altogether necessary. We were the only patrons, and the sole employee had popped his earbuds back in after taking our orders.

"As do I. Shall we take turns?"

I shrugged.

"You may go first."

"How did you find out who I am?"

"Direct. I like it. Your friend Cassandra was disenchanted — and I mean that figuratively, not literally — with the idea of being turned into a rug. But you'll be glad to know she did not give you up easily. Several of our number will bear reminders — look at me with the puns! — of that encounter for the rest of their lives."

"How did she know my name? I don't think I gave it to her."

Liadan wagged her finger at me. "My turn." She placed the same finger to her lips as if weighing what to ask, then raised the finger in the air like the idea had just come to her. "Why is Fiachra so interested in what the Guild is doing?"

I shook my head. "I don't know."

"That's what I figured."

"Then why did you ask?"

"Because I suspected it's a question you haven't been asking yourself, though you should."

I couldn't believe I'd gotten this far without considering his motives. That was a glaring oversight. "Fine. My turn."

"No, no. You just asked me a question."

I replayed the conversation in my head. I hadn't even thought before asking why. "I didn't mean that to be my question."

"You agreed to the rules. Now, you must play by them."

"Fine." Ashleigh had always hated that particular *fine*.

Despite the word conceding the point, the tone told the listener you weren't making any concessions in your heart. It's really the highest and best use of being passive-aggressive.

"What is your role in this matter?"

It was an excellent question. And not one I knew the answer to with any certainty. As I mulled it over, the words of my child — when she was feeling bratty — rang in my head. "That's for me to know and you to find out."

"What? I don't know what that means."

"It means I'm not going to tell you, and you can't make me." I was leaning all the way into being bratty. It wasn't a good look, but I was out of answers.

"The rules, Scott. I shouldn't have to remind you again."

I grinned at her. "The rules were that we would take turns asking questions. Nothing was said about answering them. If you're going to be overly literal, you have to keep things straight, Tooth Fairy."

While her eyes blazed, her voice was cold as a glacier. "I will strike you down." Liadan's skin flashed with a crimson shimmer.

By the time the barista turned his head our way, thinking his peripheral vision had caught something out of the ordinary, there was nothing for him to see but two people having a strained conversation.

Sensing the movement, Liadan looked toward the barista and flashed a smile. He hurriedly turned away and found some way to occupy himself. Her striking beauty really was almost too much. I impressed myself by having not focused on it to this point.

I hadn't truly appreciated Annie's reaction to Fiachra before, but I did now. Steel would have better luck resisting the pull of a magnet than I would have refusing Liadan if she decided to charm me.

"There's something I want to show you," she said, some of the warmth having returned to her voice.

"Okay."

"It will require us to step outside."

"In that case, I'm good. When we leave here, we will do so at separate times and going our separate ways."

"Please," she pleaded, batting her eyelashes in an overtly flirtatious manner. "I promise not to hurt you."

# Chapter 25
# Made of Metal and Light

That she even felt it necessary to voice such a promise was alarming, but Liadan was bound by her promise.

I clenched my jaw and nodded. She rose and waited for me to do the same before turning toward the door.

Once we were outside again, I doubted my decision. But it felt like we were on some kind of prescribed course, and I could not deviate from the track.

She made her way to the nearest street lamp and stood under its warm glow, beckoning me to join her. I stopped in front of her and crossed my arms. "You wanted to show me something?"

Liadan nodded and pulled out a small jewelry box filigreed in gold and silver. An intricate oak tree decorated the lid. I don't know where the box came from. I was certain that the athleticwear she had on was snug enough that if she'd had it on her before, it would have been obviously protrusive.

She watched my face as she opened the lid and exposed the velvet-lined interior and its contents.

My mouth tingled like an electric current ran through it. I withdrew backward involuntarily. "What is that?"

"We've been holding onto these for a long time."

I no longer had any room to doubt that the tooth fairy was real, and Liadan was among their number. My stomach rumbled and revolted at the revelation.

"I want to give you the gift of knowledge."

Wasn't that almost exactly what the Serpent had said to Eve in the Garden? And look how that turned out for everyone.

"You know what? I think I'm gonna pass."

Liadan extracted a tooth from the box, placed it on her tongue, and closed her mouth.

In an instant, I'd lost control over my body. My central nervous system had been hijacked. Liadan compelled my eyes to look into hers. "You are beginning to understand?" She touched me lightly on the nose. "I can do anything I want with or to you. Anything."

Dread and terror coursed through my veins in place of blood.

She forced me to take a step toward the curb. Then another.

The horror was that of sleep paralysis, when your mind has woken up from a nap but your body hasn't. You're telling it to move, but nothing is happening. You are occupying an immobile husk.

Except that my body was moving ... of someone else's volition.

She had me step down from the curb onto the street between two parked cars. My movements were uncertain and jerky. Like a fawn standing up and walking for the first time. Anyone who saw this would think I was drunk.

My head turned and peered up 6th Ave. The multiple bright lights of a tractor-trailer barreled down the road several blocks away, unencumbered by changing traffic lights.

Liadan turned me to face her. She stepped me backwards into the right lane. She tried to project indifference to me, but she was fully invested in this. Intensity poured out of her.

She refused to turn my head up the street again. I tried to

look around the corner of my eye. All I could make out was a great brightness approaching.

My body turned. It leaped fully into the center lane. My hips swiveled and faced me toward the monster made of metal and light. It was less than half a block away.

The truck blared its horn. Its tires and engine roared. I did not move. My skin prickled from the disturbance in the air that preceded the monster's arrival. Brakes screamed. Still, I did not move.

The lights absorbed my vision. There was nothing else. The light jolted to my right and yawed clockwise as it flew by me. I did not move. A tremendous blackness thundered past.

The earth shuddered as the tractor-trailer collapsed onto its side. Metal ground against concrete. My feet sent me the vibrations from the collision.

I collapsed. A human heap in the middle of the roadway. Carnage enveloping me.

As I lay in the street, I pushed my shirt off of my face. I had moved my hand. I moved my hand!

Rolling onto my belly, I pushed myself up and took stock of the situation. Steel pipes littered the street from me to where the truck had stopped on its side a hundred feet to the east. Liadan leaned against a tree, more or less where I had last seen her. She gave no indication that she was going anywhere. She couldn't have been more casual if she'd been taking a drag on a cigarette.

The truck driver. I ran past the trail of debris that led to the trailer and had to take a wide path, so I didn't break an ankle. I slowed as I approached the cab. With the truck on its side, the only access point was the front windshield.

The truck had come to a final rest after crashing through the granite slab that announced the existence of the Financial Center, as though the seventeen-story building was insufficient to make passersby aware of its own presence.

The inside of the cab was a gory mess. Several steel pipes had breached the cab and impaled themselves through his chest and head. They held him unnaturally in place in his seat while everything around him was askew. I turned away almost immediately.

Hunched over with my hands on my knees, I tried to keep myself together. Several drops of blood splashed onto the pavement below me. It was mine.

I snatched my phone out of my pocket and turned on the self-facing camera. Blood spilled onto the screen as I held the phone below me. I rotated myself upright. Wooziness nearly overwhelmed me. I backed up a couple of steps to lean against the corner of the truck.

The screen showed a gash above my right eye that curved downward toward my temple. Most of that side of my face was a scarlet mess.

I dropped the phone when I realized that the punctured driver's corpse was on the screen. Only when I reached down to pick it up did I see that my left arm had a piece of metal embedded in it. I stood up carefully. The wooziness had doubled down. I wasn't certain that if I tumped over, I'd be immediately able to get up again.

As I steadied myself with a hand against the truck, I began making my way around its exposed underbelly and back toward Liadan. She still stood against the tree, head cocked to the side, watching as I ambled across the street and weaved between parked cars.

When I stopped in front of her, I was no longer wobbly. Anger had replaced fear. She flicked out her tongue, which held the ashes of my tooth, then spit them out.

"You killed him." I pointed at the wreckage behind me.

She shrugged. "That's not what it looked like from here."

Liadan reached into her mouth, pulled a bit of tooth off her tongue, and flung it to the ground at my feet.

# Chapter 26
# That's My Cue

I held up my bleeding arm and turned my head to make sure she saw the bloody half of my face. "You broke your promise?"

"Beg to differ." The haughtiness in her voice was insufferable. She thought herself beyond consequences.

I was dumbstruck, standing there with my mouth agape. Liadan never moved while I floundered. Eventually, I collected enough of my wits to spit out a sentence. "You what?" Or if not a sentence, then a coherent phrase.

"I believe that the video footage will show an intoxicated man wandering out into traffic."

"But that's not what happened," I complained, and hated myself for it.

"I think we have all learned a valuable lesson today — what I am capable of. And thanks to the hundreds of millions of you who so carelessly dispose of your bones, I see an extraordinary future ahead. One in which the Fae claim their dominion over this land. We will need some help, of course. But don't you worry your little head about that. I have it well in hand."

Sirens rang in the distance.

"We will stop you," I said impotently.

"We?" Liadan laughed. "You and who?"

"Fiachra."

Her laughter increased.

"You would exchange one overlord for another? That seems rather ill-considered. I think maybe you are in over your head here, human."

"How well do you know our history?"

She shrugged. Finally, some uncertainty showed on her face. She masked it quickly enough.

"In 1942, Hitler was raging through Europe, enslaving and killing millions. The U.S. allied itself with Stalin and the Soviets to defeat the Nazis. It was distasteful, but it was the only way."

"And?"

"And I will align myself with whomever I need to so I can rid the world of you tooth fairies."

She narrowed her eyes and withdrew the small golden and silver box again. "Yours is not the only one of these I possess, you know. Ella. Ashleigh. Even Annie. Did I miss anyone else who matters to you? Maybe your parents and sister. Maybe they can all take a beach trip together and walk down to the water and keep on walking."

I closed the distance between us.

"Oh, will you threaten me now?" Amusement colored her face.

Flashing red lights turned a nearby corner as the sound of sirens magnified.

"That's my cue," she said. "Toodles."

Liadan disappeared, leaving behind only wreckage.

I looked around and decided quickly that it'd be best if I were not here when the first responders arrived. I slipped into an alley between two buildings and worked my way south. The entrance to the parking garage was about to be blocked off. And I suspected that the lightheadedness I was now experiencing was from blood loss. I needed some help.

I poked at my watch a few times until it brought up the number I wanted.

A deep baritone came through. "Yes?"

"I'm in kind of a tight spot."

"Where are you?"

I shared my location with him and, in the briefest of terms, told him about the situation. He instructed me to sit tight until he arrived.

I followed his instructions literally, slumping down the wall that I'd been leaning against until my butt made contact with the ground. The only thing that kept me conscious was the stinging of sweat trickling into my head wound. I had the sweltering humidity of August to thank for that.

But even that discomfort must not have been enough to keep me alert. The last thing I recall thinking while I waited was wondering what kind of vehicle a literal giant drives.

The answer to that question would have to wait. By the time I came to, I was already in the vehicle. It was clearly not the Fiat that my sense of humor had demanded, so that was disappointing.

"Welcome back," Athos said. My movement having clued him in to my consciousness.

"I hope I wasn't too much trouble."

"I've managed worse, but do be careful not to bleed on the seat."

I found that my arm was wrapped in gauze. Reaching up to my head, I discovered it had been tended to as well. "Thanks," I said, gesturing at the bandages.

"It'll do until we get you to a healer."

"That where we're headed?"

He nodded.

"Like a hospital?"

"No."

"Where are we going?"

He didn't answer. I assumed that was my indicator to stop asking questions.

The city's lights grew less dense as we hopped onto the interstate and headed north. I wondered if we were going back to his town of Gardendale until he took I-22 and carried us northwest.

The Brookside exit was not what I was expecting. A place known for only two things: a bout of police corruption that made statewide headlines for a while, and a seemingly misplaced Russian Orthodox church. The latter had experienced the height of its influence a century earlier when the coke ovens still burned bright in these parts.

When he pulled to a stop in front of a nondescript house in a run-of-the-mill subdivision, I looked at him with surprise.

"What were you expecting?"

"I don't know, a doctor's office or something."

"This will be better."

"In what way?"

"In the way that you need healing, and I have brought you to a healer."

It was hard to argue against that kind of logic, although I wasn't entirely sure my health insurance was going to cover my expenses. This had "out of network" written all over it.

Athos killed the engine and opened the door to his van. It wasn't until the lights came on that I could see the interior well enough to figure it out. Not a minivan, but a true van. The kind you only see being driven by families where the children vastly outnumber the parents.

"Can you walk?"

"Yes, I can walk." I said it with contempt for the question and hoped I was right.

I popped my door open and slid to the ground, feeling steadier than I had expected. The gibbous moon hung above the tree line. It was bright enough to cast its own shadows, reminding me of a story my great-grandfather used to tell about a cold night of camping in Colorado when one of his buddies had a sleeping bag — or a slumber bag, as he called it — that wasn't warm enough. He inched closer and closer to the fire, until an ember popped out, landing on the bag and burning through it in an increasingly widening hole. His buddy flopped over, and wriggled and writhed until the fire had gone out, while the two other boys laughed and cackled at their friend's misfortune. After that, they all had a miserable time. The cold one complained through the rest of the long night, ensuring that if he didn't sleep well, no one else would either.

That was the kind of adventure I could go in for, rather than the kind where fairies try to kill me.

Athos led the way to the front door, where he ducked under the portico. When he knocked at the door, I wondered what time it was. It had been a little after eight when I'd left the building. My watch said it was now after ten. There was a good chance we'd be waking the healer up unless he'd given them some advance notice.

The door opened, and a surprised "Oh" escaped my mouth. I tried to recover with an overly friendly, "Howdy."

Sam crossed her arms.

Sam, the flirt, forward woman from the Warrior River.

Sam, who I hadn't called back.

Athos looked down at me, a smirk showing his amused curiosity. It was the first time I'd seen him express any kind of joy, but I didn't really have time to explore that at the moment.

"You didn't call."

She wasn't wrong. But it wasn't for lack of good intentions.

"Yet. I didn't call *yet*."

# Chapter 27
# On the Count of Three

Sam's glare deepened. I squirmed under the pressure.

"It's been a … there's not even a word for what the last couple of weeks have been. Alarming, maybe."

"I can vouch for that," Athos said.

She turned her withering look to him. He shrugged it off. The scars that peeked out from his shirt on his arms suggested that he'd been through worse than she was offering.

"Perhaps you can piece him back together," Athos suggested, "and then you two can work through whatever offense he has caused."

"It's fine," she said lightly as she stepped aside to let us in. "I've got other irons in the fire. He just seemed like a nice boy."

Jealousy must always wait in the wings, because it pounces and pricks at the slightest provocation.

The house was one of those new-but-not-nice places that are slapped together within a couple of weeks, so that even the working class can buy new construction and firmly entrench themselves as debtors (and thus contributors to the labor force for the next thirty years). Was that too cynical? Maybe.

Anyway, she obviously had good taste, even if the interior walls weren't entirely square.

Sam led us to her dining room and directed me to a chair. I sat obediently. She took my arm in her hands and unwrapped the bandage. Blood had dried on the gauze that was up against the skin, creating an adhesive bond. She tugged at it to see how stuck it was. Pretty stuck.

"On the count of three."

I nodded.

"One … two … —"

She ripped. On two.

"Yow! What the heck? You said three."

"It's a trick I do with kids. Keeps them tensing up or flinching."

Blood poured out anew.

I looked down at it and then at Sam. "Aren't you going to get your doctor kit or whatever?"

She looked to Athos with raised eyebrows.

"He's new to all this," he said.

"New to what?"

Athos ignored me. "Just do your thing. It's easier to see the results than to explain the process."

Sam gripped my arm with both of her hands, tightly but not squeezing. Blood oozed between her fingers.

Warmth emanated from her hands like a fever. The flow of blood stopped. I'd expected stitches, maybe even staples. But not … whatever was happening.

She started scrubbing at my arm with a wet rag to get at the dried blood. I winced and yanked my arm away, anticipating a sudden torrent of pain, but none followed. I looked down at the arm. The coagulated remnant was the only evidence that moments ago, a gash had been there.

I extended my arm, which Sam took in her hands and resumed cleaning.

"Now your head."

"What did you do?"

"Magic." Her tone disguised whether she was being genuine or humoring me.

It didn't matter. If this wasn't magic, it might as well have been.

Athos said, "I need to make a call."

She pointed down the hallway. "Use the first room on your left."

He left us alone in the dining room.

As Sam removed Athos' hastily applied wrap, I asked, "Are you going to count to—Ow!"

A smile curled the corners of her lips upward.

My forehead and cheek tickled as fresh streams of blood wandered down. "Catholics pay less penance," I grumbled.

She placed one palm on my head against the wound. The other cradled the back of my head. A minute later, she hunched down in front of me, cleaning my face.

"Good as new," she declared.

Athos emerged from the room down the hall with a person who, in anyone else's company, would be strikingly tall. But as it was, the giant dwarfed him.

"Heard you found a spot of trouble," Fiachra said.

He didn't bother to adopt his human facade and currently presented as a cool purple. I'd begun to think of him as a living mood ring.

Sam didn't object to his presence or appear startled at his appearance, so I assumed this was old-hat for her. Either that or she was an extraordinary poker player.

"Let's go to the living room," she suggested. "But you two boys best not bust up my furniture."

She made a detour by the kitchen to drop the blood-soaked rags into the sink.

When she arrived in the living room, Athos seated himself

on a love seat that he fully occupied. He sat still as a picture, likely afraid that any movement would spell disaster for the furniture. Fiachra took up a plaid high-back chair that he was coaxing his skin to emulate. I sat on one end of the sofa, and Sam sat immediately beside me. I didn't know what to make of that, but it was certainly preferable to the guy in a public restroom that walks past four empty urinals to stand beside you and pee.

"Tell your tale," Athos instructed.

I told them everything. From the moment I'd encountered Liadan in the street to my phone call with Athos. Silence resonated in the room once I'd finished.

Sam stood and excused herself to the kitchen. The sounds of cabinet doors and percolating coffee soon emerged. I took it we were going to be here a while.

"How are you doing?" Fiachra asked.

I looked down at my arm, still disbelieving, as if it were an illusion that would soon wear off. "The truck driver. I know in my head that it wasn't my fault…"

"It wasn't," he assured me.

"…but in my heart," I touched my chest, "I wonder if I could have done something different. Resisted harder."

Athos nodded. "Violent death is not something one acclimates to easily. And ideally, does not become acquainted with at all."

"The point of her exercise, Scott, was that you could not resist. None of you will be able to when the time comes. That is why we must find a solution before they gather their strength and apply it."

"Is there nothing you can do to stop them?"

Fiachra shook his head. "The rest of the Fae are quite constrained in what we can do outside of Sidhe Baile. We all pre-date the covenants. And inside Sidhe Baile, they have many sympathizers. Many who whisper quietly in the night about returning the Fae to power. Who have become discontented with the quiet, idyllic lives we lead."

I considered it. Humans would not be so different if the roles were reversed.

Sam returned with coffee and biscotti on a pewter tray.

The next topic required me to wade into some uncomfortable waters. People think lawyers are always keyed up for a fight. But it's not the case, even for litigators. Some of us live our lives trying to avoid conflict. It's a weird conundrum.

I took a deep breath and looked directly at Fiachra. "Liadan says you have ulterior motives for wanting to keep her out of power."

He raised an eyebrow at me. "Of course, I do. Altruism is a fiction. Surely, you were not so naïve as to think this was all out of the goodness of my heart?"

Sam leaned forward and whispered loudly, "His face tells me he hadn't considered your motives before tonight."

I flushed red. We kept running into things I should have thought of sooner. This problem wasn't new to me. Once, when a partner was telling me about a recent issue he'd encountered in a case, I followed up with a question. He said, *Scott, that's probably the eighth question you should have asked. You blew right past the first seven.*

Right now, though, no one's motives mattered except the tooth fairies who wanted to enslave a good chunk of humanity in order to eliminate the rest. I didn't have room for anything else.

"So what's the plan?"

# Chapter 28
# Formulating a Plan

Apparently, the plan involved a passport and international travel. When I answered the knock on my door two days after my run-in with Liadan, Madeline greeted me with an eager smile. I stuck my head out past the door frame and looked to the left and right. Had to be sure no one else was accompanying her.

"Some people call ahead before they come over. It's Friday night, I could have been doing something."

"I'm a free spirit," she said. "I don't like being burdened with things like plans."

"You're kidding, right?"

"Yes. Now, are you going to let me in, or what?"

I stepped aside. Madeline came in and made a beeline for my bookshelves in the living room. After several minutes of perusing, she turned back around.

"Well?" I said.

"Well, what?"

"Do you approve?"

"I'm not judging. I only get judgy when people have out 'important' books that they've obviously never read but think they need to own to impress people. But yours are … definitely not that." She smirked as she finished the sentence.

"That last part sounded a little bit judgy. Also, I'm newly divorced and closing in on middle age. There aren't a lot of folks coming around, much less any that need impressing."

"Read whatever you want. I am kind of surprised, though … no legal thrillers?"

"Eh," I shrugged. "They're a little too close to work while also not at all resembling anything I've ever experienced. Probably like to you watching that show *The Librarians*."

"Don't you dare say anything ill of Noah Wylie." She made her hands into a heart shape.

I raised my arms in surrender. "I stand corrected."

"The same goes for Rupert from *Buffy*," she added with a stern look.

"I wouldn't dream of it."

The look on her face caused me concern that this was about to turn into one of those weirdly uncomfortable conversations where somebody tells you about their fantasies with a fictional character, then wants you to do the same. But Madeline pulled back from whatever reverie she'd been engaging.

"I'm not here just to be nosy about your books."

"I assumed as much. Do you remember where we left off?"

"Yeah, you had to do some research about Great Britain."

"Close, but no cigar," she said with way too much enthusiasm. "Oh, do you want to know where that idiom came from?"

"Not really."

Her expression soured, but only for a moment. The joy returned when she started telling me why I was wrong. "Not Great Britain. That doesn't include Ireland. And we need to go back in time about two thousand years because whatever happened was before the Romans got there. So it's like a black hole of information. We're not going to find anything on this side of the Atlantic."

"So we're at a dead end?"

"Nope. Pack your bags, dude. We're going on a field trip."

"No, *we* aren't. It may have escaped your attention, but I have a kid and a law practice."

"The kid doesn't even live with you."

The blood rushed to my face as quickly as it drained from hers. She covered her mouth. "I'm so sorry. I didn't mean—I'm sorry."

I pushed away from the shelf I'd been leaning against and looked around to see if there was anything she'd brought in with her that she would want to take when I ushered her out.

Tears sprang to her eyes, and she begged my forgiveness.

I would be the planet's biggest hypocrite if I didn't pardon someone for shoving their entire foot in their mouth. My own had spent considerable time there from adolescence to the present. I slipped onto the chair next to where she sat cross-legged on the couch. "Where are we supposed to be going?"

She sighed. "Dublin."

In my surprise, I made a noise that tried to be a word but never got there.

"Can you make it work?"

I flipped through the calendar on my phone. "Dunno. I can maybe move some things if I can conjure up a good enough reason."

Her posture slowly improved from the slump it had taken a minute ago. "Can I make a suggestion?"

"Alright."

"You've got an aunt who helped raise you. She moved to … let's say … Wales, in her later years. Now she's taken sick and has a grim diagnosis and you need to visit her before she passes."

I considered it. "Couple questions. Why Wales?"

"Nobody knows anything about Wales. They won't ask as many questions."

Made sense. "Next. You came up with that awfully fast."

"That's not a question, but I'll answer it anyway. I'm a librarian. I have access to a lot of stories. It's useful."

I realized I was going to have to rework the adjectives that I have readily available in my mental inventory for librarians. *Crafty* definitely had to be added to the list.

"What's in Dublin?"

"The Book of Kells, but that's really only a waypoint for us. I don't get the sense that's where we'll wind up."

"Why's that?" This was starting to feel like a deposition with a witness who actually listened to their lawyer (a rare enough occurrence) and answered only the very specific question that was asked instead of elaborating.

"It's not something I can identify yet. But I hope to have something a little more concrete before we go."

"It kind of seems like we're going across the Atlantic on a whim."

She furrowed her brow at me, and the playfulness left her voice. "Just because I don't have a fully formulated answer yet doesn't mean I'm operating on a hunch. What I have are a dozen wisps of information and the name of a librarian in Ireland who DM'ed when I started asking certain kinds of questions in a librarian's forum."

"Are you sure it's safe to be asking around about this?"

"Are *you* sure it's a good idea to be second guessing everything I do?"

I'd struck a nerve. "Sorry."

"Look, I get that this is way more personal for you since your kid was kind of threatened and you were almost suicided, but if you want to be involved in this — and I assume you do or what the heck — you're gonna have to trust someone. And as things stand, I'm the person best positioned to help you, okay?"

"Okay."

"Okay. Great." Relief washed over her. "I didn't have a backup plan if that went a different way."

"I don't think there's much in the way of backup plans for any of this as best I can tell."

"Oh. Yeah. No. You're definitely right. We are plowing new ground here." She took a deep breath. "I mean, nobody's seen anything like this in a couple thousand years."

The only time I'd felt more overwhelmed than this moment was when the hospital sent us home with Ella. What was I supposed to do with a screaming love goblin? No one had trained me for that. And we had to keep it alive. At least Ashleigh had some kind of instinct that had kicked in. I was mostly driving blind through a hurricane.

"So, when do we need to leave?"

She looked at her watch. "The sooner the better."

"Like a couple of weeks?"

"Umm, no. A couple of days."

I consulted my calendar again. "I've got Ella tomorrow and Sunday."

"Monday then?"

"I guess so. How long will we be gone?"

"Dunno," she said with a shrug. "I wouldn't pack more than you can carry on your back, though."

**Chapter 29**
# Shattered Adolescent Dreams

Madeline giggled. "You know I wasn't being literal, right?"

I looked at the hiking backpack that took up nearly the entirety of my leg room on the express bus. I'd considered getting rid of it many times over the last fifteen years since adulthood had set in and stuffing my travel clothes into an oversized pack became increasingly less acceptable.

"Well, you see, when you said that I should only pack what I can carry on my back, what I assumed you meant was that I needed to be able to carry it on my back."

She shook her head with a grin. "At least tell me about all your patches."

The front of the pack was covered in the flags of various states and countries, most of them showing significant weathering. "How much time do we have?"

"It should take about twenty minutes to get from the airport to our stop for Trinity College, so you've got about fifteen minutes left. And I expect to be riveted to my seat by your storytelling. Go."

"No pressure then. After college, two buddies and I had saved up enough money to go backpacking through Europe for a

150

couple of months. We got a Eurail pass and saw as much of western Europe as we could in the ten weeks that we had."

"Yeah, that's not storytelling. That's just summarizing, and barely that."

"When we were in Greece, we went to the beach. And it turns out that most of the women who were there were very comfortable with topless sunbathing."

"And?"

"And the ideas that I'd been stowing away since boyhood about what a nude beach would be like were shattered. That was the day I learned that most people look better with their clothes on."

"Most, but not all?"

"Correct, and the problem with those who look good without clothes on is that it can make things very uncomfortable for a young man who has to then refrain from observing them."

She laughed. A big, hearty laugh. The chatter that surrounded us in something that barely resembled English as I knew it quieted momentarily before resuming.

"Can I make a request?" I asked as the city around us took on the very Dublin qualities that I remembered from my youth.

"Within reason."

"Coffee."

"Reasonable and doable."

"I know we were supposed to sleep on the flight and that's why we did the overnight, but that was … challenging."

"What? You don't sleep well when you're mostly upright in confined quarters and a cabin full of strangers?"

"Surprisingly, I do not."

"Fair enough."

"Want to hear another story?"

Madeline yawned and nodded simultaneously.

"After my senior year of high school — which was a rough year in a lot of ways, mostly of my own doing — I came to

Dublin with a group from my church to do some mission work. One day, we came downtown to do some sightseeing. I was feeling like a fifth wheel with my friends, who were paired up with girlfriends, so I did my own thing. After a while, I'd seen what I wanted to see, so I sat down on a bench and pulled out the book I was reading, one of Tom Clancy's Jack Ryan books. Pretty sure it was *Patriot Games*. Anyway, in the book, the characters were in Dublin. And there was this big gun fight on the very street I was on. I forget the name of the street now. It's like Champs-Élysées is to Paris, as *blank* is to Dublin." I paused to see if she could fill the gap in my memory.

When she shook her head, I continued.

"Anyway, there was this firefight. So it was pretty cool that I was reading that part of the book at that moment. And there was this tiny part of me that expected to hear gunshots erupt around me and see people screaming and scrambling for cover."

The bus lurched to a stop, and about a third of its passengers stood up to disembark.

"This us?"

"We're next."

I hauled my backpack up and turned sideways in my seat so I could set it quasi-behind me. My legs scrunched against Madeline's.

"Not one for personal bubbles, huh?"

"Sorry. I didn't think that through. A little out of practice."

"I mean, they say you shouldn't travel alone with a guy because he might try to put the moves on you and it will get really awkward, especially if you reject him. But I gotta say, I didn't expect it this early in the trip or in quite this manner. And honestly, I thought I'd probably aged out of this situation."

My cheeks flushed, even though I knew she was just messing with me. I groped for some way to change the subject. "My pack is a lot lighter this time than when I came in the Oughts. I had about a hundred rolls of film with me, and I was carrying a dozen books at any given time. Bezos hadn't invented the Kindle yet."

"You must be older than that boyish face lets on. I thought I'd noticed a few gray hairs sprinkled in there."

I smacked my head on the back of the seat in front of me in exasperation.

"Oy!" Its occupant fussed at me.

I grimaced. "Sorry."

Madeline buried her face in her hands and shook silently, trying to contain her laughter. As the bus passed over the River Liffey, I said, "I may just ask the driver to let me out here so I can jump off the bridge and be done with it."

Madeline grabbed my arm with one hand as the shaking intensified. When a couple of big guffaws escaped, her cheeks reddened too. Now, we were getting closer to being on equal footing again. After another minute, she had restored control and sighed. "You know, we are why people hate Americans, right?"

"I thought it's because we're always meddling in other people's affairs."

"Nah, I really think it's because we are bad guests."

The bus stopped and "Trinity College" flashed on the display.

"That's us," she said.

On the city sidewalk, I realized I was totally unprepared for the Irish climate. The temperature was at least thirty degrees cooler here than at home. The hairs on my arms poked out at odd angles like a thousand small tentacles in search of warmth. I had no coverage to offer them. My breath hovered in the air as I waited for my compatriot to get off the bus.

Madeline tried to roll her suitcase beside her as we jostled through the busy morning crowds. After it slammed into several shins, she allowed it to trail in her wake. Once we pushed into the campus, the crowds thinned, and the cacophony of the city grew muffled. Green lawns stretched beside us and met a patch-work of buildings, both ancient and modern.

Blue signs told visitors where to find what they were looking for. Not one of them failed to point the way to the Old Library, home of the Book of Kells. As we closed in on the heart of campus, the new, smooth walkway gave way to ancient stone pavers. Madeline's arm that guided her suitcase looked like the pistons in an engine as she bounced over them.

I grinned at her. "So tell me now about how dumb my back-pack is. 'Cause I gotta tell you, I don't think *my* organs are getting rattled all around or anything."

She stuck her tongue out at me.

"Nice. If you were Ella, I'd have to send you to timeout for that."

"Well, you're old enough to be my son, so no more getting fresh like you were trying to on the bus."

"I—" I started to protest but bailed on it. Then I did some quick addition. It would have taken an early start on producing progeny, but she was technically right. And as those great sages who wrote *Futurama* once said, technically correct is the best kind of correct.

# Chapter 30
# Several Possible Evils

At the entrance to the Old Library, a man greeted us each by name. He was stooped and appeared to be as old as the library itself. He wheezed his way up the three steps that led into the building.

"Welcome to Trinity College Dublin. I am Eamon." A wry smile crossed his face. "I sound like a tour guide. Come this way."

I had to disagree. The only guide I'd seen leading a tour was several generations younger and substantially less emphysemic.

"Haman will take your luggage for you."

After the university student that Eamon indicated had relieved us of our possessions, I put my hand on Madeline's elbow and whispered, "This is the guy who slid into your DM's?"

She nodded curtly.

"If y'all have an old-fashioned librarian hook-up later, you better make sure he's got his oxygen machine handy."

She jabbed an elbow into my chest hard enough to leave an impression.

Once we were inside, the man's tottering shuffle steadied as his posture straightened, and he gained a good six inches in height. It was like watching the transformation of (spoiler alert!) Verbal Kent at the end of *The Usual Suspects*.

Since we were trailing our host somewhat, I waved my hand in Madeline's peripheral vision to get her attention. She looked my way. I pointed at Eamon and tried to use my arms to ask what the heck had just happened and why he had done that. I'm not sure the entire question translated into frantic gesturing.

She mouthed, "I don't know." But I got the sense she was blowing me off.

His voice too became sturdier as we made our way to the Long Room. "This library has existed since 1592, nearly thirty years before the Colonizers first sent people to the Americas."

He glanced over his shoulder at us. If he was looking for camaraderie over mutual disdain of the English, he was barking up the wrong tree. I was pretty indifferent about them. I had some thoughts about what a jumbled mess the common law judicial system we'd inherited was, but I didn't think he was interested in that spicy take. That said, I've been to Louisiana, and the tortured Napoleonic system they have there isn't any better. So maybe we'd gotten stuck with the lesser of several possible evils.

The Long Room was incredible enough that it pulled me out of my legal rabbit hole. Two floors of ancient manuscripts under a vaulted barrel ceiling. The smell was intoxicating. That much old paper gives off a scent that is almost magical unto itself.

I tuned back in to Eamon to hear him say, "This room is home to more than two hundred thousand books. The entire library houses over six million. We are privy to every book published in Ireland and the U.K."

Madeline didn't hide her awe.

"How many books does the Birmingham library have?" I asked.

"Fewer. Far, far fewer. And we have to fight to keep the budget to buy every single one of them."

Eamon asked, "Your government does not care about books?"

Red streaks peaked out from under the collar of Madeline, and she fidgeted with her hands. "Our local politicians have little more foresight than a locust and spend the bulk of their time in office either making sure they get re-elected or handing out favors and contracts to the people who got them elected in the first place."

"Maybe politics is a topic best avoided?" I offered.

"Access to books is not politics," Eamon countered. "It is a matter of providing for the general welfare of the people. And unless I am wrong, your federal constitution and many of your state's constitutions imbue their governments with this directive, no?"

"It may have escaped your attention," I said with a grimace, "but we've had a rather difficult time living up to those ideals."

Madeline scoffed. "Not true. The venerable forefathers were just super good about not saying the quiet part out loud. And I'd say historically white dudes have done an excellent job of looking after their specific welfare, to the exclusion of women and POCs."

I had no response to that. Neither, it appeared, did Eamon. A silence descended on us.

"So … have you read the new Jack Reacher book?"

Madeline glared at me.

"I am less familiar with that wing of the library," Eamon said earnestly. "But I can direct you toward it, if that is your wish."

"No," Madeline said. "He's just being a jackass. I haven't known him long, but it appears to be his natural state."

Eamon raised his eyebrows at me. I shrugged. He smiled. "As much as I am enjoying this discourse, which is far more engaging than the usual questions I would get from tourists if you weren't here, you did not come all this way to converse with me."

"You mentioned that you might have answers to questions I was asking about the Fae."

The old librarian looked suddenly uncomfortable. I asked if he was okay, and he replied, "I would rather we not even mention them by name."

"That makes you uncomfortable?" Madeline asked.

"They are an extraordinary pain in the arse. I would not do anything to provoke or summon them."

"That may make this conversation difficult."

I had an idea. "Do we need to use a code word for them?"

He waved my suggestion off like it was a troublesome gnat. "No, no. We won't do anything as silly as that. Forgive an old fella's superstitions. Yes, I may have answers for you. What do you know of the Book of Kells?"

I knew only what I'd seen on signage since arriving at Trinity College, so I deferred to Madeline, who I hoped had a more intelligent answer than anything I could muster. She didn't disappoint.

"The Book of Kells contains the four Gospels and was written in the early 800s AD. There is some question about where it was authored. In the 1600s, the Abbey of Kells was destroyed, and the book was moved to Dublin, and eventually to Trinity College, where it has remained ever since."

"Well said."

"I know more," she added as eagerly as a schoolgirl wanting to impress the teacher.

He nodded.

"It is an illuminated manuscript, meaning that it contains illustrations to accompany the text. In 1953, it was divided into four volumes, two of which are always on display here in the Long Room."

"Shall we go see it?"

The younger librarian's smile was as broad as any I had seen from her.

Eamon led us to a glass case that housed two volumes of the Book of Kells. The pages being displayed showed extraordinary works. A full page of John the Beloved surrounded by intricate designs and Celtic symbols. Another page contained words framed by symbols and fanciful animals.

It was an incredible work of art, but I had no idea what it had to do with fairies. I was pretty familiar with the New Testament, and none of the apostles mentioned anything about Fae folk. Demons, yes. Fairies, no. And Ireland certainly wasn't on their radar.

Still, I didn't want to ruin anyone's fun. Though I was jonesing for that cup of coffee I'd mentioned on the bus.

I asked, "Where do you keep the other two volumes?"

"In a safe room filled with argon gas. Along with the fifth volume." A shy grin crept across his face with the revelation.

Madeline and I exchanged astounded glances.

"You sly bugger," she said.

Eamon raised his eyebrows at her.

"Should I not say that?" If she were a turtle, she would have pulled her head almost entirely back into its shell.

"Not in polite company, you shouldn't. Fortunately for us, I am a librarian, and no one who knows us has ever leveled that accusation."

Relief flooded her face. "You're right about that, boss. But you wouldn't believe the number of people who expect me to be prim and proper because I'm a librarian." Madeline couldn't contain her eagerness even long enough for a smooth segue. "So about that fifth volume ..."

"Shall we go?"

Madeline was positively giddy. "Does a bear sh—"

"Not in Sidhe Baile, it doesn't," I interrupted. "She has a chamber pot."

# Chapter 31
# Within the Vault

The entrance to the safe room was out in the open and not disguised as something else. There was no book on a shelf that, when tilted backward, revealed a secret door. There was just a spoked wheel on a door built into a wall that revealed it was a safe.

When I expressed my surprise, Eamon said, "People expect a vault at a library like this one that serves as a repository for ancient documents. There is no reason to hide it or make anyone curious about its location. That would only cause them to go wandering about in search of it … in places we would rather them not go."

Eamon flattened his hand against a biometric scanner beside the vault door. After reading his fingerprints and palm, it emitted a satisfied chime and several bars disengaged with a thunk. He pulled the door open by the wheel and gestured us into the vault.

When he closed the vault door behind us, the locking mechanism re-engaged. If you were at all prone to claustrophobia, this would have been the point where it kicked in.

I had not expected a changing room, but on one wall was a

series of cubical cubbyholes. "You'll need to disrobe here."

"Excuse me?" Madeline said.

Eamon chuckled at his own joke. "I'm kidding, of course. But we will be putting those on." He pointed to some gear that looked like someone had stolen it off the set of a sci-fi movie. "The next room houses several ancient texts. To protect them from humidity, the room is sealed and filled with argon. Obviously, we can't breathe that, so we'll be wearing these encapsulated suits with their own air supplies."

I raised my hand. "How do we get in without letting all the gas out?"

"There is an antechamber between that room and this one. It was made to occupy two, so three will be snug. Once we have our suits on and turn on the oxygen supply — do not forget to do that — we will enter the antechamber and close the door behind us. All the air will be sucked out of the chamber. There will be a series of lights telling you what is happening. For the couple of minutes when we are in a vacuum, your suits will balloon out. Do not be alarmed. The lack of external air pressure pushing on them allows for this effect. The chamber will then fill with argon gas, and a door will open to the vault."

"What would happen if my suit got a hole in it?"

The old man nodded. It wasn't the first time someone had asked this question. "You would likely asphyxiate and perish."

"Has that happened before?" Madeline asked with moderate alarm.

"Not to anyone authorized to be here."

Sounded like there was an interesting story behind that cryptic response, and we weren't going to hear it.

Eamon took us step-by-step through getting suited up. It's not something you'd want to do with any frequency. It's fairly tedious. And you'd better go in with someone you trust because they do the final zip-up that keeps your lungs from getting sucked out through your trachea when the air gets pulled from the room.

The suits had their own comm systems, which made sense. If something went wrong while the antechamber was in vacuum status, there wouldn't be any other way to communicate with your partner, because no sound can transmit in a vacuum.

The most surprising part of the suits was the gloves. Somehow, even though they were completely sealed, I still had tactile sensation. I flexed my fingers and couldn't believe the lack of resistance. Eamon must have seen the curiosity on my face.

"Imagine that kevlar, nitrile, and silk cross-pollinated and produced a mutant offspring with only the best qualities from each of them."

I pursed my lips. "I'll be honest. I'm kind of getting hung up on what the reproductive organs of fabrics might look like."

I had no trouble seeing Madeline rolling her eyes, even through the suits' visors.

"Twelve-hundred-year-old vellum is a delicate thing. It wouldn't do to have someone tear a page because the gloves were too clumsy to feel anything through them. One last instruction: do not rely on visual cues and body language for communication. It is likely they will not be perceived. Everything must be verbal. Everyone ready."

"Yes," I said, my thousands of hours of depositions becoming unexpectedly useful again. *Make sure you answer everything out loud. The court reporter can't take down shakes or nods of your head. It's really normal to do that in every-day conversation, but it doesn't work here.*

Madeline nodded her head. I pointed at her and smiled. "Crap," she said.

As Eamon pressed a button to open the door to the anteroom, it occurred to me that we looked much more like a trio going to meet an alien life form or interact with a deadly virus than to see an old book.

The door opened almost noiselessly, revealing what looked like a small elevator car. We snuggled in. Eamon mashed a button and the door behind us closed. He twisted a handle on an adjacent wall, and the green light below the $O_2$ sign turned orange. A whirring sound started overhead.

I looked up as best I could, though the top of the suit hampered my upward sight lines. I imagined a giant fan sucking all the air out of the room, but it was probably more complicated than that. As promised, the suits turned us into yellow emulations of the Stay Puft Marshmallow Man.

The orange light became red.

"Good news," Eamon said. "Everyone's seals are good. Else you would be dead or dying right now."

He pressed another button below what I assumed was the designation for argon. My tenth-grade knowledge of the elements chart had lapsed. The light below it went from red to orange as a loud hissing noise emerged. As it continued, the suits resumed their original shapes.

The hiss trailed off, and the light turned green. Eamon reached out and turned a handle identical to the one he had used to close the door behind us. The only difference was that this one had Vault inscribed above it, where the other one read Library. Easy prevention from getting confused and opening the wrong door.

My brain was still expecting a cozy, softly illuminated library, so it took a couple of seconds for everything to sync when I saw a clean room to rival any scientific laboratory.

Drawers in the walls clearly identified their contents, while a counter in the middle of the room separated the vault into two aisles with a workspace in between. Three books were laid out on the countertop, but I wasn't able to focus on them yet. I was enamored by all the things we were bypassing. There was a Gutenberg Bible and one for the Magna Carta,

"The original?" I asked.

Eamon turned around to see what I was pointing at. "There were several originals. That is one of them. And to think, that bastard John was just trying to save his own neck and ended up shaping the world for the next several ages."

He turned back toward the manuscripts that were awaiting us. He swept his gloved hand over them with a flourish. "The fifth volume of the Book of Kells."

# Chapter 32
# The Fifth Volume

"There are only a handful of people who know of its existence. It is as closely guarded as any state secret."

"How is it you've decided to reveal it to us?" I asked.

"There comes a time when every secret outlives its utility. It has become clear that there is a new evolution afoot. So when Madeline started asking particular questions, and I inquired of certain acquaintances, I brought you into the fold."

"Enough jabbering," Madeline said. "Can we see it?"

Eamon smiled and motioned us over.

The fifth volume sat apart from the other two and was already opened. As we crowded around it and took in the images and unreadable but beautifully written text, Eamon pointed, and his tinny voice transmitted into our suits. "I trust this is familiar?"

Madeline's headpiece of her suit wagged from one side to another. "No."

The image he pointed at caused my heart to skip a beat, then speed up ferociously. A being that was human in shape, with skin that might have been overlaid with Joseph's coat of many colors.

"It's them." I was very eloquent in the moment. Later, I would think of exactly what I should have said that would have more appropriately fit the revelation.

"Indeed."

"It's who?" Madeline asked.

"*That* is a fairy." I jabbed my finger in the direction of the Book of Kells. Eamon's hands moved in frantic panic. Apparently, I had gotten closer than he was comfortable with.

"Please," he said. "There are no copies. No photographs. No digital imaging. If it is destroyed, it will be lost to us."

"Uh … is that smart? No offense."

"It is necessary."

Again, with no explanation. I hoped the library's other tour guides were more forthcoming with information, or else there were a bunch of disappointed tourists out there.

"No wings?" Madeline said.

"No wings," I confirmed. "Also, they're real fussy about stereotypes, so maybe don't bring that up if you meet one."

Madeline's face showed she was putting together some disparate pieces of a puzzle. "So the #toothfaced thing?"

"Yeah, I think that was the release of some animosity that had been building up for a hot minute."

Eamon turned several pages to an illustration of a fairy and a human seated beside one another on two ornately carved wooden thrones.

"The relationship between humankind and the Fae has undergone a couple of iterations since the Beginning. As best we can tell, for the first several thousand years of their joint existence, they operated under the First Covenant. It is believed that these were instituted by the Creator. We do not know what the covenant consisted of. They were either never recorded or have been lost to time. But it is clear that there was to be no procreation between humans and fairies."

Madeline laughed. "Yeah, because who hasn't thought to themselves, *I'd really like to bump uglies with a chameleon today?*"

Eamon cleared his throat and started to answer.

"I'll take this one. Madeline, I'm going to say this in the least weird way possible — by which I mean there's nothing not weird about it." A smirk presented itself at the corners of her mouth, so I continued. "I don't know if it's pheromones or what, but they are … I'm searching for the right word here … intoxicating."

"You have a crush on a fairy?"

"No. It is way deeper, more primal than that. The second time Fiachra visited me at my office, I thought my assistant was going to rip his clothes off and have at him right there at her desk."

"Oh?"

"And when he and I went out for pancakes, there were dudes *and* their wives giving him long looks."

"Uh-huh. Didn't you have a run-in with a female fairy? How did that go?"

My hand instinctively went to my healed scalp but bumped into my visor, causing me to flinch.

Eamon reasserted himself into the conversation. "Strictly speaking, the Fae don't have genders. There are beings who are masculine and others who are feminine, but not male and female in the sense that we are accustomed to. They do not have … gear. Is that what the kids call it?"

A shockingly loud burst of laughter pummeled my ears. I thought Madeline might fall over. Eamon blushed. When Madeline recovered herself, she sighed deeply, putting her hand to her chest, and looked at me. "I haven't forgotten that I'm still waiting for your answer."

"Yes. The head of the BCG, visited me one night after you and I had met, and even though she almost murdered me, I probably would have done most anything she asked of me."

She let that marinate for a minute and showed some restraint (thankfully) in not exploring exactly what I'd meant. She turned back to Eamon. "If they don't have 'gear,' as you so elegantly put it, that begs the question, why was there a rule disallowing them from having sex with humans?"

"The question calls for me to speculate, as I cannot say with any certainty."

"I'll allow it," I said. "Expert witnesses are allowed to answer speculative questions."

Madeline swung her head back toward me. "You know why people hate lawyers, right?"

"Yes. Yet, we still can't help ourselves."

"I do not think they were always physiologically different from us. There is historical evidence of the results of relations between our kind and theirs."

"Such as?"

"Greek mythology. The Pentateuch. How many examples do you want? There are many more accounts. Storytelling has been wrought with tales of humans with extraordinary abilities since before we were recording written histories."

"You think those stories are true?" Madeline asked, with no note of either surprise or disbelief. The question was one of genuine curiosity.

"There is truth in their essence, if not in their details."

"Interesting. Okay. I'm gonna have to mull that over. So what changed then?"

Even a week ago, I would have been skeptical. No, that's not a strong enough word. Skeptical makes it seem like there's still room for belief. Until Sam healed my head and arms with just her hands and set fire to the rest of my worldview that wasn't already in flames, I wouldn't lend any credence to the notion that Hercules and those of his ilk were rooted in truth. Now? What choice had I been given but to reconstruct my belief structure about what was or could be true?

Eamon said, "There was an event that brought about the end of the first iteration of the relationship."

"Which was what?" Madeline said, continuing in her role as the inquisitor.

"Which is what has brought you to Ireland." The old librarian gently turned several more pages of the book, the vellum making the softest of rustling sounds. It depicted a woman seated on a throne. A hoard of creatures and men bowed to her.

"My kind of girl," Madeline said. "Who is it?"

"Do you know?" Eamon asked me.

"No." I failed the pop quiz.

"This is Queen Maeve."

"Like from *The Boys*?" I asked.

"I do not know that reference."

"Doesn't matter. What do we need to know about her?"

"Likely more than I can tell you, I'm afraid." Eamon turned the page, revealing that the next couple dozen had been torn out of the volume.

My mouth made an involuntary O-shape. Madeline showed her surprise with several softly spoken swear words.

"When did that happen?" I asked.

"Before the book came into our possession. If I were to guess again, I suspect it was likely when the monastery at Kells was sacked, and the book was salvaged and brought to us."

"But, why?"

The shoulders of his suit rose and fell. "To answer that, I must know what the lost pages contained."

I said, "So there's nothing else you can tell us about what Queen Maeve has to do with any of this?"

"No …"

"But?" Madeline prompted.

"There are others who know more of her than I. But I can tell you about the Second Covenant, the one that currently seems to be the source of such consternation with a certain contingent of tooth fairies."

"Fiachra says they aren't governed by it."

Eamon nodded. "That appears to be true, but that doesn't mean they are unaffected by it."

# Chapter 33
# Piles of Books

"After the thing with Queen Maeve happened, humans and fairies adopted a new set of covenants, with the idea that they would constrain both and prevent whatever it was from happening again."

Madeline let out a growl. "You understand how frustrating this is, right?"

"Ay," Eamon said with a raised eyebrow. "Now imagine that for several decades, you have been one of the few people on the planet to know of this problem but have been unable to discuss it with anyone or seek help in resolving it."

Madeline looked sufficiently abashed.

"Let us go to my office, and I will tell you about the Second Covenant."

Eamon opened a separate vault drawer for each of the three volumes of the Book of Kells and placed them with all the delicacy of a mother handling a newborn.

Once we were back in the anteroom and had taken our suits off, the fresh air told me just how musky I had started to smell. Hopefully, there would be a shower in the relatively near future.

Of course, the coffee Madeline had promised on the bus had never materialized, so I wouldn't be holding my breath.

Eamon's office was only a couple of corridor turns away, and it was everything you would want from the nesting space of an old librarian. Floor to ceiling shelves overflowing with books. Piles of books littered the floor and were festooned with haphazard sticky notes and index cards covered in scrawling handwriting.

He had to clear the two visitors' chairs of their own book stacks before we could sit.

"Tea?"

Madeline and I both nodded. One form of caffeine was as good as another. Eamon put a kettle on an electric hot plate.

I was startled to see the name Raymond Mohl on top of the stack of books that been in Madeline's chair. He'd been one of my professors in undergrad.

"What kind of research are you doing?"

"Lately, I've been reading about the civil rights movement in Florida. Fascinating."

"Not our finest hour," I said.

"Undoubtedly, but it is often times of turbulence that allows brilliant men and women to sift themselves through the chaff and affect great change."

He went on for a minute, but I got tangled up in a quagmire of my own thoughts until the kettle whistled.

Eamon smiled and stood up. His joints creaked and popped as he did so. He retrieved a tea service and set it on his desk within our reach, pouring the water into the teacups. I followed his and Madeline's lead in what to do next, not wanting to appear to be the barbarian that I was when it came to tea drinking. Under normal circumstances, if my tea weren't iced and so sweet that it was basically nectar, I didn't have anything to do with it.

"Shall we get to the subject at hand?" With a cup of tea

warming his hands, Eamon settled into his chair. "The Second Covenant accomplished several things. Primary among them was creating a system of checks and balances between man and Fae. Iron became toxic to fairies, so that they could not have access to both modern weapons — modern being about the same time that Jesus of Nazareth was ministering in Israel — and to the magic that most ..." His words trailed off.

"He knows," Madeline said.

"Ah, very well. The magic that most humans cannot harness."

I tried hard not to be offended by the continued exclusion of certain information from me. It seemed like we should be well beyond that, so I put on my big boy points and moved past it. "So modern meant spears, swords, chariots, and whatnot?"

Eamon nodded. "They could not have envisioned then the effect that limitation would have on fairies' ability to evolve technologically as humans have done. Mayhap without iron and steel, we would have found an alternative, but it is difficult to image what is both common and strong enough to have been a substitute."

I thought back to my time in Sidhe Baile and realized the pre-Victorian nature of everything. Almost all that I'd seen was made of stone and wood. Whatever metallurgy the Fae had learned, they'd not found anything that enabled them to keep pace with us. At least, that was true of the very small corner of the realm that I'd seen.

"What did they gain in exchange?"

Madeline answered. "Control over any human who gave their name to a fairy."

"What kind of control?"

Sidestepping the question, Eamon requested, "Tell us what happened with Liadan."

"You know her name?"

"It has become imperative that I learn as much as plausible."

That was an understatement. For the second time, I recounted my experience with Liadan, making sure not to leave out any details. When I finished, Eamon said, "That is both instructive and disconcerting. So, the control that the Fae can assert over those of us fool enough to give them our names is not so extensive as that. We cannot disobey any instruction given by the fairy. The power recedes over time, but often not before the person experiences grave consequences." He leaned forward and lowered his voice. "The Fae are rather mischievous. There are other commandments as well that govern human-fairy relationships."

I didn't know why that warranted whispering, but I nodded conspiratorially. "Alright, you said the primary thing was this lopsided exchange. What was the other thing?"

"Before the Second Covenant, humans and fairies could travel freely between here and Sidhe Baile. The covenant shuttered the gate. Each was relegated to their own world." He shrugged and sighed, "But as with all shutters, there are cracks where the dark can seep through."

"Or light," Madeline added optimistically.

"I suppose. While there has continued to be limited interaction between the two over the last two thousand years, there is some indication that activity has increased of late."

"So that's it?" I threw up my hands in frustration. "Some people agreed to this, and everyone else is stuck with it?"

Eamon looked at me as though I'd said something particularly stupid. "You are not so naïve as that, are you? That is the way it has always been. The few make the rules for the many."

In fact, I had said something dumb.

Madeline asked, "How did they make it official or whatever?"

I knew the answer to this. We were closing in on my area of expertise. "They made a contract, didn't they?"

"Ay."

"Where is it?" Madeline asked eagerly.

"Legend has it that the contract resides in Sidhe Baile."

"You don't have it locked up in your book vault?"

"Ha. Would that I did. T'would be more extraordinary even than the Book of Kells."

"Why all the secrecy?" I said. "Why shouldn't everyone know about all of this?"

"Some parts of the world-that-was are best left in the annals of history. Though they are not forgotten. Not entirely. Fairy tales and comic books are the modern equivalent of *The Odyssey* and *The Aeneid*. The commemoration of our forsaken past."

I grunted my disapproval. "The few deciding for the many."

Eamon would not be provoked. "So it is."

Madeline steered us back to practical realities. "Where did all of this happen?"

"Here in Ireland. Sligo."

"Wha …. Really? How?" Again with the eloquence. I would never be confused for William Jennings Bryan.

"Queen Maeve. It is where she orchestrated her conquests and launched her queendom."

"Queendom. I like that," Madeline said.

"She did not come to a happy end, I'm afraid. She is still entombed in Sligo." Eamon pecked at his keyboard while we waited, then swiveled his monitor to show us a photograph of an idyllic Irish landscape with a mountain rising out of it.

"Help us out here," Madeline said. "What are we looking at?"

"Knocknarea."

"Okay?"

"Maeve is buried atop it. It was her last request — that they bury her on top of the mountain so that even after her death, she could oversee her subjects."

Madeline pointed toward the top of the screen. "Why does the mountain have a gray nipple on top of it?"

"A cairn, not a nipple. Her request was granted. But for the last two thousand years, everyone who has hiked to the top of Knocknarea has carried a stone with them and left it on top of her tomb to make sure she didn't come back from the dead."

"Whoa. Harsh."

"She was that hated? Or feared?" I asked.

"Very much so. She brought about the end of an age and ushered in a new one that no one was extraordinarily pleased with." Eamon looked down into his cup of tea. He hadn't taken a drink of it, and now it had turned cold. He placed the cup on his desk. "You should go to Sligo. I think there may be more answers for you there. But even if not, it would be worth your while."

I looked at Madeline, and though she too appeared uncertain, she said, "Sure. Why not?"

"Good. It is decided, then. I will text a friend of mine and have him meet you at the bus station."

"Are you sure he'll be available?" Madeline said.

"Ay."

"Just like that?"

"Ay."

"I have one favor to ask," I said.

"I will help if I can."

"I would kill for a shower right now. Is there any way you could make that happen?"

"Mm," Madeline said. "Yeah, if I'm going to be stuck beside him on a bus, I'd really like for him to have a shower."

"You don't smell too fresh yourself."

"Defense mechanism," she said. "It's the only thing that keeps the hound dogs at bay."

Eamon laughed heartily. "I can arrange showers for both of you, and anything else you need for your travels. There is one thing." He stood up and shuffled to a bookshelf on the wall. Madeline and I stood as well. He tipped a weathered leather-bound book backward and pulled it out.

Eamon made his way back to us and handed the book to me. *The Complete Works of W. B. Yeats.*

"I gotta confess. I'm not much of a poetry guy."

"You haven't been reading the right poetry, is all." He took the book back and thumbed through it until he found what he was looking for. Grabbing a stray index card off his desk, he placed it in the book and handed it back to me. "Start there. You may find it interesting."

# Chapter 34
# Buried in Sligo

It took me the better part of the bus ride from Dublin to the northwest corner of Ireland to get around to the poetry collection that Eamon gave me. I wasn't intentionally disregarding the book. I mean, I totally would have. But this time it's because after the steaming hot shower and a bellyful of breakfast, I couldn't keep myself awake on the trip. My body was exacting its revenge for bad airplane sleep by forcing me to endure equally bad bus sleep.

I pulled the *Collected Works of W. B. Yeats* out of the top flap of my pack. It was easily the heaviest (and oldest) thing I was carrying. The epigraph in the front of the book was a quote from Yeats: "The mystical life is the center of all that I do and all that I think and all that I write." You don't run across the word mystical anymore, yet when I put some thought into it, I had to admit that I had encountered, and necessarily come to believe in, more mystique in my last five weeks than in any of my preceding years.

When I flipped the pages to where Eamon had left a marker, it took only one stanza to realize why this poet and why this

poem. The further I read of "The Stolen Child," the more startling I found it.

> *Where dips the rocky highland*
> *Of Sleuth Wood in the lake,*
> *There lies a leafy island*
> *Where flapping herons wake*
> *The drowsy water rats;*
> *There we've hid our faery vats,*
> *Full of berrys*
> *And of reddest stolen cherries.*
> *Come away, O human child!*
> *To the waters and the wild*
> *With a faery, hand in hand,*
> *For the world's more full of weeping than you can*
>     *understand.*

The second and third stanzas were similar, but the fourth
and final stanza was downright alarming.

> *Away with us he's going,*
> *The solemn-eyed:*
> *He'll hear no more the lowing*
> *Of the calves on the warm hillside*
> *Or the kettle on the hob*
> *Sing peace into his breast,*
> *Or see the brown mice bob*
> *Round and round the oatmeal chest.*
> *For he comes, the human child,*
> *To the waters and the wild*
> *With a faery, hand in hand,*
> *For the world's more full of weeping than he can*
>     *understand.*

I read the thing several times to make sure I caught its meaning and wasn't reading more into it than was on the page. I suppose that's what had turned me off to poetry in the first place. The patience required for reading it more than once, and the proclivity of every English teacher to preach symbolism to us that I had no natural eye for spotting.

By the time I'd finished my third reading of the poem, I rousted Madeline with a gentle-ish elbow to the ribs. She would have wanted me to wake her anyway. With her head tilted back against the headrest, the snoring was out of control.

Her eyes popped open, and she brought her head level. After smacking her lips a couple times, she asked, "My mouth is dry as a sawmill. Was I snoring?"

"Huh? No, not at all," I said, while nodding my head vigorously.

She buried her face in her hands, and a muffled "Oh, geez" emerged.

"When you're done with your self-loathing, I have something for you to look at."

Madeline pointed a playful finger at me. "I'll have you know my self-loathing knows no bounds. It is a constant companion."

"Okay. That's weird, but whatever. Read this."

I plopped the book into her lap, already open to the poem I wanted her to read.

She read it. And re-read it. The third time she read it, she followed her finger, which underlined the words as she perused them. Her finger stopped under the final period. She looked up. "He's been to Sidhe Baile."

"That's what I deduced too."

"So, what do we do with that information?"

"Same thing you get as when you cross an elephant and a rhino."

Madeline sighed. "I already know this is some terrible dad joke, but I don't know the solution, so let's just hear it."

I grinned. "Elephino." I enunciated the syllables to give the intended effect.

She grumbled, nearly in pain at the pun.

"To be fair, I heard that joke as a teenager."

"Your sense of humor hasn't evolved since then?"

"Definitely not. I still think farts are funny, too."

She rolled her eyes. "Boys are gross. You know that, right?"

"Yes." I was ready to turn back to our actual task until I realized that an opportunity had presented itself to ask about something I'd been wondering. "Is that why you …" I realized I had committed myself to this line of questioning, but I already regretted it.

She tilted her head. "Spit it out."

"… play for the other team?"

Madeline gave me a hard look before answering. "Are you asking if I'm gay?"

"Yes?"

"Are you uncertain what you're asking?"

"No."

"Celibate."

"Huh. Okay. Can I ask more questions?"

"Sure."

"Alright. Is it a religious thing?"

"No. Personal preference. Do you remember that scene in *Demolition Man* where the woman was totally freaked out by the idea of exchanging bodily fluids with someone else?"

"No, but I think I follow."

"It's not that either."

"You know, if they'd wanted abstinence to have more buy-in among teens, they should have pitched sex the way you just did."

That drew another hearty laugh. It also brought on us a bus full of Irish eyes, just like on the earlier bus.

Whatever the reason, I was sure it wasn't a lack of suitors.

She was still an attractive woman, like in how Helen Mirren has never gotten less good looking. And she was charming as could be. But if she wasn't going to elaborate, then I would bail on my super uncomfortable line of questioning. "So … Yeats. Any ideas yet?"

"How about this? He was buried in Sligo and has strong family ties there."

"Okay. That's not nothing. How did you know that? And if you say it's because you're a librarian, I'm going to throw things."

Madeline held up her phone, showing me the screen with dozens of search results about our poet.

"Ah."

A small city unfolded around us. The bay to our left gave us occasional glimpses of itself as we drove north. With a final deceleration and whoosh of air brakes, we disembarked at Sligo's bus station.

"Any idea who we're looking for?" Madeline asked.

"I wasn't given any more instruction than you were. What do Irish priests wear? Maybe that will help."

We stood beside the bus, out of the way of those who knew where they were headed. We still hadn't moved when the bus departed, though all the other passengers had long since made their ways from the station.

A man in chinos and a plaid shirt rounded the corner of the station and strode toward us. "You the Americans?"

Besides his clothing not being at all what I expected from a parish priest, the next thing I noticed about him was that his teeth were as yellow as a low hung moon.

"We're Americans," Madeline answered, "but I don't know if we're *the* Americans."

"Eamon?"

He certainly wasn't one to mince words. I nodded.

"Come."

# Chapter 35
# The Prophet's Chambers

The rector drove wordlessly west, away from the bus station and into the countryside. Sligo Bay stayed within sight on our right for the entire drive. Beyond it, islands and a range of distant mountains. A persistent green shelf obscured the view to the left. It might have been a hill, but if so, it was the longest hill I'd ever seen.

The drive took only ten minutes, but it felt every bit of sixty. Between the silence and my growling belly, it wasn't a great time. The first few times my stomach grumbled, Madeline nudged me with her elbow. It took no real effort on her part with how we were smashed up against each other in the tiny car. If we encountered too steep a hill, we could kick out the floorboards and pedal like the Flintstones.

It didn't come to that. Our dour host brought the car to a stop at a church that announced itself as St. Anne's Church of Ireland. After unbuckling his seatbelt, he said, "Welcome to our humble church. Some of the parishioners have prepared a meal for you. And after that, you can take rest in our Prophet's Chambers." He smiled a broad, yellow smile. We seemed to have turned a corner.

When I got out of the car, I noticed that the sun wasn't nearly as low in the sky as my watch said it should be. I asked our host about it, he said, "Summer days are long. You are much further north than you may have realized. At the summer solstice, there is only five hours of darkness. Conversely, winter nights are long and quiet."

Inside the church, Irish congregants doted on us and fed us full of food. I couldn't name most of it, but it was tasty nonetheless. In that way, it wasn't altogether different from a Southern potluck. Afterward, they showed us to the Prophet's Chambers, a two-room parsonage for which plumbing and electricity were clearly add-ons a couple hundred years after the structure was built.

Before he showed himself out, the rector said, "Rest well. Tomorrow, we go to Knocknarea."

"Is it close?" I asked.

"A couple of kilometers that way," he said, pointing.

Madeline asked, "What should we call you?"

"Declan."

"Not Father or anything?"

He smiled. "Do either of you belong to the Church of Ireland?"

We shook our heads.

"Catholic?"

"No."

"Huh-uh."

"Anglican?"

More head shakes.

"Episcopalian?"

Same result.

"In that case, Declan will do."

A minute after the door closed behind him, Madeline said, "I wonder what we'll do about breakfast tomorrow."

I made a noise that was meant to express how full I was. "I don't know how you can think about food right now."

"Several thousand years of human evolution has taught my brain to always be in search of calories."

"Don't you think the Industrial Revolution pretty well did away with that necessity?"

She waved me off. "A couple of generations of progress are no match for survival instincts." She checked the cupboards and refrigerator in the kitchenette and announced, "We're good."

"Imagine my relief," I muttered.

Madeline snatched her bag from where she'd set it down. "Nighty night. I'll take the bedroom and let you take that ancient couch there to prove to me that chivalry isn't dead."

"Fine." I was too far beyond tired to care.

"And don't you get any ideas about hanky panky. I'm a trained killer."

I laughed, assuming it wasn't true, but also not being sure. "On a serious note …"

She let go of the handle on her suitcase and swiveled to face me. "How do we know we can trust him? Declan, I mean."

"Eamon says we can."

"And how do we know we can trust Eamon?"

"I think Eamon pretty well established his own credentials by what he showed us. But if you need more than that, I'll vouch for him." She anticipated my next question. "How do you know you can trust me?"

I nodded as she made my point for me. "No offense."

"I don't guess you do. You can chase this rabbit all the way back to its hole and question every relationship you've made since this whole thing started for you. Or you can choose to have faith in the people who've proven themselves reliable to you. And in turn, rely on the people they rely on. Besides, aren't we all on the same side?"

"How the hell should I know?" I raised my voice without

intending to, but Madeline didn't flinch. "I'm on the side of keeping myself and my family alive. But beyond that, I don't even know what the heck that means — on the same side. The guy who got me wrapped up in all this hasn't shown his face in weeks. I'm pretty sure there's somebody else's life he could have upended before disappearing into the ether."

She shifted her weight to one hip and crossed her arms. "You done having a pity party?"

I clenched my jaw. "Not yet. I've had about six tons of information uploaded into my brain, and I don't know how to sort it out or what to do with it if I do."

"You know what I think?"

I waited for her to answer the rhetorical question.

"You need to go for a walk and get a good night's sleep. No earbuds, no music. Just let your head unscramble itself. But before you go to bed, make sure to brush your teeth so they don't turn out like Declan's did."

"Right?"

"I'm pretty sure he's smoked every day of his life since he was a toddler. On that note, g'night."

Despite how tired I was, I followed Madeline's suggestion. I sat on the couch that would be my very narrow bed and ditched my chukka boots before searching out the sneakers that I'd shoved into the bottom of my pack. A walk wouldn't solve everything, but it would be a shame to be in Ireland for ... however long this was going to take, and not actually see any of it.

# Chapter 36
# The Story of the Wolf Queen

Declan's tiny car came to a stop in a gravel lot only a few short minutes after we'd left our quarters at St. Anne's. "You weren't kidding about it being only a couple of kilometers away," I said.

"No. I would find it difficult to keep watch over Knocknarea, were I any farther away." He opened his door and got out.

Madeline and I followed suit. "You mean to keep tourists from messing with stuff?"

"I do not."

I thought this conversation with Declan was going to be like pulling teeth — which is probably a poor choice of idioms, considering the context of our situation — trying to get any information out of him. I resigned myself to soaking in my surroundings.

Leaving the parking lot, we headed up a stone and gravel trail that led to Knocknarea. Grassy fields lay to our right, and cattle grazed in a pasture to the left. The thing about Ireland that people tell you (but that you can't really appreciate until you've laid your own eyes on it) is that the landscape looks like someone has turned the color dial up to eleven. The grass is a more lush green and the flowers more vivid than they have any right to be.

Without further prompting, the rector asked, "What do you know of Queen Maeve and Knocknarea?"

Madeline said, "Basically, she made a big mess that everyone else had to clean up after they killed her." She looked across to me as we walked three abreast up the path. "Is that about it?"

"Pretty much. We're missing a few key details."

"Maeve ruled from Connaught for many years. There are many tales that exemplify who she was, but perhaps one encompasses her better than any of the others."

I felt like a small child sitting on my grandparents' porch on a summer evening waiting on my Papaw to tell me about some adventure from his youth. Except that now I was walking through the very lands where the adventure had played out while hearing tales from long ago.

"When Maeve was but a princess, though not a maiden by any means, her father arranged a marriage for her with one of his allies, Conchobar. Maeve did not think Conchobar was worthy of her and soon abandoned the marriage. To appease Conchobar, who was pretty ill about the whole thing, the king gave him another of his daughters, Maeve's sister Eithene. As sometimes happens in marriages, Eithene became pregnant. Maeve was overcome with envy, despite wanting nothing to do with Conchobar. It may have had something to do with Eithene being the first child to bear the king a grandchild. You know how grandparents are."

Declan stopped to point out Judge ancient remains of a dozen or more stone walls. What had once been a village that stood at the foot of Knocknarea. Beyond this point, the path grew more rugged and began its ascent up the mountain, which was more of a large hill. It reminded me of some of the structures that we call mountains in Alabama, presumably named by people who hadn't been as far north as the Smokies or as far west as the Rockies.

"Late in Eithene's pregnancy, Maeve could abide her jealousy no longer. One morning, while Eithene was bathing in a spring, Maeve — who had a reputation as a fierce warrior — attacked. She slaughtered most of her sister's attendants and drowned her sister. She immediately fled, knowing that her father would not sit idly by. One of the surviving attendants miraculously delivered the child who, in later years, would assassinate his aunt as she bathed."

"Turnabout is fair play," Madeline said.

"So she's super-duper ruthless," I said. "But how does that get us to a connection with … everything else?"

Declan smiled knowingly. Apparently, the storyteller had more to tell. "Maeve came to be known as the Wolf Queen, because of this and other episodes where she preyed on unsuspecting sheep. After she came to power, her ambition knew no bounds, and she sought to take control over the whole of Ireland."

As the rector told the story of Maeve, we continued our climb up Knocknarea. It was a relatively short hike, and even as he talked, we came within sight of Maeve's cairn.

"She asserted her dominion over the lesser kings, not by removing them from their thrones but by requiring them to have sex with her to keep from being usurped. No one knows how much of a struggle any of them put up over the requirement — enough to placate their wives, I'm sure. Maeve is renowned to be a woman whose beauty matched her ferocity and prowess. Which brings us to her name. Maeve is its anglicized version. In its original form, her name was Medb. It shares a root with mead." He gave a cartoonishly dramatic pause, knowing the gravity of what he was about to deliver.

My belly prickled with anticipation, and from being significantly more out of shape than I'd realized. So maybe it was just a stitch in my side and nothing to do with eagerness for the moment.

"Medb means 'she who intoxicates.'"

Both Madeline and I swung our heads his way.

"She was a … fairy?!" I had the presence of mind to whisper the last word so that I didn't draw the attention of the tourists who were busying themselves with selfies and landscape photos for their social media pages.

He shrugged coyly. "If so, she was only half. There is no genuine doubt who her father was, but the name of her mother has not survived the passage of time, if it was ever widely known. She appears to have inherited the worst traits of both sides of her lineage — all the raw ambition of humanity and the malicious magic of the Fae." He shook his head as if he were telling a story from the morning news rather than two thousand years old.

I gestured at the pile of stones in front of us that stood as tall as a three-story building. "So after her nephew killed her and avenged his mother, they buried her here so she could watch over her kingdom?"

Declan snorted a laugh. "That is the polite version that we tell children."

"Well, what's the impolite version?" Madeline asked.

"The nephew that struck her down used a sling to do so. Slings cast stones with great force, but they are not always lethal. That is why David decapitated Goliath afterward. No sense giving the giant an opportunity to recover. As Maeve was dying from the wound, her last demand was that she be buried atop Knocknarea so that she could gaze down on her enemies until the end of time."

"Even that is not the truth, is it?" Madeline's voice was several degrees colder than I'd heard it before.

"Pardon?"

"There will be no pardon for you, watcher." Her posture was no longer that of a carefree librarian, but of a predator.

My mind reeled. Clearly, I'd missed something. Maybe lots of somethings.

"I truly do not kn—"

"No. No more lies." Anger shrouded her voice. "She was a blood sacrifice. Tell him."

Declan closed his mouth definitively. He too had transcended from priest to warrior, and circled methodically toward higher ground. Tourists skittered away from the three of us, aware that a disturbance had boiled up.

"What the heck is going on?" I blurted out, as lost as I'd ever been.

"Poor Scott," she said with mock pity. "You can't see it, can you? This cairn is no mere tomb of a long-dead queen. This is the site of her murder, the forging place of the Second Covenant, and undoubtedly, the veil that separates us from Sidhe Baile."

# Chapter 37
## Sorely Displeased

Madeline's skin flashed crimson before evolving into a brilliant scarlet. "This place," she spat on the ground, "is the birthplace of all the oppression of the Fae for two millennia. But now it will give rise to a new era, one dominated by us."

"Madeline?"

Her eyes blazed to match her skin. "Do not call me by that name any longer. I am Madailín, first among the Bone Collectors."

I elected not to tell her I couldn't hear any difference between the two names. The timing didn't seem right for that conversation, though I couldn't help myself but to poke at an obvious wound at least a little bit. "So you're the first tooth fairy?"

She closed the ground between us much faster than expected. It wasn't until she lifted me into the air by my throat that I recognized Madeline Madailín had increased in stature. Her skin fluctuated from red to purple in rhythm with her heartbeat. Where she grasped me, her hand and wrist were a cool blue.

"I thought you needed me?" I croaked.

She laughed harshly. "Liadan would be sorely displeased if I ended you. But you are not irreplaceable. There are others with your skills and over whom we could assert sufficie—"

Madailín dropped me at the same time as I heard a deep thunk. She grunted and jerked forward. While her balance wavered, I ripped myself from her hand and scrambled away.

I moved to a spot that was far enough from the fray, then spun around in case Madailín had followed after me. Several rocks from Maeve's cairn swirled in front of Declan. His hands weren't touching them. They were just suspended in midair, as though gravity had no claim on them. This was some new sorcery I hadn't encountered yet.

I realized that I'd made a mistake a minute ago. I'd said to Madailín that her side wanted me. That had been true when everyone believed her to be aligned with Fiachra and Athos. But it had no reason to be true now. Unless she'd misspoken too. But that seemed unlikely to me. If both sides wanted help, that made for an interesting position to be in. I'd have to explore that later. Weird things were happening in front of me.

Also, how did Fiachra not know that Madeline was Madailín? That was a glaring oversight. She must have been embedded earthside for years, perhaps decades.

Declan flung a stone at Madailín. His hands didn't move, so I don't know how he did it, but suddenly, a rock flew toward her. She pushed off to her right, but not in time to evade the blow. She swatted at it with her hand to deflect the impact. Even though her face was already red, the pain was evident on it.

She drew the hand in and examined it. Blood dripped onto the ground. Madailín cupped her hand to keep the blood from pooling around her. She looked back up at Declan, appraising him as an adversary now.

More stones swirled hypnotically before him, a moving shield. The cairn rattled nearby as though whatever was going on with the rock shield was only the preamble.

I looked around for tourists, but only saw their backs heading down the trail toward the car park. That was for the best. It surprised me that not one of them had stuck around to film this and post the next viral video. Momentary internet fame was a powerful motivator. But not enough so to risk death ... at least in this instance.

Madailín withdrew an obsidian knife that she had somehow stashed within her waistband. Its sable blade glistened in the morning light.

She swung her right arm outward, flinging the handful of blood at Declan. The liquid easily permeated his stone shield. When he raised an arm to cover his face, breaking his concentration, the stones clattered to the earth.

In a heartbeat — Declan's last — Madailín threw the knife and buried it deep in the rector's chest. He looked down in surprised horror and grabbed at the bone handle. There was no strength left in his hands. He looked at Madailín and stumbled several steps toward her.

As he approached, she deftly sidestepped him and gave him a shove. Declan crashed into a pile of rocks and moved no more.

Madailín's breath came in heaves as she looked across the body at me. She was a leopard, ready to pounce if I made any wrong move. Whether it was cowardice or something else, I recognized my hopeless situation. Slowly, very slowly, I raised my hands to my shoulders in surrender.

Madailín grinned, then squatted down and rolled the rector onto his back. She grabbed the knife by the haft and rocked it back and forth while twisting. The sound of ripping muscle was intolerable, even at a dozen yards away. When she yanked the blade clear of where it had been lodged in his chest, blood welled up and spilled over his shirt.

She lifted his arm and used the sleeve of his shirt to wipe the blood off the blade before sheathing the weapon.

Once the initial horror subsided, I had a thousand questions, but no words to ask them. At last, I spit out, "What the hell?"

Madailín's smirk returned to her lips. "You'll have to be more specific."

I pointed at the rector's corpse.

"Casualty of war. I have been a librarian for a long time, but I have been this …" Madailín held out her arms, reveling in the skin that had retaken its natural hues. "… much, much longer."

"So … what? You're with Liadan?"

She sneered. "Liadan is an eager puppy, but a useful one, mind you. She has gathered numbers for the cause and given it a face. It existed long before she came on the scene. It's just that most of us have been doing the decades-long work of finding answers and reassembling a forgotten history, while she's come along to play stage actor and plagiarize speeches."

"Y'all don't have answers for these things in Sidhe Baile either?"

"Those who lose wars and find themselves subjected to the wills of others do not have the luxury of dwelling on the particulars of the paperwork."

"But *you* have dwelt on it apparently."

"Very much so. We Bone Collectors are a happy accident. A new breed of fairy born out of the brazenness and ignorance of generations of humans for whom fairies were only stories. You know by now that the old ways do not consider us. But they constrain us to one degree or another." She said this last part with regret, then added cheerily. "We're going to fix that, and you're going to help."

Blue lights blinked in the distance as the wail of a siren made its first appearance.

"Looks like it's time for us to go," Madailín said, "unless you'd like to explain *that*." She flung a hand out toward Declan.

*Yeah, officer, an evil fairy killed him with a knife made of stone because she's allergic to metal. Oh, and he's some kind of sorcerer. No, really, it was wild.*

"Wait. How am I supposed to help?"

She smiled without any joy in it. "You're going to do that thing you do and draw up a new covenant for us."

"I'm no—"

"We don't have time to get into the finer points of this right now." The siren had increased in volume and one police car had multiplied into several. "Shall we find out if my theory is right?"

"What theory?"

"That this is the gate between your world and mine."

"Have at it, I guess." What else was I going to say?

Madailín turned her back to me and strode toward the cairn. At its base, she kneeled and pushed her hands into the soft earth. That she never even bothered to look back over her shoulder to make sure I wasn't sneaking up on her was somewhat emasculating. But she wasn't wrong. I had no intention of attacking her. Of course, I didn't plan on handing unbridled power to the tooth fairies either, so I'd have to come up with something.

# Chapter 38
# Poor Choice of Words

The mountain shuddered beneath us, becoming a giant massage chair that made my footing feel unsure. Madailín remained hunched over, pouring all of her attention into the earth. I stood a couple dozen yards away doing nothing, except trying not to fall.

Suddenly, she jumped up and twirled around. "Something is down there."

Knocknarea stilled.

"What is it?"

"Dunno. But I felt it. Big magic, for sure. Old magic."

I had to avert my eyes from Madailín. In her excitement, Madailín's skin was cycling through the entire ROYGBIV spectrum, like an over-stimulated cuttlefish. It was vertigo-inducing. I held up my hand to block my view of her.

"Sorry. Out of practice. Alright, you can look again." It was weird for the same voice and personality to be coming out of a person who looked so different and was, by any metric, an enemy.

I lowered my hand tentatively. She was a muted teal now.

The police had vacated their cars and were now making their way up the path toward us. "Ready to go?"

"Do I have a choice?"

"Not really. I was being polite."

If nothing else, living in the South for so long had taught Madailín how to use politeness as a weapon.

She looped her arm through mine like I was escorting her to prom. A familiar sickening feeling overwhelmed me as the world exploded into the blurred colors of a nebula. We landed softly in an ethereal world.

If we had been in the Smoky Mountains, they would have called the mountaintop clearing we landed in a bald. I don't know what the name for it is in Sidhe Baile, likely something difficult to pronounce.

Madailín breathed in deeply through her nose. "Doesn't it smell amazing?"

"I mean, it just smells like wet grass."

She glared at me. "You know what's wrong with you humans?"

I started to offer an answer, but she didn't wait for it.

"Your sense of smell sucks. It's a miracle predators didn't extinct you all when the world was still young, before you'd developed all your weapons and tricks."

"Have you ever read about what cities smelled like before modern plumbing and before vehicles replaced horses? There's an argument to be made that lack of smell was conscious evolution."

I chastised myself for engaging in this playful banter with her. I couldn't break myself out of it. Brains aren't equipped to deal with a sudden switch from friend to enemy, with a murder following closely on its heels. Maybe other people's are. Mine was struggling to keep up, which firmly established that a career in espionage had never been in the cards for me.

Madailín took off walking along a mountain path that led into an evergreen forest. "Can I ask a question?"

"Sure. You're not a prisoner."

I stopped in astonishment. "I'm not?"

"No, you are. That was a poor choice of words. My apologies. But you are free to ask if you like."

"Nice," I grumbled. "If you needed all this information, why did it take you so long to get it?"

"We were playing the long game. When you're not confined to a lifespan of, say, eighty years or so — just by way of example, you know …"

"Uh-huh."

"… then you can develop things at your leisure. There wasn't any urgency about it."

"And now?"

"Well, Liadan went and created some urgency. Not only did we need information, but the keepers of knowledge had reason to put their pieces together, too. Until now, everyone was content to let the Respite lie. The humans were firmly advancing and had left us in their past."

"Except for fairy tales," I said.

"Yes, the collective memory of us was reduced to children's stories. And while that was … irksome, it also provided the benefit of enabling us to work in the shadows because those who believed weren't watching, and those who didn't know there was anything to believe in found rational bases to ground the occasional oddity in."

I didn't think any of this was useful in any way, but having a conversation was far better than walking through Fern Gully in solitude. She probably wouldn't think that's a funny reference. I kept it to myself.

"I can't tell how you feel about Liadan."

"Kind of a mixed bag. She's a precocious little firecracker who has more ambition than anyone not running for elected office. Although she is a politician of sorts. Just more of the authoritarian dictator than one pandering to the electorate. She has definitely put a whole bunch of things in motion, so in that way, she's very utilitarian. But, man, is she hard to deal with. Of course, if you tell her I said anything negative about her, I'll have her fairy gestapo cut out your tongue."

"Not if the fairy gestapo gets you first. Autocrats aren't big on dissenters, you know."

Madailín stopped abruptly. Her hand went to her waistband and hovered there. Woodland insects paused their melody, as though holding their breaths to see what the moment held. "I hadn't considered that you might turn on me."

The intensity in her eyes was sudden and ferocious. Her skin tones shifted from cozy greens to colors on the warmer end of the spectrum. I took a quarter step backward and bumped into a tree. I let it support me. There was no more adrenaline in my body, apparently, so the surge didn't happen. Instead, my legs felt like overcooked linguine. "Well, between the two of you, you're the only one who hasn't tossed me out in front of a tractor-trailer, so that's definitely a point in your favor."

"But you would say that. You'd say whatever you need to right now to keep from ending up like Declan."

I shrugged and forced myself to stand a straighter. "Until, like, an hour ago, I thought we were on the same team. And even though you've kind of betrayed that — or maybe you haven't because you're being true to something deeper. Honestly, I'm getting kind of confused about what it says about you — but whatever. Anyway. I still feel a kinship with you. So let's take advantage of that." At a minimum, she was the lesser and more rational of two evils.

"Okay?"

"Okay, I want to make sure that my family isn't harmed, and you—"

"You still consider your ex-wife family?"

I sighed. "It's messy and hard to disentangle. I loved her for a long time, and she's Ella's mom. And I was with her through some of the most significant parts of my life. So, yeah, she's family."

"Not to mention …" Madailín made a circle with the thumb and forefinger of one hand, and shoved the forefinger of her other hand in and out of it. She grinned wickedly.

I shook my head. Maybe fairies' incapacity to have sex caused them to act like adolescent boys about the issue. "Yes, that's certainly a complicating factor."

She began walking again, apparently having reached a decision about my fate. But curiosity colored her face. "Have you two had sex since the divorce?"

"Not since, but … I'm not talking about this with you."

"Why not?"

I scoffed. "It's personal, and we're not exactly bosom buddies."

"How personal could it be? Dudes try to put those things anywhere they can. I bet you've thought about that hot little secretary of yours with those long legs of hers." She paused. I didn't take the offer to respond. Not an admission I was ready to make. "And you've already said you'd have done whatever Liadan wanted. We both know what that meant. Besides, I need something personal from you. Kind of like an assurance that we can work together."

"So you're extorting me for stories about my sex life?"

"If that's the way you want to see it."

"Fine. We haven't done it since the divorce, but we did once toward the end of things, when the writing was on the wall. It was … hateful. And weirdly, it kind of sealed things."

"Kind of light on details."

"No, that's all you get." I said firmly.

She shrugged and walked in silence.

After a minute, I said, "I need a promise from you that if I don't turn on you, you'll keep anything bad from happening to Ashleigh and Ella."

She stopped and turned to me. "You need to understand, once made, there is no undoing a promise with a fairy." Her voice was grim as death.

"I understand."

"Give me your left hand."

I held it out. She took hold of it and turned it palm up. Then she pulled the obsidian knife from her belt for the second time. The slash was so quick, I didn't even know she'd done it until blood began welling up from the fault line across my palm. She handed me the knife and held her left hand out. I made the same quick slashing motion across her hand. A crimson river appeared.

Madailín clasped her hand to my forearm, and I gripped hers by instinct. Where her hand was, my skin took on her coloring, like her blood had leached into my arm. Her forearm paled to reflect my pigmentation. When everything returned to normal a second later, she released my arm.

I looked down at my hand and found that the cut that had been there a moment ago was gone and hadn't left so much as a scar.

She gestured at the bloody smear on my arm. "There's a creek up ahead. We're going to need to wash that off before we get where we're going."

"Which is?"

"The warehouse."

# Chapter 39
# The Most Alluring Woman

The warehouse wasn't a sheet metal building that you find in every industrial complex in America. It was a cave that had been excavated out of the side of a mountain. An enormous cave. The entrance was unassuming, being only as wide as two people walking abreast. The entryway descended through a cascade of natural steps that had been augmented to decrease the risk of slipping on wet stone and breaking a tailbone. Sconces bearing torches lined the walls alternately on the right and left, leading to a cavern that opened up like the rotunda of a capitol building.

The contents of the caverns looked like something right out of an Indiana Jones movie. Row upon row of enormous warehouse shelving lined the chamber. On the far side of the cavern was a tunnel, though I couldn't see where it led. As best I could tell, there were only two points of ingress and egress for the chamber.

It wasn't until we reached the floor of the cave that I could make anything out of the black lettering on the sides of the crates. At the head of each column was a placard with the name of a continent. Asia had a much smaller contingent than I would have expected, given its population. Maybe the tooth fairy hadn't permeated the zeitgeist there like it had in the West.

The crates at the head of each column didn't have lids affixed to them yet. They bore the current year, month, and date, as well as other markers. The ones from North America were designated with MX, USA, or CA, followed by Aa-Af, Ag-Al, and so on.

"Intake," Madailín said.

"What?"

"The bone collectors. This is where we bring the previous night's haul. From here, they take it back and sort it for all the active LOTs. Then once somebody has lost their last tooth, they're no longer in LOT status, and they get archived."

"LOT?"

"Losers of teeth."

I grimaced. "Oof. That's clunky."

"Hence the acronym."

Calling these things crates is a disservice to them. Every one of them was a work of craftsmanship. Dovetails and dowels eliminated the necessity of nails but required more care and attention to go into the making of them. But how they did all that without iron tools, I have no clue.

I walked up to one of the crates and looked in. It was packed full of small burlap pouches that were tied off with ribbon. When I picked one up, I thought it was empty at first. Then I felt the lump inside. A tooth, of course. I couldn't make out the scribble on the pouch, but presumably, it contained all the identifying information so that the tooth could be sorted appropriately.

Holding the pouch in my hand, I looked at the hundreds of crates around me. It wasn't until this moment, armed with the knowledge that these crates would be taken to other cavern chambers to be properly sorted for long-term storage, that I internalized the scope of this operation. And not only the scope, but what it represented. A shiver worked its way down my spine. How many millions — or was it billions — of people could the BCG subject to the same control that Liadan had lorded over me? And what did the BCG intend to do with its power? This wasn't altogether different from the weapons storage that the United States and Soviet Union amassed during the Cold War.

"Didn't Ella lose a tooth recently?" The voice was not Madailín's. I clenched my jaw in the way that my dentist had fussed at me for doing because it was wearing grooves in my molars. But at this point, I would rather ground them to a powder than keep them in my head where someone could weaponize them against me.

I turned slowly and found that Liadan and a multicolored contingent of the BCG had joined Madailín. Each of them wore a black armband with a red tooth on it. The callback to the Nazi regime couldn't have been more obvious. As I watched, Liadan gave an armband to Madailín. "Welcome back to the fold. You have been away too long. Your service for the Greater Good is commendable."

The lackeys spoke their gratitude and various other platitudes to her. Madailín nodded her thanks as she slid the armband up her left arm.

Liadan returned her attention to me. A dozen yards separated us. As she closed the distance, she transformed her complexion to match my own. Freckles sprinkled over the bridge of her nose and cheeks, and auburn hair spilled onto her shoulders. She was the most alluring woman I'd ever seen.

She didn't stop until she was much closer than my personal bubble of space dictated was appropriate, but I didn't move away. Couldn't move away. When she placed a hand lightly on my chest, a collection of butterflies erupted in my belly. She snagged a button on my shirt and pulled me gently toward her until our chests touched. Her lips brushed my ear as she whispered , "I don't need your teeth to make you do what I want."

I shoved her away at the shoulders. The underlings scurried into action toward us. Liadan raised a hand to stop their advance, and her cool blue face grinned wickedly at me.

I was disgusted with myself and would definitely add this interaction to my self-flagellation pile, which had grown large and unwieldy over the years. When Ella once asked me, *What's the worst thing you've ever done?*, I cast a glance toward the jumbled mess of misdeeds and knew there was too much to unpack, so I deflected the question.

"You know what's funny?" she said. "You know it can't be done. Not because of some arbitrary rules, but biologically. Yet, you still want to. What do you think that says about you?"

I already knew what it said about me, but I would not let her goad me into a reaction. Not over this. I stood unmoving, jaw still clenched.

"Fine. Be like that," she said whimsically. "I just wanted to play." Liadan sauntered back toward her underlings and Madailín. "So, you want a tour?"

I glanced at the shelved stacks that surrounded me. "Think I'm good. I get the general idea of it."

"This? No, there's much more to our operation than the Repository. There are the labs and your quarters. And the grounds themselves are quite lovely, though you likely saw that on your way in."

"I'm free to walk around? I thought I was a prisoner."

Liadan shook her head. "Not a prisoner. More like a diplomat who's being ... retained so we can accomplish certain objectives."

I crossed my arms. "So a political prisoner, then."

Liadan huffed. "How is this supposed to work if I keep trying to be positive about the situation and you keep reducing it to its ugliest form?"

"You mean, how I'm just calling things out like they are instead of covering them up with flowery words?" I was feeling a little plucky now.

"Fine." She strode toward me, gesturing for her party to follow. She snatched my arm as she passed me and spun me around. "We will dispatch with any pretenses. You are here until you can figure out how to get me what I want. And in the meantime, I want to give you some motivation to comply."

"What is it that you want?"

"Everything. Every single bit of it."

# Chapter 40
# More Animal Than Human

They were more animal than human at this point. I couldn't imagine what the tooth fairies had done to them. But I got the sense I wouldn't have to imagine it. Liadan was either going to tell me or experiment on me in a similar way.

After leaving the sorting chamber, we had walked through a dozen other caverns, delving deeper into the mountain's heart. I wasn't claustrophobic, but you don't have to be for the sheer volume of rock that surrounded you to begin having an effect.

The last couple of caverns we passed through had been smaller and held no boxes. One held a flat, stone table that was about eight feet long. It was covered in stains matched by similar markings on the floor. Menacing leather straps hung down at its sides, and it appeared to be more altar than table.

Several bronze tools lay atop the table. As we walked, I identified a long pair of forceps, a hammer that looked like an overgrown meat tenderizer, and several other things that my dentist used but whose names I didn't know. I turned my face away, comprehending now the source of the stains.

Even if there were another route to our destination, Liadan's election to bring me this way wasn't happenstance. I was fairly certain she didn't do anything haphazardly. Every act was directed toward her goal of shifting the balance of power in favor of the Fae, and more specifically, the bone collectors. She wouldn't be content unless she aggregated power so that she could wield it.

There is something admirable — though perhaps that is the wrong word since it evokes positive connotations — about those who dedicate themselves so singularly to a cause. Most of us are incapable of it as we have competing obligations — family, careers, hobbies. But for this tiny contingent, their entire existence is wrapped up in a focused endeavor. While we have some of the greatest advances in science and medicine to thank for such folks, they have also caused an inordinate share of human suffering. No cost is too great for them to achieve their end, particularly when others are footing the bill.

A final narrow corridor led us to a low-ceilinged chamber that was unremarkable but for the pits that had been dug into the floors. Nine of them in all, three equal rows.

Liadan gestured for me to approach the closest of them. As I neared its edge, she held a torch over it. Upon being struck by the light, the man occupying the pit whimpered and galumphed across his confines in search of a shadow to hide in. Finding none, he crawled under his gray blanket and continued making mewling noises. I watched as Liadan withdrew the light and moved toward the next pit. The man peeked out from under the covers like a child checking to see if a storm had passed. His face was lumpy and disfiguring.

Liadan and her herd of miscreants awaited me at the neighboring pit. This man waited on hands and knees. "Water?" He croaked, and flinched as he did so. A dog that had barked and knew the swat of a newspaper was coming. His chin and lower jaw were smeared with dried blood.

The commotion caused one of the pit dwellers to cry. A woman by the sound of it. Liadan moved toward the sound.

"I get the idea," I said.

"Maybe you do, and maybe you don't," she shrugged. "Come."

Reluctantly, I did as she bade me.

The woman sat with her back against the wall of her cavity. A child huddled against her, and she wrapped her protective arms around the boy. Under normal circumstances, he would have been several years too old to allow anyone to see him cuddling up with his mother. It would have meant death by embarrassment among middle grade boys. But there was no normalcy to be found here.

When she recognized that my skin was pale rather than Skittles-flavored, she cried out for help. "Get us out of here. Please," she begged. "Take the boy and leave me." She tried to push him toward me, but he clung even more tightly to her.

"Quiet," Liadan said. "Or *I* will take the boy."

The woman bared her teeth at the imposing fairy, then clamped her hand over her mouth with its several missing teeth.

I tried to make eye contact with Madailín, but she actively avoided looking in my direction. I wanted to assume the best of her and believe that she too was horrified by all of this, but I really had no basis for that assumption, other than naively hoping for the best in people. Nothing about my surroundings said that had any grounding in reality.

"Can I tell you what is interesting about our lab rats?"

The question was rhetorical, so I didn't bother declining the offer. I didn't want to know, but that was hardly of any consequence.

"I can make them—" she interrupted herself and put a palm to her forehead. "Let me refresh your memory first. About a week ago, you and I met in Birmingham, and you very nearly stepped out in front of a big truck."

"I recall."

"Well, confession time — I made you do that." She paused

for a reaction, but I held my tongue. "We have learned, through extensive testing, that the only way to force a human to kill themselves is to do it in a manner that is painless or mostly so before the fatal event occurs."

Her use of clinical language to describe things made it somehow more horrible.

"It turns out that if you force humans to self-mutilate, there is a pain barrier we cannot compel them to cross. They shut down and become entirely useless for a time. We have tried enchantments and medications to knock down the barrier, but the best we are able to do is push it back further, not eliminate it. You may be disappointed to hear that women generally have a higher threshold than men. Or maybe that is not a surprise to you."

It wasn't a surprise to me. Ashleigh's labor with Ella had been a long and arduous thing. Despite her many protests that she couldn't do any more and could they just do a c-section already, she persevered and delivered the baby. And within minutes after Ella was born, the joy superseded the pain, however great it still was. If that side of procreation were left to men, humanity would have gone extinct shortly after Creation. So no, it didn't surprise me.

"Here's where things get really interesting." While Liadan had been putting on a show for much of the time she'd been addressing me, she was genuinely excited about the experiments. Her cadence sped up when she talked, and there was a spark in her eyes. It couldn't have been more alarming. German scientists in the 1940s probably exhibited that same enthusiasm. "When it comes to strangers, I can make any one of these humans do nearly anything I demand. Under our control, they don't even flinch at mutilating another human — the lack of regard for others of your kind is distressing."

I kept my mouth shut so as not to say anything that would prolong the lecture.

"Now, when I try to get that mother to harm her child, she has the resistance of a mule. No amount of compulsion can break her will. It's extraordinary. We have done a significant amount of testing on this front. The closer the familial relationship, the more stout the resistance. The further we get from the nuclear family, the easier it gets to break down the subject and force them to act as required. It does appear to take a significant toll on the subject, as many are almost entirely … depleted afterward. Some recover. Others don't. However, we have found that some thrive under these conditions, regardless of the relationship. Like they've been waiting on this opportunity their entire lives. And now, their conscience doesn't even have to bother them over it, because their actions are beyond their control."

By the way she talked, they must have been torturing people for years. Hundreds of people. I could feel myself disengaging, trying to form a layer of separation between the atrocities and myself. "Why are you telling me this?"

"Well, first of all, the advances we're making are extraordinary. You were our first field test, and it went swimmingly." She dropped her cheery tone. "Second, I thought you were astute enough that I didn't need to be more overt with my threats. If that's not the case, please let me know."

"I hear you."

"Great! Let's show you to your quarters."

# Chapter 41
# No Knocking This Time

I had been expecting my quarters to be a pit that closely resembled the one my human brethren occupied. So when Liadan's goons dropped me off at a cabin with little fanfare and no instructions, I hardly knew what to do.

It was a one-room building, so there wasn't much exploring to be done. A bed, a rocking chair, a small fireplace, and a table with a couple of chairs. Laura Ingalls Wilder would have been content. On the table, there was a basket filled with breads and baked goods. They smelled extraordinary. Carbohydrates are my favorite food group.

There was no way I was going to touch them. Fiachra's commandments scrolled through my brain like a news ticker. My belly grumbled to verbalize its discontent with the decision my brain was making.

If I was going to eat, I would have to forage. That was certain to go poorly, but I would give it a shot. I pulled open the cabin door. The sun was well into its downward arc, so any excursion would have to wait.

Meanwhile, I had to figure out how to pass the time with nothing to eat and nothing to read. It would be a long evening.

It might feel less long if I had a fire, though. I stepped through the still-open door to find wood stacked neatly on the south side of the cabin. I then vainly felt in my pockets for a lighter that I knew wouldn't be there. I couldn't be sure the fairies had left me a flint and steel either.

Several glasses and other dishes sat on a shelf in the cabin. I grabbed a bowl and glasses and headed outside. Looking through the bottom of the glass, the world around me became a distorted jumble. Maybe it would do. I gathered dried grass and small strips of wood fibers from around the woodpile and wadded them into my bowl, then spent most of the next hour doing my best Bear Grylls impression. I discovered that while Ella and I had watched countless hours of survival shows, implementing the fire-starting techniques we'd observed was more challenging than I'd appreciated.

After some time, I figured out the right distance away from the kindling for the glass to make a tight beam. Smoke eventually made way for embers, and embers into a flame. I carried my small bowl of fire into the cabin and set it in the fireplace. I hustled around, gathering various size twigs, sticks, and logs until I had a proper and sustainable blaze going. It was tempting to whoop and dance around, yelling "I have made fire!" like Tom Hanks in *Cast Away*, but since humans have been making fires for untold thousands of years, I thought maybe I should derive less satisfaction from this primitive chore.

Closer inspection of the drawers below shelves where I'd found the dishes — one of which had been sacrificed for my general welfare and become part of the fire — revealed a couple of quills, a well of ink, and a stack of rough paper. I moved them to the table and began scratching around, first getting the hang of using this kind of implement, then moving on to words.

I was here for the express purpose of creating a new contract for fairies and humans. Without having seen either of the old ones, I really had no starting point for what form it should take.

## Casual Business with Fairies

I wrote out variations on bits from historical documents that I could remember. *We hold these truths to be self-evident, that all humankind and Fae are created equal, that they are endowed by their Creator with certain unalienable Rights, that among these are Life, Liberty, and the pursuit of Happiness.* That wouldn't pass muster. It wasn't the right tenor.

I pulled from the words of Abraham Lincoln: *The world will little note, nor long remember what we say here, but it can never forget what we did here.* Ideally, there would be very few that even know about what I was brought here to do. But if Liadan and the other members of the BCG were to have their way, this was to be a lopsided contract that resolved everything in favor of the Fae. That wasn't tenable from where I sat. There was no way I could allow myself to be the one who subjected humans to become the prey of the fairies. It would be better to let them kill me. *Give me liberty, or give me death.*

There was a soft rapping at the door. I jumped up, my chair clattering behind me. I gathered up my scribblings, wadded them up, and pitched them into the fire. Then I scanned the for a weapon. I'm not sure why I bothered. Since I was being held captive in enemy territory, they could do whatever they wanted to me pretty much whenever they wanted to. And there was nothing I could do to impede that, certainly with whatever resource I found to weaponize in this cabin.

The knocker banged on the door a little more insistently.

For lack of any other options, I grabbed a half-burned stick out of the fire. It was about the size of the skinny end of a baseball bat. I strode to the door and flung it open with my brand in front of me.

Fiachra knocked it aside and pushed his way in. Athos hunched in after him.

The cabin suddenly felt much smaller, as did I.

Fiachra pointed at the useless chunk of wood dangling from my hand. "You ought not point sharp sticks at people."

"Yeah," Athos agreed. "You could really hurt someone that way."

"Not us, obviously."

"No, not us. But someone small, maybe."

"Like a child."

They grinned at each other, amused by their own witty banter.

"What are y'all doing here?" I asked.

Athos answered, "We came to jailbreak you."

"What about the covenant they want me to write?"

"I want you to write it too," Fiachra said, "but from less confined quarters where you might be inclined to make the thing a little more neutral. Seems to me you may be swayed to make a lopsided version of the covenant if they have you under their control."

"Why would that bother you? I thought what's good for the BCG would be good for all of y'all."

Fiachra nodded. "Mayhap it would. And then again, not. These things are hard to know. We have had an age of peace, if not prosperity, under the covenants. To change them so that we are at odds with the humans may work ill for both humankind and the Fae folk."

The door burst open. No knocking this time. Liadan and friends bustled in, brandishing something that looked like the bastard child of an arrow and a spear.

Athos grabbed me by the shoulder and pulled me toward himself. He kept his hand poised on me like a parent steering a child through a crowd.

As cramped as the quarters had felt before, I was now trapped in a cage with a porcupine. An angry, rainbow-colored porcupine. It seemed improbable that any of us were going to escape without getting quilled.

Athos immediately recognized Madailín, despite her altered pigmentation. He sneered and leaned forward. One of Liadan's henchmen planted the point of his weapon against the giant's chest. Several scenarios played out in Athos' eyes before he leaned away from the spear. A calculated retreat.

"He's not leaving here," Liadan said. "Not until I'm done with him."

"You're not going to like how this goes," Fiachra threatened.

Liadan raised an eyebrow at him. "No weapons, and the numbers aren't on your side. I don't think I'm the one who should be concerned."

"If you spill Fae blood, the Godmother will not look kindly on it."

"You going to tell mommy that I've misbehaved?" she mocked.

Sweat poured off my forehead, but I didn't dare wipe it, afraid that any unexpected movement might be the catalyst that sent the standoff into chaotic violence.

Instead, Fiachra was the spark. From his place beside Athos, he jumped into the gap between the opponents and spun to face us. He flung a portal open behind us and shoved Athos backwards. Athos reflexively squeezed my shoulder. My collarbone cracked under the pressure as I was pulled backward.

Madailín pounced on me like a lioness, breaking Athos' grip on me. We crashed to the ground with her on top of me.

Fiachra thudded down beside us. The portal dissipated. Three short spears stuck out of his back, their heads burrowed deep inside of him. When he breathed in, bubbles of blood escaped around the weapons.

Madailín pushed herself up and away from me. I rolled onto my hands and knees, and crawled the couple of feet to him. Dirt from the cabin floor clung to his face as the color drained from his skin. He tried to speak but had trouble mustering any sound.

I placed a hand at the nape of his neck and leaned against his face.

Fiachra gasped and whispered, "Do not falter."

He said nothing else and did not move again. When I pulled away, I saw that the blood that was escaping from underneath him had found my hands and surrounded them.

I stood up and backed away from him. My foot bumped into something that clattered and rolled once. Madailín had dropped her spear when she lunged at me. It was the only weapon left in the room that wasn't embedded in Fiachra.

"You better be very sure of your next move," Liadan said, her voice devoid of emotion. "You only get one shot."

I nudged the spear away. Sticks and stones were not my weapons. I would use words to hurt her.

Liadan commanded one of her lackeys to pick up Fiachra. He did so unceremoniously and with a grunt. The group bustled out of the door behind him. After it slammed shut, Madailín's muffled voice said, "You killed one of our own."

"He misaligned himself with the enemy. His blood is not on my hands."

But it was on the floor of my cabin. I meandered to the hearth and shoveled out some cold ashes to absorb the blood that my friend had shed, trying to rescue me from the mess he'd gotten me into.

# Chapter 42
# Leather-Soled Moccasins

The following afternoon, after having having made herself comfortable in my new quarters, Liadan said, "I thought you might do something foolish last night." She pushed the chair back onto two legs and propped her legs onto the table. I prayed that fate was as petty as me and the tilted chair would collapse under her.

As she reached forward for a handful of the blueberries that I'd foraged that morning. I hurried forward and dragged it to the other end of the table. She smirked at me.

"Arguably, it was foolish of me not to grab that spear and plant it in your heart."

Liadan scoffed. "You would never have gotten that far."

I shrugged.

Liadan hadn't yet offered any reason for her visit, and I didn't want to give her the impression that she was welcome to stay as long as she liked — though of course she would, and I had no recourse — so I remained standing. "What do you want?"

"You know what I want," she said.

"If we're going to play wishing games, let me tell you what *I* want — to go back to my normal life, and preferably to a time before I knew y'all existed." My voice was several turns of the dial louder than when I'd started.

"Says the privileged oppressor."

"Oppressor? You've killed two people I know in the last twenty-four hours. So tell me exactly who I'm oppressing."

"Your very existence is an encumbrance."

"And yours is a mistake made out of ignorance."

Silence lorded over us for a time.

Liadan slid her legs off the table and let down her chair. "Don't you feel better now that you've spoken your truth?"

"No, I don't feel better." Heat rose to my already flushed cheeks. "I've seen you and yours kill three people in a matter of days. Before that, I'd gone my whole life without seeing a freshly dead body."

"How very privileged of you," she said in a voice that was flat as a calm sea, before dismissing the accumulated dead as, "Casualties of war."

"Casu—?!" I was flabbergasted. "Are you kidding me! The truck driver? He had nothing to do with any of this."

She shrugged indifferently. "Collateral damage."

I couldn't stand still any longer and started pacing. It's why I never took stressful phone calls on a landline. I'm a pacer. Annie has even threatened to glue my feet to the floor, especially when I've been wearing dress shoes that clack on the hardwoods in the office. She bought me a pair of leather-soled moccasins for this express purpose, but it feels absurd to wear slippers and a suit. Not that I didn't do it anyway. Form follows function, after all.

"It wasn't my intent to kill the truck driver," she offered, her tone as meek I'd heard it. "I didn't think about the truck turning over like that."

"What did you think was going to happen?" I stated it like a question, but it was more a demand for information.

She didn't explain further. But she chewed on her lip, contemplating how best to get what she wanted from me. It would be a hard sell. I wasn't feeling particularly compliant.

Even so, I needed information regardless of what I was going to do with it in the end. "What is it that you want, specifically?"

"A new covenant with the humans. One that puts us on equal footing."

I rolled my eyes.

"What?" she demanded.

"I thought you fairies weren't allowed to lie. It's one of the commandments. Fiachra — you'll recall he's dead now — told me that."

"What did I lie about? I didn't lie."

"Equal footing? You don't want to be equal any more than I want a plate full of chicken livers. You think you're superior to us."

"That's not a lie. That's a bargaining position."

"A distinction without a difference."

"What does that mean?" Liadan asked defensively.

I opened my mouth to answer, then closed it again. I didn't want to get into a pedantic argument with her. It would be more beneficial to keep her talking instead of trying to manipulate me. I waved the question away. "I need to see the Second Covenant."

"You may not."

"Have you considered the idea that something other than immediate and stark opposition to anything I ask for might be a tactic worth considering?"

"I'm not just being obstinate this time."

I sat at the opposite end of the table from her. "What does that mean?"

"I don't have it. The Fae don't have it. And apparently, the humans don't have it."

"How is that even possible?"

"When you have had two thousand years to misplace it … things happen. Who knows? You will have to start from scratch." Liadan got up from the table and leaned against the wall. She slipped into her human skin, and I hadn't realized it when she was teal, but there was an awful lot of it exposed. My gaze slid over her in just the way she'd intended. "Now, that brings us to the next question — what do *you* want?"

Despite already knowing my answer, I took a long time to deliver it. Turns out the trick to overcoming her allure was witnessing her kill your friend.

"Nothing. Not a damn thing."

Her coloring faltered in her confusion, and for a minute she looked like a chameleon caught between disparate backgrounds that it couldn't emulate. She set aside the masquerade. "Explain."

"I'm not doing it. I won't be the one who changes the rules for you."

Teal skin became orange. She leaped across the room and landed atop the table, crouched in front of me. Before I could so much as flinch, she struck me in the face. Blood rushed to my cheek.

I pushed myself up out of the chair, though Liadan still loomed over me. "You think hitting me is going to make me submit to your demands?"

"I can do so much more than hit you. You have already seen what I am capable of. I have mostly been playing nice to this point."

I thought of the window stickers that used to be popular on the rear windshields of the redneck contingent of truck owners, *Ain't skeered*. It certainly wasn't true in my situation, but it seemed like false bravado was a better showing than turning into a puddle of cowardice. "You have also shown me the limits of your ability. Surely, you must know that physical torture is unreliable at best. You might get something out of it, but you have no assurances it will be what you want. I have seen that you can't force me to hurt those who matter to me. I'll have a come-apart first. So that's pretty much your whole back of tricks." I crossed my arms cavalierly, proud of the point I had made. "Which brings us to the conclusion that I'm not going to do it, and you can't make me." I all but stuck out my tongue at her.

Liadan's hands flashed towards me, grabbing the sides of my face and pulling me toward her. I grabbed her wrists. She pressed her forehead against mine. "Your problem is that you lack imagination. There's something I want you to see."

# Chapter 43
# Understanding the Leverage

The now-familiar nauseating sensation of transportation between Sidhe Baile and our dimension of reality enveloped me until I came to a screeching halt in a suburban neighborhood. It took me a minute to orient myself and realize this was my old neighborhood. Ashleigh's neighborhood.

Liadan released me as soon as we arrived. She watched my face as comprehension landed on me like a rhinoceros. When eyes made their way back to hers, I saw a woman in athleisure that would fit in on any sidewalk in the "over the mountain" part of Birmingham.

"Let's take a stroll," she said.

"If one of these neighbors is watching and sees me going on a walk in my old neighborhood with a beau—"

"Go ahead," she said as she started walking. "I'd like to hear you describe me."

I followed the prompt to walk but not the invitation to indulge Liadan's ego. "With you. They're going to text Ashleigh, and I'll have some hard questions to answer."

"I trust you'll come up with something. But frankly, I couldn't care less what the fallout is with your ex-wife. Those stakes are inconsequential compared to what we're dealing with, don't you think?" She pointed at the Wilsons' house. "How many kids do they have?"

"Three."

"Ages?"

"I don't know exactly. Two in elementary. One in middle school, I think."

"Do you know how many teeth they'll lose? How many we'll collect?"

I stopped. I didn't know. Didn't want to know.

She stopped two steps in front of me and turned back around to face me. "Twenty. Each. Want to know how many I already have?" She pulled a pouch out of a fanny pack I hadn't noticed until now.

The color drained from my face. I felt it go. I shook my head.

She shook the bag, rattling its contents, before putting it back in her pack. She pulled another pouch out and pointed two houses down.

"The Van Vleets. Two."

"I think you're starting to understand the leverage I have. Not just over your tiny street. But over this continent and the one across the Atlantic. And Australia, too. What I did to you, I did with one tooth. I have a dozen more."

"What happened to the rest?"

"What are you talking about?"

"You said you have a dozen. You've only used one. That leaves eleven unaccounted for."

She huffed. "Approximately. I didn't sit there and count them. I was making the point that—"

"Yeah, yeah. I followed the point."

"Has anyone told you that you're too literal?"

"Yep. Hazard of the profession. But I don't know if overly literal folks are inclined to become lawyers, or if we become that way because we're lawyers."

"Nobody cares," she said sourly.

I didn't care either. I was rambling because I was terrified. The full breadth of the BCG's power hadn't landed on me until she walked me through it house by house. That fear led me back to a question I'd been mulling over for some time.

"If you can do all this with things as they are, then what do you need me for? Why do you need anything to change?"

"To be clear, I don't need *you*. I need someone who can do what you do. And since someone else got you involved, you will do. But do not think you cannot be replaced. I will hazard the inconvenience if you make it necessary."

"Whatever." I was past caring about her threats to eliminate me. You can only do that so many times before the novelty wears off. "You didn't answer the question."

"Because it—"

"Hang on. Sorry. Can we go back to your side so I don't get an angry call from Ashleigh?"

Liadan grabbed a wad of cloth from the chest of my shirt and transported us back to my cabin. When she let go, I stumbled backward and began trying to flatten the crinkles. "That was unnecessary."

"Would you rather I have taken you gently by the hand?"

If we were talking druthers, I'd rather have had her head on a pike, but it wouldn't be productive to say that out loud. "Let's just get back to where you were going to tell me why it's so imperative that you make the changes you have in mind."

"Because ...." She appeared to be gathering her thoughts. For all her rhetoric and speech-making, I'm not sure she'd been asked to justify it before. "Have you ever been oppressed before?"

"Look, I'm a white dude. Any discrimination I've experienced pales in comparison to what just about anyone else has had to contend with. My kind have had it relatively easy."

She nodded. "Because our present position is unjust."

"You're gonna have to show your work here."

"When we were begotten, it was for the purpose of serving humanity to collect their discarded bones, to the amusement of their children. There isn't a one of us who has a choice about it. This is our task, and we carry it out. As humans have continued to increase in numbers, so too have the tooth fairies." She all but spit out the last two words. "Supply and demand. It wasn't until we'd been doing it for about a hundred years that some of us got inquisitive and discovered we are sitting on a mountain full of weapons. And I will not sit idly by contenting myself to a life of absurd servitude to the virus that is humanity when I have the leverage to change our circumstances. To create a new covenant that will legitimize and vindicate us."

That was a lot to unpack. "How do the other fairies — the ones who aren't tooth fairies — feel about it?"

"They are antiquated and inconsequential. They have no lust left in their bloated hearts."

The problem with most revolutions is that the young folks driving it are full of piss and vinegar, but don't have the wisdom to execute their visions, and the old heads don't have the energy or interest to do more than sit back and quietly watch things play out in front of them. The landscape didn't look much different here. Of course, most revolutionaries don't have an arsenal of teeth that enable them to seize control of a large swath of humanity. That alone may be enough momentum to see this thing to a successful outcome. But Liadan still hadn't identified what such an outcome would involve.

"So that's the *why*," I said. "But what's the *what*?"

"Recompense." Her voice was quiet again. "I will be repaid in blood for a century of slavery. There will be an uprising unlike the world has ever seen and which it will be unable to quell. And you are going to give it to me."

My blood ran cold. I opened my mouth to speak, but she interrupted me, though still with no urgency or anger. "Do not protest. You will draft the new covenant for me, because if you refuse, I will parade in front of you the remains of every person you've ever known. I will start with Ella and Ashleigh and work my way backward from there. Do you understand?"

I nodded meekly. Hearing their names come out of her mouth broke the last strands of resistance. I was General Lee at Appomattox Courthouse. Except Liadan wouldn't be so gracious as to let me keep my sword. I'd be lucky if she didn't impale me with it.

"I need to know your terms."

She smiled and re-wrapped herself in her freckle-splashed human skin with its auburn hair. Just to make sure the impression lasted, I guess. She beamed at me with a sickening smile. "Certainly."

# Chapter 44
# A New Covenant

I requested several days to come up with a contract to govern the relationship between human and fairies, which was no small undertaking. A contract that the BCG intended would give fairies the upper hand, since at least some of their number felt like humans had shafted them the last go round a couple thousand years ago. My request for several days got whittled down to three.

The ashes in the fireplace and crumpled paper strewn about the room provided evidence that I had been failing miserably for the last two to come up with anything workable.

Aside from taking time to get water, use the bathroom, and forage the minimum amount of food I could subsist on, all my efforts had gone into this particular futility. And having not bathed or showered since leaving Dublin, I was finding my own smell pretty offensive.

It didn't help matters that I was having to write by hand and didn't have any reference materials or access to a computer. Because of course the most important document since — I couldn't even think of what hugely important document would have been most recent was going to be hand-written. Normally,

I would have just done a quick search engine query and had my answer in a couple of seconds, but under these paltry circumstances, the question would nag at the back of my consciousness indefinitely.

Regardless, this rather significant document was going to be written by a singular dude with no outside sources. What could go wrong?

There were a couple of difficulties. For one, I couldn't figure out the structure of the thing. It couldn't be entirely one-sided like the Declaration of Independence, or even its French equivalent, the Declaration of the Rights of Man and of the Citizen. It wasn't even a constitution. There was no governance. While a governing body might not be a terrible idea (not that I have extraordinary faith in governments generally), I was reticent to propose it under the present circumstances because a totalitarian regime seemed like the most probable outcome.

Throughout my dozens of try-fail cycles, something tugged at the smallest, most remote corner of my awareness. It was a long time before I became aware of the persistent nag, and longer still before I could make anything of it. Eventually, I realized that somewhere in my last conversation with Liadan she had said something that clung to my consciousness, and that was the thing hassling me now.

I got water I didn't need. I went for a walk in the woods. I did all the things that usually work when I'm trying to jostle something free in my brain. None of them had any effect.

It wasn't until I sneezed and wondered if I might be getting sick that the thing was set free. Liadan had called humanity a virus. And because my brain prefers to play leap frog rather than operate on any kind of linear path, *viruses* caused a jump to the virus exclusion that I'd written for the insurance company. From there, I jumped to insurance policies, the contracts I knew best.

Upon that realization, the new covenant took shape in my head and began pouring itself onto the pages.

## Covenanted Agreement

We agree to adhere to the terms of this covenant.
This covenant is based upon our reliance that:

1. The representations or statements made by any party to this covenant are true.
2. The covenant contains all the agreements between Humans and Fae or any of their representatives. All prior covenants, unless incorporated by reference in this Agreement, are null as though they had never been made.
3. The payment of the consideration binds the covenant, and if no consideration is paid, there is no covenant.

## Duties of the Parties to the Covenanted Agreement

The following are duties that the parties are to perform. Failure to perform these duties may result in a dissolution of the covenant. These duties apply to every section of the covenant.

1. Notify each other promptly if an incident occurs, whereby the covenant is breached. The notice must give the time, place, and circumstance of the incident, including the names of the involved persons and known witnesses.
2. Cooperate with each other and assist in any manner necessary concerning a breaching incident.
3. Promptly provide any papers or documents pertaining to a breaching incident.
4. Submit to examinations under oath by representatives chosen by the parties as often as may reasonably be required.

5. Authorize the parties to obtain necessary documents and records. If an affected person is dead or unable to act, their covenant representative shall provide the necessary authorization.
6. Produce and authorize the parties to examine any records needed to investigate a breaching incident.
7. Take reasonable steps after a breaching incident to protect against further loss or damage. Failure to take these measures will itself be a subsequent breaching incident.

## Definitions Used Throughout This Covenanted Agreement

Some words or phrases in this agreement have been defined below. Defined words or phrases have the following meanings, unless a different meaning is described in a particular clause, endorsement, limitation, or exclusion.

1. **We, us**, and **our** means the parties subject to the covenant.
2. **Breaching incident** means any occurrence that gives rise to, causes, is causally related to, or results in a violation of any of the agreed-upon terms and conditions of this binding covenant.
3. **Covenant** or **covenanted agreement** means this document, which contains the entire agreement and understanding among the parties with respect to the subject matter herein, and supersedes all prior and contemporaneous agreements, understandings, inducements, and conditions, express or implied, oral or written, of any nature whatsoever with respect to the subject matter herein.

4. **Fae** means any sentient being identified as a fairy or faerie, whether in existence at the time of the execution of the covenant or begotten hereafter.

5. **Humans** means any sentient being identified as *homo sapiens* or subsequent evolutionary mutation, regardless of race, color, national origin, religion, sex, sexual orientation, gender identity, transgender status, age, disability, genetic information.

It went on like that for pages and pages. Defining every single term. Setting out the conditions outlined by Liadan. Numbing the mind with details. And burying in the middle parts the important bits that I didn't want to draw too much attention to.

The first draft was a total train wreck. By the time I was done, it more closely resembled the scrawlings of a madman than any kind of competent or cohesive document. I circled dozens of lines and paragraphs and drew arrows to where they needed to be moved. Scraps of paper got shuffled in between pages so that I would remember to add things in with the second draft. It was a big, jumbled mess that only I could make sense of.

I mentioned aloud (several times) that this process would be a lot cleaner and faster with a word processor. The sentry posted outside my door was indifferent to my rantings.

I had just titled the second draft when someone knocked on the door, followed by Liadan grousing, "Don't knock for him."

The door swung open. Madailín stepped in ahead of Liadan. I was looking for some form of abashment in her face, but there was nothing. It may as well have been carved from slate.

"Well?" Liadan said.

I flung my hand out, gesturing at the papers scattered around the room. "It's a process."

She sauntered toward the table where I'd been writing. The table looked askew, but I'd put it midway between the window and the fireplace, so I could drag it one way or the other for lighting depending on the time of day.

When she reached out for the stack of papers that made up the first draft of the covenant, I set my hand firmly on top of it. "No."

Liadan met my gaze and tilted her head to the side.

"It's not ready for anyone to look at. No one ever gets to see the first draft," I said. "Ever."

"Superstition?"

I shook my head. "You wouldn't stop a doctor mid-surgery while he's got somebody's guts spread all over the table and ask him to explain things. You can see it when I've got it all sutured up and ready to go."

"It must be ready by tomorrow night."

"What's tomorrow?"

"Madailín can tell you. I have other matters to attend to." She finally released the edge of the papers that had remained in her grasp and strode toward the door. She stopped at the frame and said, "Do not disappoint me."

I thought it was only in movies that bad guys felt it necessary to make the last word be a vague threat. As if there were any chance at this point that I could drive from my head Liadan's exposure of the depth of her abilities.

"Is it coming along?" Madailín asked, making an effort to sound friendly. Even her coloring was soothing. But whatever sentiments of friendship I had once held had dissipated over the last couple of days. She was not on the same side as me and never had been. But there was only one of us who'd known that all along.

"What happens tomorrow?" I asked without first answering her question.

"Do you remember what I told you happened on Knocknarea?"

"The signing of the covenant."

She nodded. "But it is not just the signing of a document. There is ceremony to uphold, including a sacrifice."

"Geez. Are you kidding me? I kind of thought we were past that in the twenty-first century."

"Some things can be sealed only with blood," she said. "Is not blood atonement central to your beliefs?"

There was no arguing with that. Scriptures are pretty clear on the topic. Without the shedding of blood, there is no remission of sins.

"Who?" A knot of fear twisted in my stomach even as I asked.

"It is not for me to know."

"Who's going to be there?"

"I don't know specifically. Both humans and the Fae will have representatives to sign it. And then there will be the witnesses."

I couldn't imagine who the human representatives would be. Who even knew about fairies? Then I came back to the word *witnesses*. The way she'd said it made me think the witnesses were neither human nor fairy.

"What kind of witnesses?"

"Those who have no interest in the outcome of these events."

*Aliens?* I wasn't going to voice that question. It was a bridge too far, and I didn't want to sound like a moron. In all the confusion of the moment, it escaped me that I had met intelligent beings who weren't fairy or human.

I thought of a question that hadn't occurred to me until now. "How is it that, being a fairy, you lived for so long in our world if iron is toxic to you?"

"It has taken a toll. There are remedies that provide some

relief, but it has been like being slowly poisoned to death for decades," she said wearily. "We all have our sacrifices to make."

I plopped down in a chair, pushed my hands through my hair, and closed my eyes. "This is too much."

I heard soft footsteps on the floor and thought Madailín was going to be so brazen as to put a hand on my shoulder. When she spoke, her voice was further away than I'd expected. "Your part in all this is almost done. Do not falter now."

My eyes flashed open at the repetition of Fiachra's last words, but I was alone again in the cabin.

# Chapter 45
# Presenting an Offering

I wasn't expecting the crowd of people that had already congregated by the time I arrived. Even with small fires circling the top of Knocknarea like a living wreath, the new moon left a darkened landscape that made it difficult to discern how many people were present or who they were. What the darkness did make visible in the night sky was a billion stars, including something I hadn't seen before. The Milky Way shown as a hazy gash of light, splitting the sky nearly in two.

Madailín escorted me to the densest grove of attendees. She was curiously quiet, having spoken hardly a word since arriving on my doorstep. I had come to expect endless quippiness from her, so it came as a stark change. Maybe the gravity of the moment was getting to her.

My documents rustled in their sheepskin folio as we walked. One outsized person dwarfed everyone else attending the spectacle. As we closed ranks, I opened my mouth to speak to Athos, but he emphatically shook his head before breaking eye contact and leaning down to speak to the twenty-something guy standing beside him.

With my first interaction, I had nearly committed some diplomatic screwup. This didn't bode well for me.

Madailín brought me to a stop in front of a dark-skinned man with crinkly gray hair. He looked vaguely familiar, but I couldn't place him. The dark night, with its dancing firelight, wasn't helping matters in that regard. He introduced himself as the Secretary-General of the United Nations. The woman beside him he introduced as the Prime Minister of Ireland. Looks like the committee (or whoever arranged this) went all out for the human contingent.

Their expressions were strained. There was no joviality in the meeting. And if I had to guess, were someone to turn the lights up, it would expose the bags under their eyes. Nothing would add a few years to your face like learning that the entire species is imperiled, and it's incumbent on you to change the course of human existence.

Madailín didn't take me to the fairies, though I recognized some of them by sight. Liadan and her band clustered tightly in a frenzied knot. Another group of fairies, whose attire signaled them as dignitaries, stood apart from them. The young upstarts and the establishment. Adversaries in every iteration of society.

"What are we waiting for?" I asked.

"The last arrival." She pointed at a fairy walking up the path to the crown of Knocknarea, where we stood. A hush fell over the assembly as each group noticed her. She was unlike anyone I had ever seen. She was luminescent. Literally. Light emanated from her like a constellation. Even at this distance, awe struck me in a way that I'd never experienced.

For the first time, I was in the presence of something greater than myself. Ancient texts give accounts of people who become dumb or blind after their interactions with angels. I finally sympathized with it.

"Who is that?" I whispered.

"The Godmother."

## Casual Business with Fairies

When she crested the path and reached Knocknarea's summit, all the fairies dropped to both knees and bowed in reverence. Liadan and her gaggle of angry peacocks were the last to do so, but even they dared not be so irreverent as to remain standing. Athos kneeled and bowed his head. The Godmother paused before him, placing a hand lightly on his shoulder and leaning close to his ear. When he looked up, her light showed that tears had gathered in his eyes.

The young guy beside Athos stayed on his feet but bowed deeply. She nodded to him and moved along what was by now a procession. When she got to us, I put my hand over my heart. It was stupid. I have regretted it every moment of my life since. The corners of her mouth turned upward in amusement.

She stopped in front of Madailín, whose face was still bowed to the ground. The Godmother kneeled in front of her. She placed both hands on the sides of Madailín's shoulders and brought them both to their feet. Tears streamed down Madailín's cheeks, glistening in the Godmother's glow. The elder fairy gently whisked the tears away and whispered, "My child." Madailín's chest heaved.

As the Godmother moved away from us, I noticed for the first time that much of the cairn that perennially grew atop Knocknarea had been removed, revealing earth that hadn't been exposed in two thousand years. And something else too. I unconsciously left Madailín alone to contend with whatever had just happened to her, skirting the perimeter of the congregation to figure out what the large thing was that had been uncovered.

Since no one was paying any attention to me, I made my way to what revealed itself to be a stone table. Its bronzed top sloped toward a funnel at one end. Ornate engravings adorned the sides. My brain made the connection to picture Bibles I had as a kid. This wasn't a table. It was an altar.

In the middle of the altar lay a broken gold crown.

"It belonged to Maeve," Madailín said in a quavering voice as she settled next to me.

"It was still there after all this time?"

"When they removed the stones, they found it lying in two pieces beside the altar."

Nodding my head toward the missing rocks, I asked, "How are they going to explain this?"

"There will be much to explain after tonight. A few rocks ranks very low among them." She shrugged. "And none of it is my problem."

She flattened her hands on the altar before picking them up again and stalking off without saying anything further.

The Godmother approached with no one following her. "May I see what you have written for us?" I handed the folio to her. She pulled out the sheaf of paper. "This is considerably longer than the last one."

"You were there?" I blurted out.

The Godmother nodded. She squinted at the words on the first page. "I will need more light."

The guy beside Athos stumbled forward and cast a quick glance over his shoulder. He then proceeded toward the altar. When he came to a stop, he held his hands out in front of him and pressed the sides together, palms up as if presenting an offering. A ball of fire emerged above them and hovered above us.

"Thank you, Thomas."

He nodded and walked back to his place beside the giant.

"This will take some time," the Godmother said as she resumed reading. There was notable grumbling from among the Bone Collectors Guild, but everyone else remained solemnly quiet. I got the impression that there was only one contingent who wanted to implement these wholesale changes. Unfortunately, they were the ones who held in their grasp weapons of mass destruction.

About two-thirds of the way through her reading of the covenant, the Godmother looked at me over the tops of the pages in her hands. I held my breath. Her gaze lasted much longer than I was prepared for, both mentally and physically. I hadn't collected enough air in my lungs to comfortably hold my breath for the length of time the episode was lasting. Then there's the added stress of being appraised by an ancient and superior being.

Based on where she was at in the shuffle, I knew what she'd read. This was the make-or-break moment.

By the time she reverted her attention to the pages, the rush of adrenaline that coursed through me had dissipated, and all that was left was the limp feeling of noodles that had been boiled too long.

When she finished, the Godmother returned the covenant to its original order and laid the pages on the altar. She placed her hands on them, casting a cool light over the gleaming ink. Without looking up, she asked, "This is as you intend it to be?"

"Yes, ma'am," I mustered.

"Will you be signing it for the humans?"

I shook my head. "I drafted it. I shouldn't be the one to sign it."

She turned toward the humans. "Prime Minister." The woman stepped forward. She read the covenant less thoroughly before signing, having been strong-armed into the arrangement and knowing she had to sign regardless of its contents.

After the Irish prime minister retreated, Liadan strutted to the altar, the self-appointed representative of the Fae. She reached for the covenant, but the Godmother grabbed her wrist. Liadan's eyes widened in surprise and fear.

In a voice that scarcely rose above of a whisper, the Godmother said, "Ambition has never befitted us." The Wolf Queen's broken crown lay before us as an inescapable reminder.

When the Godmother released her wrist, Liadan made a

reasonably good effort to hide the anger and contempt in her voice. "Yes, Your Excellency."

Liadan picked up the covenant and began reading. After two pages, she started flitting through the agreement and huffing. Finally, she shoved it at me. "Show me the good part."

There was no mistaking what she wanted. I took the document and peeled off the first half-dozen pages until I came to the header, Terms and Conditions. When I returned the pages, she poured over the next several paragraphs with an eager bloodlust. After that section, she skimmed again before skipping to the last page.

"This is everything we discussed?"

"Of course," I said. *And more.*

Liadan picked up the fountain pen to add her own mark.

The Godmother said, "Be certain, Liadan. What is done cannot be undone."

# Chapter 46
# Blood Atonement

Liadan scribbled her name below her predecessor's. Dropping the pen onto the signature page, she spun and strode back to her clan. A great uproar of cheering broke out among them. As far as they knew, they had just overthrown both their human oppressors and the old guard of fairies. Liadan turned to face the rest of us, chin up and shoulders back in defiant victory. "Seal it."

The Godmother bristled at the irreverence, but did not address it. She shifted her attention and held out her hand.

Madailín stepped forward mournfully. She stopped in front of the Godmother, her dejected face cast toward the ground. The Godmother took Madailín by the hand and tilted her face upward. "It will be over soon, child."

"No," I blurted out, surprising myself at my reaction. I scooted around the altar to be on the same side as them. "No."

"It is necessary," Madailín whispered.

"Why not one of them?" I pointed at the Bone Collectors Guild.

A look of distaste settled over the Godmother. "The sacrifice must be one with substantial ties to both humankind and Fae.

Madailín was among your people many years before returning home to us. You were also a consideration and may exchange places with her if you wish."

"I will not allow that," Madailín said, her voice defiant. With her back already to the altar, she pushed herself up to a sitting position, then swiveled and lay back.

I scanned the crowd of people, none of whom were going to interfere to prevent this. We were all just going to have a ritual sacrifice, apparently.

"Step aside," the Godmother prodded me gently. "This must happen. The covenant is not sealed without it."

"It's okay," Madailín said. She laid back with her hands folded over her belly.

The Godmother pulled out a bronze knife, whose handle was ornately decorated with gold and silver, that had been sheathed at her belt. Since I hadn't moved, she sidestepped past me, making her way to a place next to Madailín's torso.

As she raised the knife high over her head, it gleamed in the firelight. The color appeared to drain from Madailín's skin, leaving her a mottled gray. I looked away, unable to bear the sight.

"Wait. Wait."

I turned in astonishment. Finally, someone had spoken up.

Liadan sauntered to the altar. She held her hand out. "Allow me to have this honor."

Murmuring broke out among the crowd.

"You impudent little imp," the Godmother said. "You disrupt this sacred moment for another of your games."

"Come now. We're fairies. Impertinence is basically our identity."

Madailín reached out and touched the Godmother. "Let her bear this weight."

The glow the Godmother exuded shifted and dimmed as she handed the knife across to Liadan, who accepted it greedily.

Liadan looked at me, seething with contempt. She took the knife by the blade and jabbed the handle toward me. Instinctively, I grabbed it. She said, "It is not I who will carry the weight of this."

Liadan reached into a bag she was carrying and withdrew the now-familiar golden box. When she opened it, a single pouch lay within it. And I well knew its contents. Despite my hopes for a different outcome, sharp-edged pangs of fear and dread cut their way through me.

She extracted a tooth and addressed the representatives of the Bone Collectors Guild. "For thousands of years, the Fae have been beholden to the whims of humankind. Only one among us has known anything but subjugation. One who could not muster the will to meet conquest with defiance. One who was impotent with cowardice. But tonight, we have rewritten the covenant. Tonight, we begin the work of remaking the world in our likeness."

Whoops and cheers followed the rehearsed delivery. This was her moment, and she had prepared for it. She waved the BCG to quiet down.

"After a small bit of pomp," she gestured down as Madailín as though she were no more than soiled clothing, "we tear asunder the veil that shrouds our worlds."

Ignoring the cheering that had resumed, Liadan turned back to me. "This is going to hurt you — both of you — far, far more than it's going to hurt me." She dropped the tooth onto her tongue and closed her mouth.

Silent anticipation fell over the gathering. Even those who hadn't seen the torture chambers and violence that I'd been privy to would not soon forget the images of the executive who'd had his teeth excised and implanted into his face. There was no doubt what was at stake, and presumably, what had been lost.

Several seconds passed, in which she stared intently at me.

Nothing happened.

A grin broke over my face as a tsunami of relief crashed into me, obliterating every other feeling, at least for the moment. I had made an extraordinary gamble that relied on two things to work out my way. One, the established Fae weren't aligned with Liadan and the BCG — that bore out when the Godmother came to the small Exclusions section of the Covenant buried about thirteen pages deep.

## Exclusions

1. No party may undertake any actions or omissions with regard to any other party that will cause or allow them harm, injury, death, or otherwise work to their detriment.
2. Without explicit consent, no party may assert, control, dominion, or undue influence over another party to cause that party to act other than by their own free will.

Every insurance policy has its limitations and exclusions. Insurance companies rely on them to mitigate their risk, just like I had done. I could concede to every demand for power that Liadan made, knowing that she wasn't going to wield it to hurt us.

I had Ella's hundred watchings of *Aladdin* to thank for the idea — the original one with Robin Williams as Genie, not the terrible remake. At the end, Genie grants Jafar's wish to make him the most powerful genie in the universe, only for the villain to find himself confined to a lantern. Liadan had just signed her own lantern into existence.

She deserved some credit, too. If she hadn't called humanity a virus when she'd taken me back to Ashleigh's street in Birmingham, it wouldn't have prompted my brain to think of virus exclusions, and I may not have thought to format the covenant in this way.

The other wager I'd made was that impatient Liadan would be so eager to wrest control and commence her reign that she wouldn't actually read twenty-something pages of dense word-vomit. Precedent was on my side here. I mean, have you ever actually read an insurance policy? They're mind-numbing for a reason.

Liadan's face said she was bewildered and confused. I took the opportunity to set the knife down on the altar and pick up the covenant, which I promptly threw at Liadan. A couple of pages separated from the pack and meandered to the ground, but she caught the bulk of it, dropping the box of my teeth in the process.

"You didn't read it, moron. You threatened me and my family and coerced me to write a contract that would endanger all of us. Then you trusted that I would do what you said."

Liadan's eyes never left me. She dropped the pages to the ground and reached behind her back. When she brought her hand back around, it carried a bone-handled dagger.

# Chapter 47
# Change of Plans

My blood nearly curdled with the sound that Liadan's scream made. As she tensed to pounce, a blur of light burst past me and crashed into Liadan, who stumbled backward as her banshee-yell was cut off. Her dagger tumbled out of her hand. The slice of earth that enveloped me was a bundle of confused chaos.

The Godmother caught Liadan in an embrace as she fell, lowering her slowly to the ground. She then released Liadan and raised herself upright, revealing the gold and silver handle of the ceremony knife protruded from Liadan's chest. I looked over my shoulder to confirm the knife was no longer lying on the altar.

Liadan gasped several times, as the Godmother stroked her face and spoke softly to her. "My strong, wayward child. I will see you again on the other side."

A shimmering tear slid down Liadan's face and into her hair as the color sloughed off her skin.

A great uproar erupted from the direction of the Bone Collectors Guild. I looked up to see them charging our direction, armed with primeval daggers and spears. A rush of bodies hurried to meet them. Mayhem was breaking out all around me when I was pulled backward over the altar by my shoulders.

Madailín dragged me to the ground. I brought my hands up in a defensive posture, not that I had much faith in them to inflict damage on anyone. My last fist fight had been in junior high, and the gym teacher had broken it up long before it had reached any kind of conclusion.

"You did not falter," she said.

That was unexpected. "You aren't angry?"

"Change is needed," she said. "But not to that degree. Stay here. I must go help the Godmother."

A bright flash momentarily lit up the night. "I think she's holding her own."

The ground shuddered with heavy footfalls that neared us. I couldn't see around the corner of the altar to make out who it was, but Madailín seemed to know. "Regardless, I'm not yet ready to meet the bearer of those steps." She crawled around the other end of the stone table and slipped into the fray.

The silhouette of a giant emerged. Athos reached a hand down to me. I grabbed hold of it, and he effortlessly pulled me to my feet. "Time to get you out of here."

"Don't we need to help?"

"You have done your part."

"Fine, but unless you've got a ride share waiting on us down there, we've got a long walk ahead of us." For the first time, thoughts of Declan and his fate on this mountain tried to encroach. I pushed it aside for the time being.

"Thomas," Athos said, "you're up."

I hadn't noticed him until now, but he literally stood in the giant's shadow.

Thomas stepped forward and caused an inky oval to open up.

"What the heck is that?" I asked.

"A door."

"And it goes where?"

Thomas said, "Where would you like it to go?"

"Home."

Thomas nodded.

"No offense, but I'm going to need one of y'all to go first. Ever since I met … basically everybody here, things have done nothing but go sideways."

"Not that this will prove anything," Athos said, "because you can't see anything once I'm on the other side. I could be taking you straight to the hellmouth. Nevertheless."

He ducked his head and stepped through, disappearing into the opaque portal just as he said he would.

I hesitated.

"There's no hellmouth. That's not a thing."

"Okay." I stepped forward and stopped.

"You just step through. Think of it like a hula hoop."

"And on the other side?"

"Birmingham."

I took a deep breath and stepped through, crossing four thousand miles in the span of a heartbeat. I thought any travel out of Birmingham that wasn't by car required a layover in Atlanta, but it looked like we'd found a loophole.

What I wasn't expecting was to step out of the dark of night into the of early evening. The contrast wasn't altogether different from walking out of a matinee movie into the sunlight. Athos pulled me toward himself, and I felt a brick wall at my back. Thomas stepped through a moment later and closed the door behind himself.

"How was it looking before you left?" Athos asked.

"They were getting it in hand, corralling the tooth fairies."

"And the politicians?"

"Fine. I shipped them off to Dublin as soon as the fracas broke out."

It took me a minute, but I got my bearings as we stood in the shadows of the building we were up against. Thomas had dropped us in the heart of Homewood. "Is this the funeral home?"

He grinned shyly. "I can only go places I can visualize or have a weirdly inherited institutional knowledge of. It's a long story. Anyway, I remembered that there was a funeral home near a bakery, and we needed a quiet landing spot so two dudes and a giant didn't pop up in the middle of things."

"Are you from here?"

He looked to the north and spied the statue of Vulcan standing atop Red Mountain, keeping watch over the valley below where Birmingham stood. A complex string of emotions played over his face. He didn't look as young now as he had before, perhaps having more life experiences than his youth would seem to allow for.

"I was born here, but we moved away when I was a kid. Most of my memories of things are hazy. But I remembered there was a funeral home by the bakery. That always struck me as odd. And I remember him." He nodded with his chin.

"Vulcan? Yeah, he tends to make an impression on kids. Mine likes to point out that is butt is pointed at Homewood."

Athos smirked. At first I thought he was smiling at the anecdote I'd shared. But a look passed between him and Thomas that suggested maybe I'd missed something. "What?" I asked.

Athos waved me off. "Nothing. It's a mostly unpleasant story for another time. We've had enough unpleasantness for one day."

Thomas asked, "Can you find your way from here?"

I nodded. I'd have to get a ride out to the airport where Madailín (who was still Madeline at the time) had left my car, but that wasn't a problem. I wondered if I could get my return flight from Ireland refunded since I obviously wasn't going to need. "Where are y'all headed?"

Thomas said, "We have some fires to put out."

The giant snorted a laugh and shook his head. "Farewell, Scott. With any luck, you won't see me again, and I can go to my quiet cabin in the Carolinas."

An unease settled on me as they prepared to leave. "So … what? I'm just supposed to go back to my old life and act like everything is normal?"

"More or less," the giant said with a shrug. "And you have yourself to thank for that. As do all these folks who will never have to know that they were imperiled. That is the nature of the deeds we do in the dark. Even the good ones."

Thomas opened a portal that they stepped through, leaving me standing alone behind a funeral home.

# Chapter 48
# Hedging with the Truth

When my phone rang, I picked it up off the arm of the sofa and turned the screen to see that it was Ashleigh. I called into the kitchen, "Ella, was there somewhere I was supposed to take you after school?"

"No." A beat later, she added, "I'm hungry."

"Hang tight. Your mom is calling." I mashed the green button. "Hey, where does your daughter store all this food she eats?"

She ignored my call and launched into a tirade. "What the hell do you think you're doing traipsing up and down this street with some coed strapped to your arm?! So help me, if you start dating some girl half your age, I will drive over—"

"Hey," I said a little louder than intended, but knowing I wouldn't be able to cut off the stream otherwise.

When Ella looked up from whatever she was drawing, I smiled at her and took the conversation to my bedroom.

"I don't know what you're talking about." I did know what she was talking about.

"I'm talking about our neighbors saw you having an argument with some girl basically in front of my house."

"Uh-huh." I used as much skepticism as I could muster. "And when did this supposedly happen?"

"Like a week-and-half ago."

"Okay, think about it. I was in Ireland. How could that have been me?" I knew I was being a jerk, but the alternative option was not better. *No, you're right. It was me. That was the tooth fairy, and she was super hot. But she's dead now, so it's okay. Oh, and she was about a heartbeat away from murdering me.* "Unless you think I've figured out how to be in two places at once."

The facts took the wind out of her sails. She conceded, "Yeah, okay. I hadn't thought about that."

"We good?"

"I guess." Her voice was timid with embarrassment.

I didn't want that, especially since I was hedging with the truth, so I changed the subject. "Ella says she's got some kind of achievement test coming up that she's worried about."

"She'll be fine. Just some test anxiety that cropped up. What are you feeding her for dinner?"

"Cotton candy and funnel cakes."

"Shut up," she said playfully.

"See you Friday."

"Bye."

When I opened the bedroom door, Ella asked, "Was that Mommy?"

"Yep."

"Is she mad at you?"

I raised an eyebrow. "Why would you ask that?"

"I could hear her. That's how her voice sounds when she's mad."

"We're fine. You hungry for dinner?"

"Can I have toaster strudel?"

So ... we weren't that far removed from funnel cakes and cotton candy. "Sure. Why not?"

She squealed with delight. "Four please."

# Casual Business with Fairies

"Holy cow."

Dinner led to Ella's shower time, which was infinitely easier now that she could manage everything herself. It also gave me time to make a phone call I'd been thinking about ever since I got back.

I searched my contacts for Sam's name and punched the video call button. I panicked, trying to figure out how to end it, but not in time. Sam's lovely (age appropriate) face popped onto the screen. She was reclined by a pool, catching the last of the day's sun. She held the phone far enough away that it caught a fair amount of her figure. Heat flushed my cheeks.

"Hey, stranger," she said with a big smile.

I waved with the hand that wasn't holding the phone. "It's … uh … Scott." I was fifteen and awkward all over again.

"I remember. Besides, the friendly neighborhood giant gave me your number in case you got yourself all busted up again and needed some attention. You don't think I'd take a video call from an unknown number all done up like this, do you?"

"Honestly, I don't know. I think I'd probably guess wrong about you on most every account."

"Good," she said with a smile. "Wouldn't want you thinking you had me figured out after only two meetings. Did you call just to chitchat, or did you have something on your mind?"

Seeing her like this, I had several things on my mind now. And none of them were the reason I called. "I got into kind of a mess about a week ago…"

From the other end of the apartment, Ella yelled, "Daddy, I'm ready to read together."

"Be there in a minute. Go ahead and brush your teeth."

"Do I have to? The wiggly one hurts when I brush it."

"Yes, you have to."

She groaned in frustration.

"How old?" Sam asked.

"Six, going on sixteen."

"Oh, you haven't seen anything yet. It's going to get far worse before it gets better ... in like fourteen years. Anyway, back to your thing — I might have heard something about that through the grapevine."

"Good. Okay. So ever since then, I've been waking up with cold sweats and having anxiety come on at weird times." My words faltered. I hated that I could see my face in the window on the screen. I couldn't have been more uncomfortable. "Look, we don't really talk about this kind of stuff in my family, so ..."

"Sounds to me like you need to see a therapist. And I don't say that with any judgment. I think most everybody could use some counseling."

"That's not something you do?"

"No. Injuries to the psyche, to the soul are way outside my ken. But I can refer you to someone who is familiar with our particular brand of problems. Besides, that's not really the direction I see us going."

"Oh?"

"No, I see us going to dinner and a movie."

"Are you asking me out?"

"Nope. I'm being really, really transparent. The rest is up to you. Now, I gotta go get into the shower before bats start swooping down at the pool." She shuddered.

"I can stick around for that," I offered.

She rolled her eyes and smiled, then hung up.

Planning dinner and a movie with someone you hardly know is tough. You can screw up either one of them pretty easily.

I stood up and headed to Ella's room. When I stepped through her door, I was hit in the chest with a pillow. I dropped to the floor and scrambled for a weapon, while getting pummeled on the back. Finding nothing, I launched myself toward her and tackled her … a little more roughly than I had intended.

Her eyes widened, and she put a hand to her mouth. "Let me see," I demanded.

She pulled her hand away. The lower front tooth that had been quite loose was now horizontal instead of vertical.

"Show me," she said with a weird lisp, since she was trying not to move her lips.

I took my phone out of my pocket and put it in selfie mode. She grinned wickedly and snatched the tooth out of her mouth, then held it out for me to see. A small tooth rested in her palm, along with the tiniest amount of blood.

A gap-toothed smile emerged as she said, "None of my friends have pulled their own tooth. They all cry about it. Do you think I'm tough?"

"For sure. Head to the bathroom, tough girl," I said, pushing myself up off the floor. "I'll get a baggy and some warm salt water for you to swish around."

I was on my way to the kitchen when she asked, "Do you think the tooth fairy's going to come?"

The question stopped me in my tracks, and goose bumps prickled my skin. I chose not to tell her I'd be taking over those duties because we don't do business with fairies any more.

# Author's Note

I never know where the inspiration for stories is going to come from. My debut novel, *Vulcan Rising*, arose out of a really strange dream and a couple of peculiar interactions with my five year old. One of my short stories, "The Murder Tree," opened with a line that I derived from an off-hand remark made by the host of a podcast I was listening to.

But this story had a different path. In the Spring of 2022, I was involved in a conversation with several other parents about the tooth fairy and how everyone handles it. The group is rather eclectic, and the responses were diverse. During the discussion, one of parents made a statement about why they don't participate in the tooth fairy myth: "We don't do casual business with fairies."

That sentence lodged itself in my brain, and out of it, this novel was born. But this is not the novel I intended to write.

After I wrote *Forging Bonds,* which completed the first trilogy of The Zauberi Chronicles series, I had planned to switch tracks. There was a horror story I wanted to write, but after outlining it and writing a chapter or two, I found it difficult to engage with. This may be hard to believe, but it was just too grim of a story.

# Author's Note

The really disconcerting part is that the story is based on a nightmare I woke up from one night.

When the horror story didn't work out, I started outlining a murder mystery novel … also based on a dream I had. But for whatever reason, the muse wasn't having it.

Next, I had in mind that I would finish one of the novels I had abandoned before starting *Vulcan Rising*. But *Casual Business with Fairies* latched onto me like a spider monkey. Even though I had only the vaguest of ideas for a premise, I began to write. Five thousand words into the story, I still had no idea what it would become, but I kept the faith that I would figure it out. I had been in a similar position with my second novel, *Seeking Sanctuary*, and I would work my way out of it again.

Something unique to this novel is that it contains more of me than any other story I've written to date. Many of Scott Warren's anecdotes and asides are my own. It became inevitable when I decided that he would be an insurance lawyer and that his professional skills would play a significant role in the resolution of the story.

*Casual Business with Fairies* surprised me at every turn. Each time I thought I had the story and characters figured out, things went a different direction. It was both exhilarating and frustrating. But in the end, I think it became the book that it was meant to be. Most of all, I hope it's a story that you enjoyed.

December 31, 2022

# About the Author

J. W. Judge lives in Birmingham, Alabama, also known as The Magic City. In his day job, he is a lawyer, practicing commercial litigation.

*Casual Business with Fairies* is his fourth novel. His first three novels are all part of the dark fantasy series The Zauberi Chronicles: *Vulcan Rising* (Book 1), *Seeking Sanctuary* (Book 2), and *Forging Bonds* (Book 3).

If you enjoyed *Casual Business with Fairies*, sign up for Judge's newsletter for information about other stories he's working on. You can also follow him on social media for updates, developments, and news about other projects. If you'd like to reach out to him by email, please do so at jwj@jwjudge.com.

Please help others find and enjoy *Casual Business with Fairies* by leaving a rating and review on Goodreads or your preferred retailer, or by sharing about it on your own social media.

# Works by J. W. Judge

*Fiction*

Casual Business with Fairies

Vulcan Rising (The Zauberi Chronicles, Book 1)

Seeking Sanctuary (The Zauberi Chronicles, Book 2)

Forging Bonds (The Zauberi Chronicles, Book 3)

The Murder Tree (A Short Story)

*Non-Fiction*

Write Your Novel One Day at a Time: How to Write a Novel While Having a Career, a Family, and a Life

www.ingramcontent.com/pod-product-compliance
Lightning Source LLC
Chambersburg PA
CBHW060912210726
48293CB00006B/2071